Something Not Broken

by

Marissa Dara Foster, MD, MS

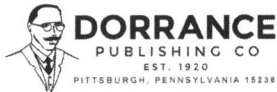

DORRANCE
PUBLISHING CO
EST. 1920
PITTSBURGH, PENNSYLVANIA 15238

Dorrance Publishing Co
585 Alpha Drive
Suite 103
Pittsburgh, PA 15238
Visit our website at *www.dorrancebookstore.com*

ISBN: 979-8-8860-4021-0
EISBN: 979-8-8860-4926-8

Dedicated to my parents,
Maurice and Carole,
with me always

For K., my sweetest truth

If sequestered pain made a sound,
the atmosphere would be humming all the time.
—Steven Levine

Unattended Sorrow:

Recovering from Loss and Reviving the Heart

Chapter 1

The unrelenting din of midtown New York City traffic suddenly penetrated the static calm of Petra's office, snapping her mind back to the present. *How long have I been sitting here?* she wondered silently, her eyes eagerly scanning the anemically adorned room, as if waiting for some response. The mug of coffee she absently cradled was decidedly tepid, and had been steaming hot when she last remembered consciously participating in the day. The pages of the manuscript she was currently editing lay out in disarray before her, depressing reminders of how little progress she had made today, or any day lately. She had been so excited when her boss, Melanie, gave her this assignment three weeks ago, her biggest one since starting at Viscount Publishing eighteen months before. There had been no sense of pressure, no pangs of self-doubt, and why would there be?

Petra had sailed through the young adult novels of her initial employment weeks, insightfully trimming and bolstering the predictably fluffy content, forging bonds with the authors, gaining the respect of her coworkers, and even becoming Melanie's pet employee and steady racquetball partner. A quick upgrade to editing a popular fitness series followed, and the long hours had been rejuvenating rather than exhausting, helped along by the fun chemistry that had quickly developed between Petra and the appropriately toned and athletic author, Mitch Gainsley. He often treated her to spa lunches and personal training sessions, and they bonded over their shared love of Jeff Buckley and French films. None of it had felt like work, and Petra often ended her jam-packed days wondering how she had gotten this lucky, earning a reasonably good salary doing something she loved and surrounded by interesting, dynamic people. So, the progression to her current task was natural, perhaps inevitable.

Fiona Finch was one of the company's most famous and best-selling authors. Her romantic historical fiction novels were huge critical and commercial successes, with rabid fans the world over, tons of merchandizing—everything from T-shirts and lingerie to cereal and dolls—and even upcoming films. The previous editor assigned to Fiona had recently gone on maternity leave, and it was rumored that with preterm newborn twins, a precocious three-year-old, and an eminent entertainment lawyer husband being courted by several West Coast firms, Kate might not ever return. There were other editors with more seniority than Petra, but she was a summa cum laude Columbia graduate, the requisite English major with the added cachet of an Art History minor.

Having spent five proliferative years at a high-profile Chicago publishing conglomerate, she was no stranger to corporate realities and the nuances of the literary world, yet at twenty-nine, was still young enough to project effortless hipness and energy. Plus, Petra had that indefinable "it" factor, a certain easy and genuine charm that made men and women fall in love with her instantly, inspiring their admiration and loyalty without evoking jealousy or backstabbing. Her appearance was innocently inviting, with her auburn pixie cut, almond-shaped dark brown eyes, ivory skin, and full pouty mouth. Petite and trim, her figure was almost boyish, taut lines softened only by her slightly ample chest. Education, experience, likability, and looks: she ticked all the boxes. There was no more ideal choice for Fiona's next editor.

So why had she hit a wall? No matter how hard she tried to concentrate, she couldn't get through more than a couple of paragraphs of the massive tome before she lost focus and entered some mindless trance. Almost three full weeks, and she was still stuck on the third chapter. The only evidence of her work: one sad, red-inked comma inserted in a run-on sentence. She was running out of ways to dodge Melanie. Menstrual cramps, migraine, food allergies, Petra had already exhausted her usual excuse arsenal. Of course, everyone in the office had been tiptoeing around her for several weeks before this unforeseen work slump, blanketing her with lots of sympathetic glances and uncomfortably careful silence ever since her break up with Tyler. Petra hadn't explained why or how it was over, only that it was.

As her fingers thumped reflexively on the beleaguered manuscript, her thoughts ambled to Tyler. Eight wonderful years, and she had ended it all in the space of a few frozen seconds. He wanted to get married, and she didn't. Just like him, the proposal was heartfelt and studied. Warm fragments of that night circulated in her muddled mind. The vintage brandy, her favorite Keats poem, his gentle and hopeful eyes, the antique ring. All so beautiful and sweet, all so perfect. That's what had struck Petra as so wrong in that moment, the reason she instinctively blurted out a simple but definite no. Their utter perfection was, for her, their undoing, the proof that something essential was inexplicably lacking. She had no earthly reason to be unhappy or unfulfilled, and yet she was, deeply, realizing it for the first time as this dream man offered her a dream life. He was faithful and supportive, always encouraging her career, never accusatory or insecure, even when she had worked so closely and socialized with the flirtatious Mitch. They always made time for each other, despite their busy schedules. Weekend trips, rural bed and breakfast inns, art galleries, new restaurants, plays. Laughter, comfort, sex, laundry, cooking. Everything was shared. But they weren't truly in love. Tyler didn't see it yet, and Petra hadn't either until that very moment when he held out the ring and earnestly searched her unexpectedly vacant face for a yes.

"Is that why I'm so distracted," she posited to herself, "unable to do any meaningful work these days, because I'm lovesick?" Petra didn't think so, as her immediately dismissive nod seemed to reinforce. As much as she had cared for and been attached to Tyler, part of her was relieved that she had woken up from their shared reverie in time to avoid an ill-fated marriage. She was a child of divorce, and didn't want to further that legacy for herself or her future children. With no alternative explanation readily apparent, she waded through her mental fog, hoping to identify and excise the source of her flagging productivity. Maybe the ending of her relationship and her burgeoning work funk were symptomatic of something deeper, the emotional equivalent of a slow leak, a hole in her psyche that had been widening unnoticed for some time, finally demanding to be filled. How had she felt complete for so long when something primal was being steadily emptied?

Once again, Petra was immersed in a timeless void, and abruptly roused by the insistent lilt of her coworker Jeremy's high-pitched voice. She must have looked dumbfounded when he announced it was almost 6:00 p.m., and a small group were heading out to McCrawley's Pub if she wanted to join them, because he inquired in a quieter, deeper tone, "Are you okay?" Petra made a pretense of gathering up her strewn pages, and assured him that she had been so engrossed in the manuscript, she had simply lost track of time. After apologetically declining his invitation, she quickly bounced into the hallway and headed for the exit to the rear elevator bank, relievedly exhaling when she had managed to escape unassailed by Melanie's increasingly urgent requests for a status update.

The sticky late May air clung doggedly to Petra's skin as she robotically walked the four endless blocks home, still caught in a frustrating spiritual self-excavation. As with the manuscript, her frantic attempts to move forward with insight and direction were akin to trying to dig out from a dirt-covered abyss, only to get suffocated and blinded by the circulating debris. After what seemed like several misplaced days, she finally entered her tidy apartment, so barren without Tyler's perennial text books and lesson plans splayed over every available surface. She kicked off her shoes and headed into the kitchen, barely managing to ingest a microwaved frozen burrito before she collapsed onto her sofa, fully dressed, uncomfortable and hot, and yet too sluggish and unmotivated to seek the cooling, clean relief of a shower and her crisp bed linens. From the edges of impending sleep, bittersweet memories of Tyler kept emerging and creeping into her mindscape, until she was too drained to resist their incessant beckoning.

My last semester at Columbia has arrived, and I am struggling through the worst class of my college career. This is the result of a challenge I had accepted from my favorite frenemy Zack, a cocky applied mathematics major, who maintained that my string of straight A's would be broken if I stepped beyond my "lightweight" academic comfort zone. To prove him wrong, I enroll in one of the more esoteric courses, The Hidden Biology of Language, which has a reputation for being especially grim and challenging. Professor Hugh Dunlap's infamy as an uninspired, oblique lecturer is soon proven to be well deserved. Three excruciatingly painful mornings a week, he disseminates dense and convoluted theories, in a shrill, quavering voice oddly reminiscent of both adolescent awkwardness and senile fragility, even though he is about forty years old and sturdily built.

As tortuous as the lectures are, made mandatory by his insistence on taking attendance and perverse fondness for pop quizzes, my greatest agony is the final paper that has loomed since the first day of class, comprising the bulk of our ultimate grade. Normally, I enjoy research and writing, but the subject matter as presented is so remote and unengaging, I can't even begin to pick a topic on which to focus. During these interminable classes, I sometimes find temporary respite in vicious daydreams, vacillating between fantasies of slowly poisoning either Professor Dunlap or Zack, undecided as to who is more blameworthy for my current misery...

And then there is a welcome surprise. Due to a scheduling snafu, Professor Dunlap has been called off to an academic conference in Geneva, leaving the class in the hands of one of his graduate students, Tyler Harrison, for two glorious weeks. The first time he strides into the cramped lecture hall, the class seems to collectively hold its breath, not sure of what to expect from this young and handsome, but seemingly diffident, teaching fellow. He stammers a bit through his introduction, staring at his feet, and nervously tousling his wavy, slightly longish black hair. Then he starts his lecture, and some strange alchemy takes over, transforming him from the inside out. He speaks spontaneously and confidently, only sporadically glancing at his notes, and his enthusiasm becomes a palpable object radiating out from him, like a series of tentacles spreading out and rescuing us from the forgotten, murky sea into which Professor Dunlap has dumped us. His steel blue eyes become almost electric in intensity, piercing and encompassing, seeing everything and nothing. I leave there riveted, still having no clue what the class is about, but now it's because the teacher is blindingly mesmerizing rather than wholly unintelligible.

    The next afternoon, I head out to the main quad to visit Tyler during his office hours. Ostensibly, it is for guidance about my paper, but I think I just want to see him, face-to-face, alone. I have taken the time to brush my hair, and wear clean, unwrinkled clothes, a rarity in my harried coed life, so I know my intentions go beyond the purely academic. As I meander the long hallways toward his office, apparently tucked away in some distant alcove, I feel excited and curious, tense in a good way. Will he be shy like he was when he tentatively stumbled into the classroom, or poised and magnetic like he was when he taught? Both facets attract me, and I'm not sure if I am ready for either side of him. Will I sit there blushing, rambling incoherently? Will he find my reticence as beguiling as I find his, perhaps wondering if I, too, have a more self-possessed side that emerges as seamlessly and beautifully as his? I arrive at his door, only to discover three obviously smitten coeds, intermittently reapplying lip gloss, checking hair and face in compact mirrors, spraying perfume, all hyped up and giggling. Instantly, I feel foolish, and not wanting to be included in some immature, hormone-driven fan club, I leave, no closer to a cohesive paper, no closer to him.

    Two hours later, I find myself at the back table of Bistro Annaba, a quasi-Arabian café, a few blocks away from the main student haunts. I go there when I need to be alone, and always find solace in their signature cardamom mint mocha lattes, which are actually pretty awful tasting, but something I nonetheless compulsively order. I sit there pensively reading one of the cumbersome texts Dunlap has assigned us, perennially stumped about what I could possibly write about, convinced I am going to fail the course. A dimness suddenly hangs over my table, and I look up to see Tyler smiling at me, bemusement subtly infiltrating his countenance. I wait what seems like an eternity for him to speak, for I am paralyzed by stifling joy at his surprise arrival.

"You're in Dunlap's class on biology and language, right? I think I saw you there yesterday, and I recognize that horrible text you're reading. I swear, that book almost made me give up on Linguistics and become an Econ major." He laughs, a little self-consciously, and I am even more disarmed by him than I had been in class. Some elemental form of communication is occurring in the wordless vacuum immediately enveloping us, as if we are primordial creatures relying entirely on sensation and instinct. My eyes respond to the wish that lingers unsaid on my tongue, clumsily landing on the chair opposite mine, and swiftly catching my intention, he sits down, the weighty creaking of the wooden seat breaking the bubble of inertia hovering between us. Our conversation quickly becomes buoyant and playful, and eventually carries us on to the tree-lined walkways of Bryant Park, the encroaching twilight and regularly stationed lamps casting amber pools of shadow that mirror the quiet warmth of our mingling body heat and growing intimacy. Animated personal sharing mixes pleasantly with relaxed quiet, and after one such lull, our conversation languidly circles back to academic concerns, namely my apprehension about the essay assignment and general confusion about the course.

"I have just one question. What the hell is the hidden biology of language?" I blurt out, my pressing need for his reassurance and support outweighing my intellectual pride. We both laugh, bonding over the confounding madness of Dunlap's instruction, but also experiencing an innocent release from the unspoken attraction overtaking us. Grasping my arm gently, he leads me onto a nearby bench, and sitting next to me so that our knees touch ever so slightly, he reaches into his briefcase, pulling out a very weathered-looking paperback book. Grazing his fingers across the cover with quiet reverence, he pauses before extending the book to me.

"Do you like poetry?" he asks, slowly exhaling after he speaks. I sense that sharing this book with me means something profound to him, that this is an almost sacred moment for us, so I simply nod as I accept the book, finding no words deserving of the exchange. It is a collection of Emily Dickinson's poems,

and I internally smile, having been introduced to Dickinson by my sensitive, art-loving grandmother, one carefree, lazy summer spent daydreaming on the Massachusetts coastline.

"Good. Now this is what I want you to do." He looks at me earnestly, and taking my right hand, places it softly over the book that presently sits in my lap, my skin tingling where his fingers remain gently adhered to mine. "Approach the poems like they are living organisms, each word a cell, an organ, carrying breath and spirit. Pay attention to how your body responds to the body of the poems, how the words enter you, how they touch you physically and emotionally, transforming your internal rhythms, heightening your bodily sensations, altering your mood, spiritually challenging you—all those intense chemical changes that two living beings can bring to each other, sublime and painful." He slowly lifts his hand away from mine, and brushing away an errant hair from my face, says, "That's your paper, and that's the essence of the course."

Chapter 2

Friday morning found Petra particularly anxious. As she halfheartedly brushed her teeth, knowing that each stroke brought her closer to the morning staff meeting, she tried to devise a game plan for seeming attentive and involved in the meeting, without summoning any direct focus or scrutiny. Would quietly taking notes, and nodding in agreement with other's comments and questions be enough, or should she bring up a completely random and irrelevant issue, like the ancient, temperamental refrigerator in the staff break room, hoping to generate further pointless discussion and deflect all interest in the status of her editing assignment? Or maybe she could pick up some designer cupcakes from that pretentious French-Japanese fusion bakery, and put everyone into a grateful and distracted sugar stupor?

Dimly amused by the stupidity of all these strategies, Petra listlessly gathered up the contents of her haphazardly placed purse, simultaneously gobbling up her stale cranberry muffin. As she swept away the remnants of her dismal breakfast, she suddenly noticed her shriveling echeveria and English Ivy plants, sitting forlornly on the windowsill, their pitiful brownness even gloomier than the desiccated muffin. Tyler was the one who tended to all things green, effortlessly accommodating their different sunlight and water needs. Since he moved out, Petra had watered and repositioned them according to her best recollection of what he always did, but she was obviously doing too much of one thing or not enough of another. As guilty as she felt over mishandling Tyler's leftover domain, she knew she needed to get to the office, and try to avoid the fallout of what she was mishandling there.

Petra arrived at the door to Viscount, bracing herself for the upcoming meeting with a long, cathartic sigh, when a light tap on her shoulder wakened her barely latent nerves. "I'm sorry, I didn't mean to startle you," said Penny, Melanie's mousy but efficient assistant, the unfailing quietness of her steps mirroring her de-mure demeanor. "Melanie really needs to see you. Go straight to her office," she whispered almost guiltily, her shy, concerned eyes amplified by her thick librarian glasses. Petra didn't know if she wanted to console the poor, sparrow-like girl or slam her scrawny body violently into the wall for disturbing her while she at-tempted to fortify her already shaky resolve.

"Okay, thanks, Penny." Petra smiled reassuringly, not thinking an assault charge would enhance the résumé she envisioned having to send out in the near future. Penny made a feeble attempt to smile back, and sheepishly opened the door, allowing Petra to walk in first. Being summoned imperatively by Melanie was def-initely unsettling, and yet knowing she could no longer forestall the inevitable was also a minor relief for Petra. The short walk to Melanie's office gained an air of fi-nality, and like a death row prisoner resigned to their fate in the gas chamber, Petra felt the emerging freedom of no longer having to devise creative escapes. The door to Melanie's spacious and bright corner office was open. With her cream linen sleeveless dress, hammered steel cuff bracelet, perfectly arranged ash blonde bob, and lightly tanned skin, Melanie blended into the beige-toned, sleek minimalism of her workspace. The only splash of color was a large purple and forest green Jackson Pollock-esque painting, but even that intensity was eclipsed by the light insistently bathing the room from the imposing panoramic windows, augmenting the prevailing monochromatic landscape.

Turning away from her computer screen, Melanie relaxed into her chair, and curiously appraising the ambivalent figure in her doorway, said simply, "Petra," gracefully cueing her to close the door and take a seat. Melanie waited for Petra to situate herself in the coldly elegant chair stationed before the stately marble desk, continuing to study her with that unnervingly direct gaze that con-veyed composed authority and astuteness, or as her coworker Jeremy quipped, "I'm smart and sophisticated, but don't fuck with me." Perceptively gauging Petra's unvoiced acquiescence to whatever she had decided, Melanie proceeded to direct the conversation.

"Okay, let's just get to it. You are a brilliant editor and you've continually impressed me with the caliber of your work. You are ambitious, but also supportive of others. You're witty and fun, and everyone loves you. I respect you as both an individual and a colleague, and I do consider you a friend. But at the end of the day, this is a business, and how you've been treating this assignment...well,"—

shaking her head in obvious disapproval—"it's not good for business." Melanie paused, and Petra knew it was not an opening for her to reply, but rather a space meant for her to absorb the gravity of what Melanie was saying.

"Compared to some others, you have not been here that long, but I took a leap of faith giving you this important account, trusting that you would continue to be professional and dedicated and *involved*. That's what we promised Fiona, when the three of us met back in March. That you would be readily accessible, giving your all to the manuscript and to her. Now I'm getting angry calls and texts from Fiona, that she can't get ahold of you, that you never respond to her messages. I also haven't been able to get any updates from you. I was forced to tell Fiona that you've been taking care of a sick relative, hoping to salvage her confidence in us. I know that woman is insufferably high maintenance, but you knew that when you took the assignment, Petra, and you agreed to meet her demands, which you have grossly failed to do. Do you comprehend how improper your behavior has been?" Again, Petra knew any response was unwanted.

"Clearly, something serious is going on with you. I think it's more than you and Tyler breaking up. Whatever it is, you need to figure it out, and move past it. I want you to take a brief sabbatical, fix this problem. Travel, visit friends, volunteer at a soup kitchen, have a hot affair, meditate with a Hindu master, do *anything* that will help you recalibrate. Your job will still be here in a couple of months, but I'm expecting that this episode will never be repeated, and that you'll once again perform at your optimum level. Otherwise...." With this, she stood up, and walked over to Petra, reaching for her hand as Petra rose from her chair, clasping it decisively within both of hers. Eye level with her star employee, Melanie showed a trace of empathic interest, urging her firmly, "Please, Petra, find some peace."

Petra nodded gratefully, and was about to exit in shamefaced silence, when some impulse unexpectedly engulfed her, and she heedlessly uttered, "But I won't be back." Melanie dropped her hand, uncharacteristically thunderstruck, a guttural sound of disbelief barely escaping her slackened mouth. Petra continued, seemingly possessed by a reckless need to burn every bridge at Viscount. "Melanie, it's incredibly generous of you to offer me time off to sort through things. You're right, I am experiencing a crisis, and I have no idea where it's coming from, or how to approach it, but I do know that when I manage to unravel it, when I get on course again, I won't be led back here. I'm sorry for letting you down, but whatever I need now or in the future, it's not in this building. Thank you for your mentorship and support, but I've gotten all I can from this job. This isn't where I want to be."

She confidently marched out of Melanie's office, walking the path to her own office for what she knew was the last time. Sitting down at her desk, she felt no regret that she had slammed shut the door to her future at Viscount, but wistfully thought of Jeremy and Rianne, wondering if she'd ever go out for happy-hour margaritas with them again, and laugh about their dramatic dating woes and sardonic political perspectives. She knew she could probably catch them before they dutifully headed to the morning meeting, and though she wanted to see them before she left, she had said her share of goodbyes in the last weeks, and couldn't tolerate any more just now. So, she instead retrieved her only personal belongings, a framed picture of her and Tyler visiting his brother's upstate farm, and her Italian word of the day desktop calendar, putting them in her valise while removing Fiona's neglected manuscript. Petra left the pages defiantly on the top of her otherwise empty desk, no longer having to hide her futile efforts.

Walking out of the building into the warm and breezy day, Petra felt proud of herself for not being intimidated by Melanie, for realizing it was time to move on, and acting on it. Prior to these recent lightning-quick decisions about romance and career, she had tended to be very considered in all her judgments. Maybe this uncharacteristic behavior proved she was on the verge of a breakdown, in the middle of a potentially disastrous existential upheaval, but at least today in Melanie's office, doing what she wanted to do instead of what was expected of her, it felt like a victory of some kind. Petra had been coolly definitive and concise, much like Melanie herself, and she couldn't help but take pleasure in having rattled her ex-boss's glacial constitution.

This satisfied euphoria surrounded her the entire walk home, and when she reached her building, she was too antsy to sit alone and idle in her apartment. So, she walked to the subway station, not knowing or caring where she was headed, just needing the noise, stimulation, and even the annoyance of strangers to feel connected, or at least less isolated and disengaged than she'd lately been experiencing. The train wasn't terribly crowded this time of day, just after the early morning rush, but there was still amusement to be found surveying her fellow passengers. Petra loved that the city and its transit system were home to such disparate people, bringing shiny Park Avenue penthouse dwellers a breath away from shower-deprived homeless nomads.

One nearby couple particularly entranced her, for they seemed like the tattooed and pierced version of she and Tyler when they first met. These two were about nineteen or twenty, each absorbed in their philosophy texts, but absentmindedly entwining their feet, and reflexively leaning into each other, like some inner beacon always called them back to each other, tethering them unconsciously. Their natural intimacy made her sentimental for her own days of romantic innocence, so she found herself traveling to Columbia's sprawling open campus, where so many of her dreams had crystallized and begun manifesting, or so it seemed at the time. She timidly hoped being back there would recover some of her lost passion, giving her the drive and direction she desperately craved.

Strolling leisurely by the places that had been so familiar to her, Petra's wishes for inspiration slowly gave way to dreary disappointment. Who was she kidding? That time in her life was gone, never to be recaptured. The rosy aspirations that had bloomed during her college years had largely been fulfilled: the stable, loving relationship, the challenging and rewarding career. And now she had nothing, only a pile of messy ashes and waning energy to clean it up. What was the point of starting over if she didn't truly know what she wanted, couldn't trust her own goals and desires? Masochistically clinging on to her sour mood, she ventured to the site of Bistro Annaba, the place where daydreaming, flirtation, contemplation, and ambition had so magically intersected for her all those years before. She already knew it no longer existed, as she and Tyler had sadly discovered during one of their return visits to NYC after relocating to Chicago. Back then, it had been replaced by a chichi children's clothing boutique, and she and Tyler had deflected their profound melancholy at the loss of "their place" by making fun of the grandiose moms plunking down hundreds of dollars on shoes and apparel their innocently oblivious toddlers would quickly outgrow.

Now, the shopfront had metamorphosed into something even more predictably dreadful, the ever-present Starbucks. It was approaching late afternoon at this point, and Petra somberly watched the steady stream of customers entering and exiting, the usual mix of sleep deprived students cramming for upcoming finals, harried workers fortifying themselves for their tedious evening commute, and shiftless wanderers just looking for a place of momentary rest. Her thoughts floated to Mr. and Mrs. Azani, the parental, warm proprietors of the erstwhile café. Had they seen their American dream fulfilled, she wondered, and contentedly headed back to their native Turkey? She imagined them living in a sunny cottage near the beach, fishing, collecting shells with their grandchildren, welcoming family and friends for relaxed and lingering Sunday meals.

Petra's tranquil smile soon faded, though, as callous reality crept in, and she bleakly accepted that this kindly, hard-working couple were probably forced out of their beloved livelihood by ever-increasing rent, and now spending their golden years alone and forgotten in a dumpy, decaying tenement in one of the outer boroughs. Wanting to end this torturesome trip down memory lane, Petra opted to return home. She called for a Lyft rather than return to the subway, because she didn't want to be reminded of the optimism she felt earlier in the day, or that young Goth couple, so contented and blissfully unaware of the cruelties the deceptively fast-moving train was hurtling them towards.

Her doorman, Fritz, smiled at Petra as she entered the building, and though in the past she had enjoyed chatting with him as her busy routine shuffled her in and out the door, her face and body currently registered the tiresome events of the day, and he remained in benevolent silence as she trudged forward to the stairs. Entering her apartment, she slammed shut her door, hoping to leave behind the pessimism and angst that had clung to her steps, but the darkness seemed to follow her in, resting upon everything in her home. Even her favorite quilt, draped over her sofa, which she had cherished for all its fraying edges and faded smudges, now appeared simply tattered and dingy, a taunting remnant of the warm comfort she might never have again. The smell of a neighbor's cooking began wafting into her open kitchen window, her stomach growling in angry awareness that it had been ignored since breakfast, but Petra's cabinets and refrigerator had grown sparse. Deeming the jar of pimentos, wilted lettuce, and box of spaghetti unappetizing options, and not having the clarity and patience to choose and wait for take-out, she drank some water, and returned to the living room. Roughly yanking the ragged, provoking blanket off the couch, she wrapped herself in it, and fell asleep on the floor.

After those exquisite moments in the park, Tyler offers to walk me home. I don't recall what we say on the way, if we speak at all, but I do know how insulated I feel from the cold air and the potentially threatening shadowy figures that inhabit the now fully darkened streets. Everything about Tyler—his questioning intellect, poetically deep insights, lean, muscular frame, penetrating and sensitive gaze—conveys permanence and strength. There are remaining traces of the shyness I had noticed when I first saw him in class, like the way he'll suddenly turn towards me as if gripped by the urgent need to say something, but then look forward again, an unsureness hiding in the bend of his beautiful smile. But even these delicate hints of self-doubt make him all the more impressively masculine, like a mythological hero that gains potency and credibility by revealing his flaws. He begins holding my hand as we get closer to my building, as if he wants to savor the sense of us becoming one before we withdraw to our respective dwellings.

We arrive at Hogan Hall, the campus residence I share with three other seniors, my closest college friends. As we look at each other, attempting to make casual conversation while the thin distance between us crackles with the promise of sex, I try to distract myself by flicking off a piece of lint from his tweed coat, but this outwardly harmless gesture only heightens the tension, and without warning, we are feverishly interlocked, kissing and frustratingly groping through all the outer layers that have kept out the still raw late winter wind but are now barriers to our union. The embarrassed giggling of passing teenage girls encroaches on our island of intimate fixation, and we once again become rooted in the outside world. In an instant, practical concerns storm my awakening brain. Has anyone cleaned the bathroom recently? Did I leave dirty underwear on my bedroom floor again? Are any of my roommates home? Becca was probably spending the night at her boyfriend's; Liz would be studying in the Science & Engineering library until it closed at 11:00 p.m. What about Mena? She had a headache when I saw her this morning. Is she sleeping, or watching TV and eating Thin Mints in the common room? Do we have to stumble through a perfunctory introduction when all I want to do is rip off his clothes?

Tyler and I transition to the steps leading up to the front door of the dorm, and sit there in a foggy hush, for he, too, seems to be rifling through his own mental inventory, quietly conflicted and anxious. At this point, I drop the keys I have been absentmindedly twirling. Stirred by the clattering, we both reach down to retrieve them, our hands crashing together, locking eyes, and wordlessly hearing the same command. He wraps his arm around my back as we stand up, taking our time walking up to my apartment, because right now, we are more imperative than time.

I can't remember the details of what happened that first night, but I can vividly recall what it felt like, giving myself to this man while also taking him, this stranger that I had somehow always known. It was explosive and feral, thrilling and unrestrained, sticky and flushed, everything naughty and pleasurable that flashes in your mind when you first develop an attraction for someone. That heady surge contained something unexpected, though, a softly familiar comfort, a delicately warm peace beneath the surface blaze.

We fall asleep easily, erotically spent like the new lovers we are, and as unselfconsciously attuned as lifelong best friends. I awake before him, hard gray early morning light peeping through the irregular cracks of my misshapen blinds, immediately remembering my usual morning-after ritual of rising early, brushing my teeth, arranging my hair, and splashing cold water on my face, then slyly slipping back into bed, so that I appear effortlessly fresh and dewy. Looking over at Tyler, though, his face so sincere and pure even in its sleepy stillness, these seem unnecessary and artificial maneuvers, so I fall back asleep, puffy and rumpled, yet securely nestled against his protective warmth.

Chapter 3

Knocking, impatient and loud. "Who the hell is that?" Petra angrily hissed, back and joints achy from hours tossing against the inhospitable wooden floor. Barely awake, mind still fuzzily tracking between dream life and real world, she fumbled for her phone to check the time. It was dead, and she realized that not wanting to communicate with anybody or anything outside of her gloomy sphere had precluded the need to charge it. The obnoxiously insistent assault on her door continued, and realizing that her intercom had never sounded, she figured it must be an annoying neighbor, looking to borrow coffee or gripe about some immaterial building issue.

"Fuck off, loser" she said slightly louder than intended, when she heard a familiar voice saying, "Petra, is that you? Open this door right now!" in that emphatic and worried tone reserved only for mothers.

"Mom?" she uttered with uncertainty. For a bewildered few seconds, Petra wondered if she had been in reverse hibernation, and awoken during the holiday season, when her mother made her usual jaunt from Maryland. She envisioned her mom standing outside her door, windswept silvery blonde hair halo-like against winter blushed skin and emerald green peacoat, impossibly balancing various ornately wrapped presents while gracefully sipping a hot caramel cider and impatiently pounding on the door. Wiping her clammy brow, Petra realized she was still smoldering in NYC pre-summer hell, and scrambling to her feet, she rushed to quiet the infernal rapping. Opening the door, she saw her mother, a whirl of manic concern, frothy with question.

"What are you doing here? Did we have an appointment to get together?" Petra asked, lethargy draping over all her words.

"I didn't think I needed an appointment to see you," her mom said, more worried than offended. "I had an appointment with Dr. Zahadi for a medical facial, and I wanted to surprise you at work, take you for an early lunch, catch up, shop. The receptionist at Viscount told me you haven't been there for about two weeks. I tried calling you and texting, I got no response. I was scared, Petra. You didn't mention anything about having left Viscount when we texted last week. And during our last phone conversation, I knew things with Tyler were over, but you told me everything was still great at work. What is happening?" She moved to hug Petra, who dully turned away without noticing. Sitting down in the plush patterned chair opposite the sofa, she gazed with loving watchfulness as her daughter plodded back onto her makeshift bed.

Petra's mouth opened, intending to respond in a snarky, deflective way, but no words materialized, so she just stared at her mother, with a defiance meant to cloak her internal chaos.

"It's that Mack character, isn't it?" her mom demanded.

"Who?"

"That exercise Lothario that was all over you. Pretentious pig. He's the reason you're out of a relationship and a job."

"His name is Mitch," Petra offered in exasperation, "and he has nothing to do with anything. I haven't spoken to or seen him for months."

Unconvinced but not wanting to provoke a fight, she responded, "Well then, what is the reason for all these changes? Why did Tyler leave? You never told me what happened between you."

"I don't want to talk about Tyler. It just wasn't working."

"Since when?" she pressed.

"Mother," Petra snapped, "enough! Are you here to badger me?"

"Okay," she replied as calmly as her growing worry would allow. "We won't talk about Tyler. What about your job? Was it your choice to leave?"

Remembering how tenaciously protective and overinvolved her mother could be, Petra carefully weighed her words before speaking, knowing she wanted to quell the inevitable cavalcade of frantic inquiries without having to offer explanations she herself was lacking. "I found my last assignment a bit challenging and I needed some time to…" pausing to think, Melanie's calculated wording sprung to mind, "recalibrate."

"Re-cal-ib-rate?" Her mother repeated it back laboriously slow, handling

18

the word like a bomb that needed to be carefully approached to prevent an explosion. "In practical terms, what does that mean for you?"

Petra had a sudden image of her mother and Professor Dunlap verbally jousting, looking for shrouded motifs in each other's phrasing, jabbing each other with pointed words until someone was rendered into a bloody silence. The garish absurdity of these thoughts spiraled Petra into a brief laughing fit, broken abruptly by her mother's apprehensive frustration.

"This isn't amusing, Petra. I don't know what I walked into here. When I saw you at Easter, you and Tyler seemed as stable and happy as ever, you were beaming about editing that big author's next book. Now it's a few months later, he's gone, and you're not working, you're giving me vague non-answers, and you don't seem to be doing anything but vegetating on the couch. Your hair is greasy, you look pale and malnourished. This apartment smells musty; it's hot and dark. I've never seen you like this. I love you, and I'm scared. How can I help you if you don't tell me what's going on?" She slumped into the chair, and closed her eyes briefly, taking in a deep breath, and exhaling in an extended helpless sigh.

When her mother peered directly at her once again, Petra could almost see the cauldron of emotions boiling over within her, spilling out of her mom's eyes as invisible teardrops, sadder than any actual tears Petra had ever cried. She was reminded of one of Tyler's favorite Wordsworth poems, containing the line, "Thoughts that do often lie too deep for tears." So many times, he had sat in the chair Petra's mother now occupied, meditating on that poem, wandering through some faraway world known only to him, with the heavy thud of the closing book always carrying him right back to Petra. The looming lines of Tyler's phantom frame receded into the flesh figure of Petra's mother, still waiting for an opening to redirect her wayward daughter to solid ground.

Moved by the density of her mother's caring, all the more striking in the absence of Tyler's weighty attention, Petra felt herself uncapped, a shaken soda bottle messily bursting. Divorced from conscious effort, she began discussing Tyler, repressed emotions and concealed impressions returning from exile like haunted refugees. "He proposed to me, Mom," she began in a melancholy whisper, and allowed the unsettling specter of Tyler to disperse into the room. She envisioned his beautiful and open face as he presented her the engagement ring, unknowingly walking off a cliff, and she wished she could yank him out of that night and protect him from loving her.

Her mom nodded in mute encouragement, and Petra haltingly continued. "It was so lovely and thoughtful, and I couldn't say yes. I felt choked by unhappiness almost as soon as he took out the ring, and to me that meant that we weren't right for each other. How could I be in love with him, meant to happily commit, if his sweet, wonderful proposal suffocated me?"

She paused to catch her breath, her heart fluttering again as her tortured mind plunged her body back into that cruelly dichotomous moment when something seemingly abundant deprived her of everything. The bleak calm of depression settled back into her, and she continued, "I thought I was confident in my decision to break up with him, but then I lost my footing at work, and I don't know if that's because I regret the breakup, and really am in love with him, or if I feel guilty about it and am punishing myself, or maybe I'm just not used to being alone. My worst fear is that everything is coming undone because of some deep sickness in me that's been festering for a long time. Maybe I've ignored it for so long that it's too late for me to get better."

Her mother's round face dripped with sympathy, a warm sticky bun of sweetness, and she got up and knelt before Petra, clasping her hand, willing her maternal affection into her daughter's watery, limp fingers. "My lovely girl, you're not sick. Maybe it's as simple as being overwhelmed by the impending responsibilities of marriage and an advancing career. It's understandable that you'd want a break, to step away from too many changes all at once." She lightly brushed Petra's hair with her feathery, soothing fingers, as she always did throughout Petra's childhood, coaxing her restless child into a placid sleep, then and now.

*****

Hours later, Petra idly yawned awake, the extended nap briefly disorienting her. She heard movement nearby, and instinctively thought of her mace spray, stowed inconveniently in her forsaken work valise. Just then, the cottony jasmine scent of her mother's perfume permeated the air around her, mingled with an earthy sweetness emanating from the kitchen, and she sunk back into her sluggish gloom, quietly glad her mom was there even if she couldn't summon the energy to feel or even appear happy. She surveyed her surroundings from her sofa cocoon, finding the drapes and blinds were open, the lilac candescence of dusk seeping through the windows, romantically muting the lonely pallor that had settled on the apartment in recent weeks. The air was coolly invigorating, the mechanical whir of the air conditioner made less harsh by her mom's gentle humming as she puttered by the stove. Even the overlooked plants appeared fresher in the comforting aura of Petra's mother. The hypnotic cadence of her soft singing made Petra think of her mother's given name, Calliope, Calli for short, and how appropriate it was for her to be named after the Greek goddess of music and dance, regardless of whether her name had determined or foretold her musical grace.

"Oh good, you're awake, just in time to eat," Calliope called cheerfully from her helm at the stove, having sensed Petra's drowsy stirrings on the periphery. "I'll bring it over to you in a minute."

Petra didn't remember her last full meal, and her physical need for sustenance was superseding her lack of appetite. "What are you making? I have no food in here."

"Yeah, I noticed. I went to the corner grocery while you were resting, and picked up a few of your favorites. Do you have a tray, sweetheart?"

"On top of the fridge, I think." Probably placed there last by Tyler, she mused, after preparing one of his decadent Sunday breakfasts in bed. "*Ugh*," she soundlessly moaned, "*why is he still everywhere?*" shutting her eyes tightly, as if she could unsee visions more powerful than physical eyesight.

"Okay, here we go," Calli sunnily announced, rerouting Petra's attention. "I know you always loved breakfast for dinner, so, voilà."

Petra stared down at the artfully arranged tray, the crystal tumbler filled with orange juice, glistening, plump raspberries and blueberries verdantly punctuated with fresh mint, and a formidable pile of cinnamon pancakes, laden with chocolate chips, their velvety interior lapping up the oozy spill of maple syrup and whipped cream. She marveled at how her mother could array even a cheap napkin to make it appear elegant. A hungry, grateful grin spread over Petra's dry lips, and she barely managed to thank her mother before she dug into the sugary feast. She was savoring every succulent morsel, as if she had never tasted food before, when her mother's phone began ringing, the unmistakable tune of "I Got You Babe" shrilly announcing that Beau, her stepfather, was calling. He and Calli had been married for five years, and the personalized ringtone had followed a short time later, but Petra still rolled her eyes whenever she heard its ridiculous jangle. For a moment, Petra felt her petulant inner child emerge, and she wanted to rebelliously push the food away, and storm into her bedroom, but the seductive lushness of the half-full plate pulled her back, and she started eating again, the thick sweetness easing the bitterness she felt towards Beau.

"Hi, Cubby, how are you?" her mother playfully purred, practically somersaulting into the phone.

With that, Petra's fork tumbled onto the tray. "Is that not *the* stupidest pet name?" Petra asked herself in a low, jeering voice. "What the hell does it mean anyway? Ugh, I don't even want to know." She derisively muttered under her breath, "Oh Cubby, Cubby. Calli and Cubby," contorting her face into saccharine expressions that corresponded to the haughty disdain her mother's relationship with Beau always inflamed within her.

To be honest, Petra didn't really have a compelling reason for disliking her stepfather. Her parents had divorced when she was in high school, and it had been long overdue, as both had seemed absent from the marriage long before they physically disbanded. No huge fights, no financial struggles or infidelity that Petra was aware of, nor physical violence or alcohol abuse. Just two people who eventually found themselves with nothing they wanted to share with each other, and nothing in particular to say. Petra's relationship with Tyler began almost simultaneously with her mom and Beau's romance, and it had struck her as embarrassing and improper that she and her previously reserved fifty-something mother were experiencing butterflies and starry-eyed fumblings at the same time. Her distaste for their coupling was amplified by Beau's overtly gracious, drawling Georgian manner. To Petra, he was like a central casting reject from *Gone with the Wind*, too stereotypically Southern to realistically portray a Southerner.

Petra's rumination on Beau's irksomeness continued until she heard her mother say, "I know it's late, but don't worry, I'm not driving back tonight. I'm going to stay at least until Monday, maybe longer. My daughter needs me." Despite the impending darkness, and the roughly four-hour distance between NYC and her mother's Maryland abode, Petra hadn't considered that her mother would be staying the night, let alone several days. She had been disappearing into blue solitude for so many weeks that she felt uneasy at the prospect of several sun-soaked, coddling days with her mother. If your nighttime eyes needed to readjust to bright light, why not your dimmed spirit, she wondered?

Saying goodbye to Beau, Calli turned elatedly towards Petra. "It's settled, just you and me, kid! I am so excited to spend time with you!"

Calli's joy was so pure that Petra felt prickles of guilt offering any opposition, but she couldn't resist. "Umm, time together would be great, but you and Beau didn't plan on this, you don't have any clothes with you… isn't this an inconvenience? Please don't feel obligated to stay. I'll be fine."

Ignoring the subtle innuendo to vacate, now, her mother reassured, "You are never an inconvenience, darling. Besides, you know I always carry an overnight bag in my car. The Girl Scout in me, always prepared." Petra looked at her dubiously, to which Calli quickly retorted, "I know I was never a Girl Scout, but I would've made a good one. Anyway, let me grab my things from downstairs, I'll be right back."

She quickly exited, tossing a kiss over her shoulder, the honeyed intensity of her exuberance and perfume lagging behind. Petra was truly torn between blubbering child wanting Mommy and tormented adult needing her quiet space. "Shit" was all she managed to articulate, and then louder and more desperately, "Shit!" She had always been close with her mom, and the prospect of more cozy homemade meals and handholding was soothing, but a large part of her wanted to recede back into her unraveling blanket, and to confront, or avoid, her unraveling world alone, on her own terms. Calli personified inquisitiveness and airy luminosity, and Petra was afraid of the sleeping demons her mother's piercing attention might release from their dusky prison. She closed her eyes, and rummaged through her knotty brain, trying to ferret out reasons that would spare her mom's feelings while guarding her own protective denial. Drawing a blank, she pulled on one of the blanket's loose threads until it roughly broke, and she shuddered involuntarily, subtly aware that any healing growth for her would crawl out from some kind of death.

Petra heard friendly chattering in the hallway, and Calli soon reappeared, carrying an oversized duffel, a large tote bag, and a roomy bucket purse, while pulling a wheeled suitcase. "Fritz is a godsend. He walked me to my car, and helped me carry my bags all the way back here. So nice." Smiling with gratitude, she arranged her luggage neatly, while Petra silently calculated just how many days' worth of clothing and accessories were contained in all those bags.

"Mom, that's a lot more than an overnight bag." Petra was too worn out to verbally challenge her mom's claim that she had come into the city hoping only for a beautifying facial and an impromptu lunch, and yet had shown up with enough luggage for a month-long stay. Had Tyler called Calli, and encouraged her to check on Petra, perhaps convinced she was crumbling without him, or maybe

23

out of genuine concern? The idea of Tyler coaxing her mother into some clandestine recon mission was galling to Petra and yet weirdly consoling.

Calli read the drift of her daughter's thoughts as if they were blazingly etched upon stone tablets, and shrugging her shoulders, admitted, "What can I say? Motherly intuition. And let me save you the trouble of trying to get me to leave. Where do you think you got your stubborn streak? You won't change my mind. Anyway, I think we should go to a museum tomorrow. There's a Middle Eastern textile exhibit at the Met." She continued, gaining gleeful momentum with each word, "Then we can eat at Veselka, or that kitschy place with the mannequins and Christmas lights, what was it? Umm…Trailer Park Lounge, that's it. But I'm more in the mood for Veselka. Oh, and maybe Beauty Bar for drinks and manicures? What do you think? It's not like you don't have the free time. If you're going to be jobless, broke, and single, at least you can sponge off your mom, right?"

Petra grudgingly chuckled at her mom's lighthearted teasing, and the promise of vibrant art, doughy Ukrainian delicacies, and tipsy self-pampering did seem more appealing than the fretful, solitary blackhole of her recent days. "Okay," she tentatively said, to both her mother and her own reluctant self. Folding back into the stiff, inhospitable embrace of the couch, Petra was ready to sleep again, somewhat daunted by reentry into regular life after so many shapeless hours.

"Oh no. You are not spending another night cramped on that couch, in dirty pajamas." Calli grabbed two sleekly feminine bottles from one of her bags, and coming over to Petra, helped her up, and walked with her to the bathroom, which she had superficially cleaned as Petra napped. "You are going to take a nice hot shower, and then sleep in your bed. Here, use my vanilla-sage body wash. I'm putting this mandarin fig body lotion on the sink, put it on while you're still damp, so your skin can really soak it up. Now go," she caringly instructed, pausing to kiss the top of her daughter's head, so vulnerable with its unwashed, matted hair.

The tickle of tumbling warm water, the frosting-like thickness of the soap, golden against her pallid skin, its deep buttercream scent absorbing into the steam, encasing her in an aromatic lacy orb—it all felt hedonistic and yet fundamental, the luxuriant pleasure reminding her that she needed to rejoin the living world. Petra pictured herself in a lush rain forest, apprehensions surpassed by rushing streams and penetrating shafts of liquid sunlight. Lying down in the tub, face up, she let the pulsating water splash against her, each unruly tuft of fluid an awakening pinch, cleansing her of physical and emotional grubbiness. She felt herself becoming all ages at once, malleable newborn, temperamental adolescent, wary adult, reflective elder, and it was both frenzied and cathartic. By the time Petra left the shower, and was obediently slathering on her mother's luxe body balm, she still had no grasp of her current predicament, or what secrets might be crying out from her inner self, reaching out from the past to smash the present, but she was determined to start moving again, no matter where those steps led her. Slipping into a thin cotton nightie, she collapsed into her bed, top sheet and comforter rolled down by her mom, smelling like a spiced creamsicle, and hungering for a soft, warm place to melt.

We arrive at the house in which Tyler grew up, a sprawling, white farm-house in Bedford, New York, as clean and classic as him. We've been together for nearly two months, and our relationship is organic, taking on a life of its own. We never define it, never have to, we just are. Neither of us has claimed the other as our boyfriend/girlfriend. Our union exists above categorization, rendering any labels superfluous, as unneeded as identifying ourselves as living beings. Our belongings have effortlessly migrated in between our apartments, toiletries and clothing not intentionally brought, but decidedly left behind. I don't remember spending many nights apart after our first intoxicating sleepover. We are both busy in our last semester, with classes and plans for post-graduation careers, but are perceptive enough to give each other space even as we share a bed. We fit into each other's social circles, we have meshing entertainment and cultural aesthetics. There is no reason for separation.

Tyler has suggested spending the weekend at his family home. His parents are visiting friends in San Diego, and we both need a reprieve from late semester craziness and the relentless buzz of the city. Arriving in mid-afternoon, the spring sky is still optimistically bright, and he has planned to show me around the quaint town—small arthouse movie theater, the moody, artisanal coffee shop, welcoming boutiques, homey bakery—but soon after entering the sizable yet inviting house, with its rustic, shabby chic décor, we are entwined on the den's pillowy alabaster couch, lost in its soft enveloping hold. We aren't even outdoors, and yet just being in this suburban enclave with the faint flavor of rural countryside, we feel like we are drinking in fresh mountain air, lazing together in that sun-drenched room.

We probably grab something to eat in the spacious, cherrywood kitchen. I am struck by the neatly arranged, well-stocked cabinets and pantry, how they evoke feelings of maternal proficiency, making me miss my childhood home, sold soon after the divorce, and giving substance to Tyler's mother, a woman I have yet to meet but who seems ever-present in all the carefully placed objects. By early evening, we are sitting together in the large claw-footed tub in the master bath, the water never seeming to get cold, as if passing clusters of minutes are merely seconds. Holding court on a nearby shelf is a collection of luxurious bath goods, elixirs and oils in crystalline bottles that stand in stark contrast to the unpretentious, lived-in vibe of the house. Tyler notices my attention being drawn to one of the bottles, its pale, flaxen contents provocatively glistening in a slender, baroque flask. He reaches for it, removing the stopper, and placing the decanter beneath my nose. A contented murmur escapes from me as I inhale the scent, redolent of morning dew, honeysuckle, and sandalwood. He pours a steady stream of the oil into the bath, and then empties some more into his hands, caressing it into my arms, and then my inner thighs, in deepening, sensual strokes. So much of the bottle is emptied, but I know he isn't being wasteful or entitled. It is a manifestation of his devotion to us, an anointing of our bond. He wants me to know that he will hold nothing back from me, ever.

Chapter 4

Having enjoyed the ultimate guilty pleasure breakfast, hot buttery chocolate croissants and cream drenched brown sugar lattes, and done some unhurried
window shopping, Petra and her mom arrived at the Metropolitan Museum of Art
at eleven o'clock. Standing before the mammoth steps, Petra felt like a battered
veteran returning home from a battle that was still raging, safe momentarily but
who knew for how long? Still, the guarded hopefulness was a welcome change
from the listless negativity of her days prior to Calli's visit. Art had always been
central to Petra's life: sketching, dabbling in ceramics and painting, haunting mu-
seums and galleries, always reading up on new artists. When she had chosen a
minor in Art History, it had nothing to do with practical concerns for future job
marketability. She took those classes simply because she wanted to. They tapped
into a reservoir of perception, feeding her enthusiasm for literature, making her
more creative in her essays, keeping her passionate about living. Entering the front
lobby of the Met, she grabbed for her mother's hand, eager to explore this link to
her previous self, to begin this cautious rebirth. Map held between them, they
headed for the fabric exhibit.

The Persian textiles were contained within three adjoining rooms, each
cloth so intricate, so finely detailed, that Petra found herself engrossed, getting lost
in the dazzling jewel tones, and shaded interplays of pattern and texture. It was
like looking into a massive kaleidoscope, and she was almost dizzy from the intense onslaught of stimuli after two weeks of seeing only the confining tedious
walls of her apartment. She was still a muted, unsure version of herself, but feeling
increasingly relieved to be breathing in life again. After thoroughly digesting the
assortment of exotic drapery, Petra and Calli moved on to the interlocking

chambers of classic paintings, leisurely winding through the maze of sensory candy. Petra especially loved the variety of female depictions in the canvases, the ethereal goddesses, the beatific Madonnas, the plush, rotund nudes, the contorted, mocking abstractions. These diverse renderings of feminine physicality anchored her back into her own body, making her want to regain lost sinew and color after her prolonged stretch of neglected nutrition and exercise.

Mother and daughter continued on in tandem solitude, providing each other the comfort of proximity and space, when Calli suddenly burst into unabashed enthusiasm, "Petra, look! It's our favorite!" She impatiently led Petra by the hand to an immense painting, an epic masterpiece saturated with fiery ruby and orange hues, its depiction of violence and fear so striking that the figures in the piece appeared to be flesh-and-blood actors eternally suspended in a gripping stage performance. It was the *Rape of Tamar*, by Eustache Le Sueur, a French seventeenth century artist. Petra followed her mother's lead, fondly recalling the hours they had spent staring at it during at least a half dozen previous visits. Petra had inherited much of her mother's artistic sensibility, and upon first sight, they had both entered into the painting, traveling beneath the brutal outward theme, seeing the masterful dance between technique and artistry. Color and light, shape and form, wondrously capturing emotional complexity, transmitting all the dark beauty and despair of existence. Not having seen their beloved portrait for several years, they decided to pause at a nearby bench and savor the reacquaintance.

A very attractive Mediterranean appearing female sat next to them, sketching intently. She seemed young to Petra, barely drinking age, and yet very self-assured in both her drawing and comportment, making precise determined movements with her pencil, occasionally pausing to scan her surroundings with bored superiority. Unnerved when the sketcher's condescending gaze perched upon her, Petra returned to the painting, and now the recoiling terror of Tamar began to overshadow the optical richness of the piece. She saw only a vulnerable victim, so different than the arrogant girl next to her, and alarmingly similar to herself. But why did she feel oppressed and at risk, Petra wondered? That's what she still couldn't figure out. The painting was becoming discomfiting in its unwelcome resemblance to her emotional plight, and Petra couldn't bear to look upon it any longer. Closing her eyes for relief, she breathlessly uttered, "I just want to be myself again." Petra hadn't realized she said it out loud until the girl beside her snickered with amused disdain.

Calli laced her arm with Petra's, and sympathetically responded, "Aah, sweetheart, you are still you, and that is a wonderful thing. You just got a little sidetracked by old issues, but you will get through this. You're very strong."

Petra felt irritation slowly pulsing up from her gut. "What do you mean, old issues? What are you talking about?"

"Oh, Petra, don't get defensive. You know that you've had a tendency to self-sabotage in the past." Petra looked at her blankly, so Calli continued, "Did you forget junior high, your advanced math class? The whole first month, you cried that it was too difficult, that you were going to fail, and you refused to do any homework, left your tests blank. Once your teacher and I got you to calm down, and do your assignments, you got straight A's for the whole year. Or high school, when your art teacher chose you to paint the mural for the main entryway? You demanded to be taken off the project, convinced you'd make a crummy painting that everyone hated. You refused to paint it until your teacher thought of making her nine-year-old nephew with special needs your assistant. Through teaching him, you were finally willing to paint, and that mural turned out to be breathtaking."

"Seriously, Mom? Why don't we go back even further. You know, I dropped out of Girl Scouts too, when I got frustrated selling those damn cookies. Maybe that's the root of my problem."

Pausing just long enough to shoot the still-snickering sketcher a knife-like warning look, Calli continued, "Fine, be sarcastic, but I'm serious. Here's a more recent example. Tyler." She raised her eyebrow, gently challenging Petra, knowing that her daughter's curiosity would offset her desire to terminate the conversation. "You wanted to end things a few months into your relationship because you felt you were too in sync, too quickly. I'm not a psychologist, but I think you get frightened when confronted with potentially amazing things. Maybe you think you don't deserve them, or that they are too good to be true, so you want to cut them off before they get taken away."

Petra flashed Calli an exasperated look, no longer aware of the snide girl and her bitchy sketching. She wanted to argue, to say that her mother was over-analyzing, being judgmental and unhelpful. Yet, no clever comeback or defense emerged. She knew her mother was right. Some unknown but very real source of doubt burrowed inside her, insidiously reappearing, fleetingly kept at bay but never completely crushed. A silent tear of admission trickled down Petra's cheek, liquifying her anger, and Calli stood up and nodded towards the exit, reinforcing her daughter's tenuous steps as they left the cavernous museum. The atmosphere had gotten progressively muggy, but Petra found the close dampness reassuring, a balmy hug wrapping around her after the vast coolness of the Met.

"I think we could use a nice lunch," Calli suggested. "If we go to Veselka, I am definitely having the potato and mushroom dumplings with sour cream. And we can share those cherry cheese blintzes." Petra had always loved Eastern European comfort food, and was dreaming about which high carb, dairy-rich confection she would choose, when Lexi, Tyler's previous girlfriend, unexpectedly leapt into her mind. Lexi was some ethnic mix of that area, primarily Ukrainian or Russian, and Petra envisioned her in all her apple-pie prettiness, big aqua eyes and wide rosy cheeks, pouring buckets of sympathy on Tyler, offering to fill the void left behind by "that awful Petra." Nauseated by that mental picture, Petra decided that anything remotely Slavic would be unpalatable.

"No, I don't want to go there. I haven't been outdoors in forever, and I need the sunlight and the fresh air. Since we're here at Central Park, let's just grab something, and eat outside. I think that food truck across the street is selling empanadas. We can grab some and walk around the park."

"Yeah, that's fine. I'm just happy to be with my beautiful daughter. Anyway, I won't be seeing any empanada food trucks in my small town, so why not?"

A short while later, the fragments of their to-go meal resting in their paper napkin covered laps, Petra and her mother sat on a bench at the entrance to one of the park's wooded footpaths. Although a refuge of lushly green nature, the park still pulsated with the city's brisk rhythm, and they both watched the unfolding live action production with rapt attention. Laser focused runners swiftly careening somewhere between work and home busyness; trust fund debutantes and underprivileged inner-city teens all wearing the same fashionable athleisure and world-weary expressions despite the economic gulf separating them. Droves of tourists trying to survive within the high velocity of urban existence, while straining to capture it all on camera; bohemian free spirits living in the moment, absorbing all the commotion and channeling it into emotive poetry, painting, music, and dance. Hard and soft, concrete and otherworldly, undeniably mingling in their seeming disconnectedness. Petra didn't know where she fit into this lovely mayhem anymore, but she was eager to start finding out.

It was Calli who finally turned away from the diverse pageantry, feeling the weight of unspoken intentions. "Petra, about before, I'm not trying to hurt or insult you. I just—"

Petra interrupted her gently, picking up Calli's hand, "I know Mom." Nodding slightly, "I know. There are patterns that I have to somehow uncover and get free of, and I will, but I need to do it in a way that's right for me. Be there for me, like you've always been, but trust me to handle things at my own pace." Calli nodded, her loyalty and compassion potently soundless.

It is early June, and Tyler and I have completed our Columbia education, his PhD and my bachelor's degree. The formal graduation ceremonies are over, as well as the festivities with family, and now we are having a private celebration in his apartment, where I have been staying since moving out of my dorm. I have tried to re-create his grandmother's banana pudding, and he is making my favorite, Shepherd's pie. Cardboard boxes litter his already cramped apartment, as he is getting ready to move to Chicago for an adjunct professorship at the University of Chicago, continuing his focus on developmental linguistics. I am staying in NYC, looking for an apartment close to my upcoming job at Ruby Dell, a boutique publishing firm on Madison Ave. I interned there the summer before my senior year, and they had guaranteed me a position as an assistant editor once I graduated, so moving to Chicago with Tyler has never been broached by either one of us. I consider this romantic meal a goodbye, poignant but necessary. We are literally heading in opposite directions, and I don't think a long-distance relationship is feasible.

As much as I dread being apart from him, can't even remember what being pre-Tyler Petra feels like, I am almost relieved that geography has made the decision for us. In our three months together, we have quickly reached a profound physical and emotional intimacy. Our sex life continues to be unbridled and exciting, but we have also become buddies, totally at ease with one another. Holey, shapeless pajamas and grimy ripped socks, retainers and athlete's foot ointment, all in plain sight. Childhood bedwetting confessions, embarrassing acne stories, unrequited infatuations, we have readily shared everything. Every door seems to be wide open already, and if you're going to be confined to one house for the rest of your life, shouldn't some rooms be left unexplored, leaving something to discover later? Sure, it has been liberating being so naked in body and soul, but I fear that we have peaked too soon, and that the only possible forward movement is to speed downhill…to crash. Maybe my parent's lackluster marriage and eventual divorce have jaded me, made me a romantic fatalist, but I am concerned that lying beneath our instantaneous closeness is a complacent familiarity, just waiting to implode into disregard, boredom, and infidelity, our previously amusing, adorable quirks becoming nothing but annoying turnoffs. I don't want that...who would? Our time together has been so heart-stoppingly exquisite, so absolute, why not let it go before it lets go of us?

I fidget upon a stool as he arranges the Shepherd's pie, my eyes boring into his back as I gulp my red wine, wanting to blunt the fury my verdict is unleashing within me. The alcohol swirls my thoughts even more...I am crazy about this man, but we can't sustain this, it's just too much, it happened too quickly, we got carried away by the sex, and started spending way too much time together, it was a fantasy, definitely incredible, mind-blowing, mmmmmmm, I want him now, I wish he'd toss that damn Shepherd's pie onto the floor, and bend me over the counter, then I want to nuzzle against him, breathing in his muskiness, falling asleep in his arms... Stop it, stop! The fantasy is over; it's time to get real again.

Placing the casserole in the small, antiquated oven, Tyler reaches for the cheap wine resting on the tiny splintering table, and pouring himself a healthy glass, sits next to me. His nearness whips up already frazzled emotions, and I want to be as close to and as far away from him as possible. He goes into his pocket, and pulls out a small object, wrapped in crinkled tissue paper and tied with a blood-red string. He's proposing!, *I think in terror, mixed with the slightest hint of gladness. Okay, just open it, be calm. My unsure fingers fumble with the string, until a speckled, slate gray sphere tumbles out. "Oh, it's a rock." Now I am just confused. His steady gaze is inscrutable, calmly detached. I feel a vibrational pressure to speak, and my words clumsily drop like the rock itself. "This is, uh, quite lovely, I like the depth of color. Umm, it's a volcanic stone from the Pompeii exhibit we went to at the Museum of Natural History, right? Wow, this is...oh...uh, how thoughtful of you." He quickly explodes in a fit of uncontrolled laughter, throwing his head back, and wiping the glee-induced tears from his cheeks. "My gosh, you are so cute, Petra. I was going to give you this first," and he reaches into the crammed junk drawer beneath the tabletop, handing me a card with a floating cherub hovering contentedly in an otherwise empty ether, "but I wanted to see you struggling to appear excited about a rock." In a daze, I open the card, his clear, crisp handwriting momentarily lulling me. The ink is deep and leaden in color, matching the rock, its heft adding weight to every word.*

Petra,

This rock is from my backyard at home. When I was eleven years old,
I was going to sleepaway camp for the first time, and I was terrified.
The car was packed up, and I didn't want to leave. I cried and begged
my mom to let me stay. She hurried into the backyard, and returned
with this stone.

She placed it in my hand, curling my fingers around it, and she said,
"Whenever you feel far from home, hold this, remember that home
is always with you," and she placed her hand over my heart.
A few weeks ago, I was finishing up a paper on ancient word roots,
and I came across the Greek word for rock, Πέτρα. This is the root of
your name.

Petra means rock. I realized then how much I love you.
We haven't been together very long,
But you're the foundation of everything I want to build.
You are my rock, the only home I'll ever want or need.

Chapter 5

The remaining time with Calli was a gladdening blend of fattening food, urban meanderings, and therapeutic reorganization. Petra's refrigerator was full, her stomach was satisfied, her apartment and mind increasingly bright and decluttered, and her muscles tired but regaining strength after long, active days. Seeing her daughter's spirit and body mending, Calli was relieved, and began making plans to leave. "This has been wonderful, I needed this as much as you did," Calli expressed as they collapsed onto the sofa after a day browsing through Soho and catching an early evening jazz concert in Tompkins Square Park. "How old do you think that bass player was? He looked barely sixteen. I wonder if he ran away from home? I should've given a bigger tip," Calli mused.

"You are such a mom."

"Guilty. I admit, I do want to stay here and hover, but I'll probably just get on your nerves. I can only bribe you with pancakes for so long. Anyway, I should probably head back tomorrow. I have to get organized for my trip up to Grandma's."

"What trip? Did something happen to the house?"

"Not really," Calli said, now pensive, and taken to some location outside the room. "Aunt Chloe and I have decided that it's time to sell it. We weren't ready after Grandma died, but we've had so many problems with tenants, and there's just too much upkeep. It's better if we put it on the market. We stored a lot of her things in the attic, and we're going to sort through everything after July 4th."

Years of glittering summers and storybook Christmases instantly came alive within Petra, a warm stream of silky soft images carrying her back into her grandmother's arms. Making homemade donuts, running on the beach, hot cocoa after Midnight Mass, nighttime folk tales…spending time with her grandma had been like wandering through a gumdrop forest with a fairy godmother, honeyed and magical. The past enchantment followed Petra into the present, and she made a snap decision, "I want to help you, I'll go up to the house, and we can go through Grandma's things together. It's too much for you and Aunt Chloe to do on your own. I'll feel so close to her, being around her books and old records, all the knick-knacks and photo albums. She'd want us all to be there. Maybe Connie and Russ can come too. I never get to see my cousins anymore."

An uneasy smile spread upon Calli's face, and her voice emerged with an artificial politeness, "Yes, that sounds nice, but I was planning to set aside some of Grandma's things for you. Chloe and I are going to give ourselves a couple of weeks to go through everything, we can manage just fine. You've got your own stuff going on now, honey, and you don't need to concern yourself with anything else."

"I know you're worried about me, but I could use a change of scenery. I want to do this."

"Oh honey, I realize you had wonderful times there with Grandma, and it's understandable you'd want to revisit that, but this really isn't that kind of trip. God knows I love my sister, but let's be honest, she's problematic. She's always thought that I was Mom's favorite, and that you were unfairly pampered, at the expense of her children. I know I'm going to have to soften a lot of her wounds, and you coming…I'm just afraid that will stir up her resentments even more. I promise, I'll make sure you get something special of Grandma's to hold on to," Calli explained, summarily patting her knee. "Okay." Petra detected no trace of a question in her mother's last word, no room for debate. So, she compliantly nodded, fully aware that her mother's obstinance pointed to something more ominous and complicated than Aunt Chloe's jealousies, but intuitively wanting to shield herself and Calli from whatever it was.

The next morning, Petra awoke to yet another fragrant gust seeping deliciously under her bedroom door. Stretching indulgently, one last press against the satiny solace of her sheets, she felt at once sad her mom would be leaving, and excited about independently finding new direction, unknown paths stretching before her, alluring in their mystery. Fuzzy steps in her fluffy slippers, she entered the kitchen, and saw her mother expertly drizzling some tawny glinted liquid over a steaming plate. A wistful glaze fell over her fatigued face, knowing that without the cosseting presence of either her mother or Tyler, she'd be doomed to lifeless breakfasts of yogurt, cereal, and insipidly sweet grocery baked goods.

"There you are. I was just coming in to wake you. Since I'm leaving today, I wanted to make you something extra special for breakfast. Apple cinnamon crepes with homemade butterscotch sauce and almond Chantilly cream… which is just a fancy way of saying whipped cream with almond extract. What do you think?"

"Despite the threat of a diabetic coma, that sounds like an amazing breakfast." Thank you for spoiling me, Mom. I'm really going to miss you."

"Me too, but you know that you can come stay with me whenever you want, right? You can job search and post your CV as easily from Maryland as here."

"Yeah, that's true," she said unenthusiastically, reminded of the daunting flip-side of the unknown. When you don't know what you want, how do you even begin the process of getting there?

Wanting to break the sudden dreariness, Calli placed the syrupy meal in front of Petra, who contentedly devoured every gooey morsel, her universe temporarily confined within the sumptuous plate. Petra remained at the table after she finished eating, her mother refusing any help cleaning up, and herself too lazily sated to argue. As Calli was drying the last of the cookware, she stopped for a moment, and called out to Petra, a bit timidly, "Honey? I didn't mean to put pressure on you before. When you are ready to look for work, you will. You can stay with me just to unwind, to recharge. Consider it a spa getaway. I made Beau put together a Zen space for me in the garden. It's so peaceful. I've got pictures if you want to see." Not pausing for an answer, she grabbed her phone, and began scrolling through her photos. Handing the phone to Petra, she waited expectantly for a reaction.

Petra saw various sunshiny images of a bubbling stone fountain, a serenely knowing Buddha statue, and a handcrafted bamboo bench, surrounded by a verdant rock garden. "Beau did all of this?" she asked incredulously. Calli nodded, and Petra was impressed in spite of herself. "Wow, it's beautiful." Maybe good old Cubby isn't that bad after all, she grudgingly considered.

"I hoped you would like it. I think you'll find it inspiring. You could get back into drawing and painting. Oh, that reminds me…." She quickly darted to one of her many bags, all standing at attention by the front door. Rummaging through her tote, she emerged with what appeared to be a large, spiral bound notepad. "I came across this in the back of my hall closet when I was packing to come here. It's your old sketch pad. You always loved drawing, and I thought maybe you'd like to start again."

Petra took it from her mother, silently deciding whether she was pleased or annoyed to be seeing her sketches again. The past few days had reawakened some of her latent drive, but she still felt miles away from her regular self, and she worried that her old drawings could be heckling reminders of her vanished creativity rather than inspirational incentives. Despite her misgivings, she flipped through the handful of completed drawings, long forgotten, but now vividly rematerializing before her, the scope of the sketches extending beyond the limits of the page, to the early adolescent girl intently drawing them, serious and slightly awkward, but budding and hopeful. The drawings were mostly snippets of Petra's Massachusetts upbringing, buzzing suburban parks, autumnal apple orchards, majestic rafting adventures, ice skating on ponds stilled by grasping Northeast winters. She scanned them with vaguely sentimental interest, until she reached one of her grandmother. The woman's kind, reassuring smile was subtly outshone by the sulky shadings of charcoal, rendering the portrait a foreboding pallor. Petra impulsively shut the portfolio, thus shutting out her own qualms about reengaging her artistic nature.

"Thank you, Mom. I think I will start drawing again."

"Good, that makes me happy. By the way, did you notice that girl sitting next to us at the museum? Did you see her sketches?"

"I did see her, but I didn't look at what she was drawing." Petra realized that she had been so distracted by the girl's conceitedly restrained manner, in contrast to her own self-doubting turbulence, that she hadn't actually looked at her drawings.

"Friggin' stick figures, lopsided rainbows, misshapen hearts…stuff a kindergartner would be embarrassed to take credit for. Meanwhile, she's sitting there like she's the fucking heir apparent to Da Vinci."

"Mom," Petra laughed, "you never curse."

"That bitch deserves four letter words. I heard her snide chuckling; she's lucky I didn't punch her smug, talentless face. Asshole. Everything she pretends to be, you already are." There it was, pure mama-bear protectiveness and unapologetic bias, and Petra suddenly felt bad for that puffed-up girl, so obviously unsoftened by maternal care. Grateful for the replenishing balm of her own mother's visit, Petra walked Calli and her entourage of luggage to the nearby parking garage that housed her car. They hugged, and held back tears, sharing intentions to see each other again before summer's end.

Reentering her apartment, Petra felt strange being alone again, but knew she was getting back on track, and not about to re-wallow in dirty pajamas and spartan meals. Ambling over to the couch, she noticed several neatly arranged piles of clothing and towels. "Oh Mom, you did my laundry." Gathering up the first mound, she noticed the familiar red, nubby cotton of Tyler's sweat pants and the muted black of his worn-out T-shirt. "He must have worn these on his run the morning before we broke up," she reflected. Petra imagined him getting up early that day, running through Greenacre Park, full of nervous anticipation, rehearsing the proposal, so naively oblivious of the train wreck awaiting him. She buried her face in his clothes, molecules of his musky scent stubbornly clinging on to the laundered fabric. The rest of the day, she busied herself, beginning to respond to weeks of emails, texts, and voicemails, paying bills, reading, treating herself to Thai food, and yet those clothes ran after her, as if Tyler were still wearing them.

It has been an unusually cold and wet spring, and the only bright spot is my grandmother's visit. I hadn't realized how much I miss spending time with her. Grandpa died unexpectedly a few months before, and my mom thought Grandma should spend Easter with us in Massachusetts. My freshman year of high school has so far been anticlimactic. The honor's courses I'm taking involve lots of home-work but aren't particularly enriching or thought-provoking. I am firmly ensconced in the middle tier of popularity, socializing mostly with my familiar and safe clique of junior high pals, no dangerous poetic loners or exotic foreign exchange students to spike the tedium. No handsome jock from the upper classes has detected my reclusive beauty, whisking me from teenage obscurity into raucous parties and midnight joyrides in his fast convertible. But I still have my art, and Grandma is glad to be my model. She sits at the kitchen table, sorting through dry beans for her famous chili. Her face portrays calm involvement in the task, and that's what I mean to capture, but something unintentional creeps into the movement of my charcoal stick, a vapor of melancholy falling onto the page. The finished portrait is endearing and tragic, and I'm not sure if the faint, sneaking sadness comes from her or me, or is something repressed between the two of us. We both look at the sketch, smiling uneasily, and feeling unspoken relief when I safely shut it away inside the pad.

...I am doodling on a napkin, a naked couple facing each other, locked

in frightened solitude, on a raft teetering in the middle of an opaque, choppy ocean. Tyler and I have been in Jamaica for a couple of days, and we are idling on a white sand beach, sipping rum punch from an oversized goblet, our bronzed necks adorned by adorably garish shell necklaces. Peering over at my scribbles, he's almost awestruck.

"Wow, that's incredible. How are you doing that with a cheap pen and a wrinkled napkin? That's the most arresting and optimistic depiction I've ever seen of...love."

I become awestruck as well, because no other person has ever understood my most exposed art in this way. Similar pieces of mine have been described as disturbing and cynical. Only Tyler has ever delved so perceptively into my artistic vision, experiencing my work as if we two inhabit the same soul. The drink and the napkin are now placed aside, and we are imprinted upon the supple sand, Tyler and I, deliriously lost in our own fathomless sea.

Chapter 6

Opening her eyes while nighttime darkness was being gradually inhaled by the first wobbly breaths of morning light, Petra felt the echoes of her dreams upon her, and she knew that she had to see Tyler. It was barely 6:00 a.m., and hours away from casually appropriate texting time, but she was already saturated with nervous energy, and unable to fall back asleep. She brewed some vanilla praline coffee her mom had purchased, and plopped onto her couch, compulsively checking the time on her phone, seconds pushing sluggishly through quicksand. She had no idea what she wanted to say to him, if there even was anything to say, but she could barely wait for the chance to say it. Should she invite him over? Was it better to call or to text? Maybe he had blocked her. No, he wouldn't do that, she was sure, if only because he was too responsible to miss a potential emergency call. He might hate her but he'd want to know if she was hit by a car. Texting, that was probably best, she thought, less intrusive than the perhaps unwelcome assault of her voice.

After a halfhearted attempt at reading a romance novel left behind by Calli, and a forced breakfast of peanut butter-laden English muffin, she took a prolonged shower and tried to choose the right ensemble for their potential meeting. A gauzy summer dress and shimmery makeup might carry too many brazen, manipulative overtones, like "I'm so happy I dumped you," or "Forget what I said and undress me now," while drab sweats and lack of grooming could scream *Girl, Interrupted* instability and helplessness. She settled on brown mascara, clear lip balm, cream capri pants, and a sleeveless lime green top that tied at the waist, subtly feminine but unfussy. As she rummaged through the bottom of her closet for tan canvas flats, her hand knocked against the cold plastic of a storage container.

Pulling it out, she immediately recognized the stash of mementoes from her travels with Tyler. Twisted against one of the clear sides were the Jamaican shell necklaces, resembling bitter orphans who long ago gave up hope for a happy home. Almost automatically, she placed the box in a nearby Bloomingdale's shopping bag, and walking into the living room, retrieved Tyler's sweatpants and shirt, placing them atop the box. Petra then texted Tyler to meet her at the Bluebird Café, and exited her apartment without waiting for a response.

*****

An hour later, Petra was nursing an iced matcha latte at the Columbus Circle eatery, eyes anxiously revived from meditative staring whenever the door opened. Tyler hadn't replied to her text, but she trusted that he was coming, relying on his ingrained kindness to overcome whatever bitter satisfaction he might take in imagining her alone, insecurely waiting for him. She had hoped to get there before him, so she could at least appear outwardly settled, furtively stashing away any nervous twitches inside the sturdy bones of her chair. As she waited, she became increasingly frustrated with herself, aware that by indulging the whim to contact him, she had created this annoying anticipation. Wondering if she should just give up and close this chapter of her life for good, her eyes fell upon the faded red flabby pants sagging into the bag, and her eyes moistened, as if Tyler was also unalterably loosening and shrinking away. The coarse yanking of a chair threw her, and she saw him, situating himself with an air of impatience. With a fed-up twist of his hand and an arched brow, he beckoned her to speak.

A barely audible "Hi" was all Petra could muster.

Waiting a few more seconds for her to continue, Tyler pressed, "All right, what do you want?"

Petra had expected some hostility, being that his initial pained shock at her rejection had hardened into sullen silence the next morning as he packed his things, followed by steely indifference when he had dropped by on subsequent occasions to collect his mail and other belongings. Then, there had been no contact at all, until now. Still, Petra had hoped that the time apart had somewhat softened the blow of the breakup, and that they could begin salvaging the friendship aspect of their once intimate relationship. He was her best friend, and she desperately missed him.

"I came across some of your clothes, and, um, you know, travel souvenirs we picked up over the years, and I thought…maybe you might want them?" she practically stuttered without any conviction.

The entrancing seduction of her recent dreams was boiling over into reality, being this near to him again, and she wanted to reenter those celestial memories with him, to invite him back into their sheltered past, but she resisted, scared of acknowledging depths of feeling she had contradicted when she refused his proposal. He observed her with mild distaste as she struggled to quell her teeming impulses, shifting uncomfortably in her chair as she reached for the shopping bag. He took it from her irritably, tossing the tattered clothes onto the table, then grabbing the bin of keepsakes. He shook it towards her as he spoke, the festive vestiges of their former life a grenade in his angry hands, his quiet fury blasting into full-on rage.

"You think I give a shit about ratty workout clothes and tacky shell necklaces we bought when we were drunk in Jamaica? What the fuck is wrong with you?" he loudly snarled, slamming down the container. The young mother breastfeeding at the next table stared in uncomfortable fascination, and the Bible-camp-looking teens on the opposite side murmured in shocked disapproval, but Tyler's rage was well beyond the influence of decorum. "You crushed me, Petra, you demolished the entire foundation of my life, what I thought was *our* life. For eight years, everything I experienced, all of my plans, my decisions, you were at the center. Good and bad, I wanted to go through it with you. You gave meaning and substance to my accomplishments, to my dreams. I knew I wanted to marry you that first evening I ran into you at that café, when you made me drink that disgusting mint coffee. I thought, if I could be having this much fun under these fluorescent lights, in this uncomfortable chair with this horrible coffee, it must be the girl. I'm already falling in love."

"Tyler," she interrupted, "let me—"

"No, I am not listening to anything else you have to say. It's my turn. Your reason for ripping us to shreds? 'There's something missing,'" he scornfully imitated her, stilting his voice and raising his pitch, "'and if you're honest with yourself, Tyler, you'll see something was missing on your end too.' Where the fuck do you get off telling me what I feel? I have no idea what's gotten twisted in your head, Petra, but just because you're in denial about what we meant to each other, don't expect me to be."

43

With that, he rose abruptly, and extended one last barb. "I took everything I needed from that apartment. Whatever else you find, burn it for all I care, but don't reach out to me again." And then he was gone, again.

She wanted to run after him, but couldn't. She had nothing but empty promises and selfish regrets to offer him. Whatever psychic unease had contributed to her walking away from their relationship was still there, and until she uncovered the root of that pain, she couldn't make a real commitment to Tyler or anyone else. She grieved for him, still needed him, more than she had let herself accept, but while she was in limbo, she couldn't expect him to tread water beside her. Petra desired to exit the café and leave behind the unsettling encounter, but malaise pinned her to the chair, and she stared into her glass, the latte now awash in melted ice cubes, gray and swampy. Choosing to sip it anyway, she remained unaware of passing minutes, until a gently persistent tugging pulled her back into the restaurant.

Looking up at her with pale emerald eyes was a chubby, redheaded toddler, smiling in recognition that was lost on Petra. The child motioned for Petra to pick her up, so she did, placing her on her lap, transfixed and confused by this little dumpling of a girl who charmingly dropped from the sky. A harried, sandy-haired male ran over, apologizing and scooping the child out from her newfound perch.

"Dani, you can't run away from Daddy," he said with firm affection as he stroked her round, pink cheek. Turning to Petra, he added, "I'm so sorry," then pausing in contemplation, "You know...you kinda resemble my wife. I think Dani thought you were her mom." He chuckled embarrassedly. "Well, anyway, um, have a good day." He scurried off with his daughter, lovingly cooing through wispy kisses, "Silly girl, that wasn't Mommy." Putting her down, he grabbed a cardboard takeout tray of cotton-candy-like frozen potions, and held Dani's hand as she stared longingly back at Petra, her small clunky steps unwillingly carrying her out the door.

Petra's heart was pinned in that closing door, sorrowful for the exits of both Tyler and that angelic tyke. She helplessly realized that she didn't know where either had gone, and though she didn't fit into their lives, she greedily wished she could have both next to her now, the comforting distraction of tiny clinging arms and carnal masculinity. All she had, though, was the lingering whisper of the toddler's soapy clean bubblegum scent and the cast-off, flimsy relics of a dead relationship. Standing up and grabbing her purse, she accidentally knocked the bin of keepsakes off the table, the shell necklaces rattling against the floor. Observing the scruffy red sweats in front of the empty seat where Tyler had been, she smashed her foot into the tangled necklaces, the pulverized granules reminding her that everything returns to sand.

The long walk home was taxing for Petra. It was oppressively hot, the air around her saturated with humidity and Tyler's boiling rage. Sweat poured down her back, her feet were killing her, and Tyler and Dani's faces raided her mind, one blighted by scorn, the other pained by innocent wanting. Petra felt like she had somehow failed them both. *Don't reach out to me again... silly girl, that wasn't Mommy...* reverberated like obnoxious jingles in her ears. *Hmmm,* she mused, *who exactly was this doppelgänger Mommy?* Petra saw this phantom lookalike effortlessly prancing about from Mommy and Me yoga classes, preschool fundraisers, and lunches with other fashionable city moms, and she felt the urge to slap her familiar face for the boastful reminders of what Petra didn't and might never have.

Becoming exhausted physically and emotionally, and not wanting to backslide into indolent depression, she stopped in a small bookstore, run by the same aging hippie for as long as she could remember. The store was a mix of vintage books, antiques, art, psychedelic accessories, and new-age paraphernalia. First edition Poe and T.S. Eliot, Tiffany lamps, mood rings, Waterford crystal, Indian incense, Botticelli prints, vinyl Wagner concertos, tie-dyed shirts, and sage smudge sticks all had a home here, which is why Petra always gravitated to this multidimensional haven whenever she was feeling herself displaced, uncategorized.

"Petra! It's been so long. Come here!" exclaimed Ginevra, the earthy owner, wrapping Petra in a cyclone of ginger patchouli and paisley fringe, her effusive and long bear hug bordering on inappropriate but exactly what Petra needed. "How are you?" and not giving her a chance to answer, immediately continued, "You look like you need an escape. I have just the thing." She took Petra by the hand, and led her to a corduroy papasan chair in the back corner of her shop, shortly returning with chamomile tea and a weather-beaten book of Celtic folktales. A smell of dankness, cedar, and clove emanated from the pages of the leather-bound book, and Petra imagined that it had long languished in the library of a forested Irish estate, pipe smoke and fog from days past absorbed into its flesh. Petra began poring over the assorted vignettes, short stories accompanied by small black and white drawings, fairies and banshees, leprechauns and sea sirens, haunted castles and enchanted woods, coalescing before her. Gleefully adrift in this mythical universe, Petra closed her eyes, and soon floated into her own ghostly dreamworld.

The night Tyler gave me the rock was unlike any other. I don't recall if we ever ate the Shepherd's pie or banana pudding, but I know I wanted to consume him, and be consumed, after I read his gorgeous letter. I couldn't believe that just seconds before reading his melodic words, I had been determined to end our relationship. Chalking it up to my emotional growing pains, I internally recommitted to him, and threw myself into our union. Whatever more sinister psychological forces might be lurking behind my doubts, I wasn't aware of them, and at that moment, I refused to look any deeper.

We have loud, unapologetic sex in the kitchen, the living room, even on the fire escape, not concerned with or even aware of any life outside of us. His written admission of love is the first time that word has been shared between us, and still neither one of us says it out loud. Verbalizing "I'm in love with you" isn't necessary, as we are already within, above, and under its spell. Love positively envelops us.

We are undressed and pleasurably leaning against the sofa when Tyler brings up my relocating with him to Chicago for the first time. His uncle is a literary lawyer, specializing in contracts and copyright concerns for authors and publishers, and has connections at Watermark, a Canadian-American publishing giant with a bustling Chicago branch. "I gave him your résumé, and he can get you an interview. He thinks you'll have a great shot, especially after spending a few months here at Ruby Dell. Obviously, you are going to blow away everyone at your new job, and you'll get an amazing letter of recommendation. I can handle being separated from you, Petra, but only if I know it's temporary." Maybe it is the naked relief of being re-anchored to him after the close-call of a breakup, or just the hallucinogenic haze of multiple orgasms, but my proud feminist independence and self-reliance are now distinctly MIA, and I believe that my place in the world is wherever he is. Within a year, I am an editor at Watermark, and inhabiting a Chicago loft with Tyler.

During the interval we are apart, we make sure to see each other at least once, sometimes twice, a month. These visits are always too brief for both of us, yet so dizzyingly intense that they have to be fleeting or we would collapse from the drain of unrelenting ecstasy. Whether East or Midwest, the hours pass as a blur of hyperactive sexual intimacy, with concerts, plays, or art exhibits gratuitously wedged in. When March arrives that year, I notice I have missed a couple of periods, and a home pregnancy test confirms what I already suspect. Pregnant. Follow-up with my OBGYN reveals that I am seven weeks along. I walk home in a daze from that Friday afternoon appointment, torn between guarded excitement and nervous expectancy. Luckily, I have the whole weekend to grasp my newly altered state. There is never a question of not having it—Tyler and I are so bound to each other that concrete manifestations like house and children are inevitable—and it is this certainty that I will accept this child that has made the nebulous seedling disturbingly and wonderfully real to me. I already love and dread this hidden being, immense in its blueberry-sized tininess. It embodies my affectionate union with Tyler, all our tacit hopes, but is also the catalyst for a cascade of decisions I am not prepared to make: marriage, maternity leave, career vs. motherhood.

My most pressing concern is how and when to tell Tyler. I am not leery of his reaction, I know he'll be terrified and ecstatic like I am, I just want to announce it in a way that honors the magnitude and splendor of this event. Should I blurt it out over the phone, suddenly brandishing the grainy ultrasound image during Facetime? He'll be flying in to see me two weeks from now, maybe I can cook him a romantic dinner, and present him with a gift-wrapped baby goodie, something adorably tiny, special, and tangible, echoing our little treasure. I ultimately decide to hold off on telling him until he arrives.

One late night almost a week from my doctor's visit, I wake with an excruciating pain ripping through my belly. I lurch into the bathroom, and scream when I see intrusive red droplets scarring my underwear. As quickly as it began, it is over, and I leave urgent care that frosty Friday morning with the numb realization that I am as intact as before but now achingly incomplete. The rest of the tired weekend, I abbreviate calls, Tyler's and everyone else's, by claiming to have the flu. Diving into vats of ice cream and self-pity, I pace and sleep, ruminate and sleep some more, holding *on to my pain selfishly, not ready to invite anyone into this private netherworld. Gradually, overwhelming loss and quiet relief mingle uncomfortably, giving birth to profound guilt. Had my inner conflict caused the miscarriage? Had the developing baby felt my misgivings and rejected me as maternally unfit?*

Sunday drags on, until the mid-evening sun fully slides down, and I instinctively steady myself for the next day's work routine. I don't want the specter of this horrific loss to invade every aspect of my life, so I make the conscious decision never to tell anyone about this mixed interlude of amazed anxiety and frustrated hope, especially not Tyler. He is so emotionally generous and authentic, and

I couldn't bear the burden of his grief and mine, his relaxed, even features distorted and strained by powerless empathy and stoic resolve.

Petra opened her eyes, subsumed by the book store's yawning papasan chair, and uncontrollably wept for her lost child, haunted by its legacy of almost and never. Ginevra had patiently awaited her wakening, and was almost a half hour past regular closing time, but didn't rush Petra out of her smoggy, sad emergence from sleep. After providing a fresh cup of herbal tea, and another enthusiastic hug, she escorted Petra out into the still sunlit early evening, insisting that she keep the Irish folktales for as long as she wanted. She clutched the old book to her chest the whole walk home, a subliminal barrier against the inner devils she sensed stirring within.

Chapter 7

She awoke before sunrise with the book opened against her stomach. She had obviously fallen asleep enthralled by its faraway fantasy. Automatically, she looked for her sketch pad, finding it on her living room table. She picked up a broken and irregular nub of charcoal, and began expressing the pictures that were already drawn inside her mind. The lines seeped like fluid onto the paper, and almost by magic, she was looking at two completed pictorials. One was a discarded castle, a burning sun corroding the ruins into the ground, and the other an unlit desolate forest of gnarled, decrepit trees and haggard, creeping animals. They both possessed a horrible beauty, grotesque and captivating, and Petra marveled at the strange familiarity of these pieces. It seemed they had always lived on the surface of the paper, tattooed in invisible ink. Pragmatically, she figured the eerie Celtic tales had wandered after her in sleep, waking up in her sketches. Regardless of their origin, she treasured them as proof she was carving a new path, far from the disappointing confines of Viscount publishing, into a newly creative, unrestricted expanse.

Wanting to display them, badges of her newly burgeoning life, she needed just the right frames, too distinct to be mass produced. Petra immediately thought of the Cozy Eclectic, the home accent boutique Tyler's mother, Delaine, had recently opened in alleviation of her post-retirement ennui. The store was on the very strip in Bedford that Tyler had introduced to Petra a lifetime before, during her first visit to his childhood home. She hadn't spoken to Delaine since she had ceased being Petra-and-Tyler, but she had seen enough of the woman's gentle composure over the years to trust that she would be warmly received despite the awkward circumstances. It was mid-morning, and she felt eager to share her creative harvest with Delaine. Fashioning cardboard, wax paper, and a garbage bag into a secure means of transport, she carefully arranged the two sketches, then rapidly dressed and scheduled a Lyft into the cleansing stillness of sleepy suburbia.

In less than an hour, Petra was standing in front of Delaine's store, her sketches impatiently prompting her to enter. Once inside, she was buffeted by the fertile scent of a nearby eucalyptus plant and the train of arctic gusts from the air conditioning vent. A couple of customers were roaming around in casual appraisal, and Delaine was playing idly with a pencil as she scanned what appeared to be a ledger. Reacting belatedly to the opening and closing of the door, she looked up, a nearby stained-glass mobile scattering swatches of violet and ruby translucence over her stylishly messy golden-brown bun and light olive skin. Her surprise instantly dissolving into delight, she purposefully walked to Petra, and gathered her up in a motherly embrace.

"Sweetheart, I am so glad to see you," she expelled in a relieved murmur, softly pulling out of the hug to face Petra directly. "How have you been?"

Petra mildly shrugged, the disorganized tangle of her recent emotional fluctuations strangling any potential responses. No words could fully contain the scope of rocky terrain through which her mind had lately been trekking. Uncertain and craving assurance, she admitted, "I was afraid you wouldn't want to see me, after…everything, that's, umm…you know…me and Tyler, it's just…I mean, I think he hates me, and I understand if you do too."

Just like her son's, Delaine's deep-set, slate blue eyes were bottomless canals that ebbed and flowed with her every emotion, and now they surged into twilight infinity pools. Placing a protective hand on her shoulder, Delaine delicately spoke, "Petra, I don't exactly know what happened with you and Tyler, but I do know that I love the both of you, and whatever this is, you two will travel through it in the way you are supposed to. I'm not going to lie, Tyler is hurting, and that kills me, but I can see that you are hurting too. I'm not looking to blame anyone. And believe me," her body relaxing into a long exhalation, "Tyler couldn't *ever* hate you, even if that was his greatest desire."

Petra wanted to believe her, but Tyler's scornful parting words echoed in her ears, the harsh sound vibrating into her hands, causing her to drop the plastic bag housing her sketches.

"What's this?" Delaine asked as she rescued the bag from the floor.

"Oh, that's actually why I came today. I started sketching again, and I wanted to show them to you, and find the right frames."

Delaine led them to a nearby bronze embellished end table, where she carefully undid Petra's improvised packaging. Laying them out on the oblong glass surface, Delaine surveyed them with rapt discernment. "Petra, these are stunning. Unbelievably so. Let me check the back, I have some vintage frames I just picked up at an estate sale."

Her deliberate steps receded, and were brashly replaced by a nasal voice stabbing the previously subdued air.

"Oh my, are those originals?" the words bounding out from a manicured, coiffed fiftyish woman, blonde and attractive in a frosted, artificial way. Leaning over to see the sketches, she pushily nudged against Petra, oblivious or indifferent to her unwanted intrusion into Petra's personal space.

"What?" Petra responded in annoyed confusion.

"Are those the originals of the artist?" the blonde woman replied, slowly enunciating every word as if she were speaking to someone mentally deficient.

"I did them this morning," Petra said, turning away sharply, hoping the questioning lady would get the hint that the conversation was over.

"Well, these are nice re-creations. Are they for sale?"

"I don't work here, and I haven't a clue what you're talking about. I didn't *'re-create'* anything, I sketched them on my own this morning."

"Really?" turning to face Petra, the word drenched with accusation, and folding her arms, the woman continued, "I saw these exact drawings years ago at a gallery in Cape Cod. The artist was a man, a pretty big deal in New England in the late eighties. Preston, or Thompson, something like that. Really, you don't know who I'm talking about?"

Delaine returned just then with two baroque mahogany frames, and catching the tail end of the tense discussion, asked "What's going on here?"

With a sarcastic chortle, the customer said, "Nothing," and then appearing suddenly bored with the nuisance of Petra, she pointed impatiently towards the rear of the opposite wall, and demanded, "How much is that Cuckoo clock?"

Taking the woman's cue to follow, Delaine laid down the frames on a nearby chair, and rolling her eyes, quietly mumbled to Petra, "Cuckoo clock, fitting choice."

Petra's faint smile faded when she looked back at her drawings. She had felt so proud of them just a few moments before, sure that she was on the precipice of a very creative, enriching rebirth. Now, she felt like an imposter, cheaply peddling someone else's talent as her own. But how could that be possible, she marveled. She wasn't even alive in the late eighties, and she had never come across similar drawings at any gallery or museum that she could recall. The pictures in the Celtic book from Ginevra were along the same gothic lines, but they were different than what she had drawn, and had nothing to do with some New England artist from decades ago, if he actually existed. Petra knew rationally that she shouldn't let some vapid stranger get to her, but the brassy woman had struck a nerve, even though Petra didn't know where the nerve was located or why it was so susceptible to injury. Petra picked up one of the frames, so sturdy despite years of use, its hard-won scratches and nicks making it all the more exquisite, evoking satisfied years that filled its empty center even without a picture.

"So, what do you think? Aren't those frames lovely? Your drawings would look beautiful in them," Delaine offered, placing an arm around Petra's slouched shoulder.

"I don't know," Petra said, eyes downcast, releasing the frame from her tight clasp. "I agree, the frames are beautiful, but I'm not sure if my sketches should be framed. I kind of just threw them together."

"Petra, what did that awful woman say to you?"

"I don't know," she repeated. "She seemed confident that she had seen my drawings before, that they were originally done by some Massachusetts artist."

"Don't be silly, you're letting that upset you? I probably shouldn't insult the taste of someone who just spent money in my store, but please, she was a complete Real Housewives of New York wannabe. Money to burn and not an ounce of breeding or class. I'm sure she doesn't know the first thing about art, she couldn't distinguish between Color Me Mine and the Venus de Milo."

Petra nodded in acquiescence, but internally, her self-doubts were mounting. She reached again for the scraggly frame, needing to share in its resilience.

"You can leave your sketches with me," Delaine patted her back as she spoke. "I'll have new glass fronts inserted in the frames, and the wood can be buffed and shined. It shouldn't take too long to complete."

"Just replace the glass, nothing else. I like the imperfections."

Delaine nodded in understanding, and then added suddenly, "Oh, before I forget, I want to give you something." She walked towards the register, and shortly returned with the same book she was examining when Petra entered the store. "Here, I'm entrusting this to you."

Perplexed, Petra accepted the taupe leather journal, "I thought this was your business ledger, why are you giving it to me?"

"It's a journal of Tyler's poetry. He wrote these when he was in high school. I found it a few weeks ago during my spring cleaning, and I didn't realize what it was until I opened it. I was reluctant to invade his privacy, and left it alone, but for some reason, I saw it this morning before I came to work, and just decided to bring it with me. Then, you showed up out of the blue. You know that I don't believe anything is just a random accident. I feel you are supposed to have this. Something tells me you and Tyler will both benefit from you reading his poems."

Soon after, Petra was being shuttled back to the waiting dusk of NYC. The Lyft vehicle had no working AC, so windows and sunroof were all wide open, and the rush of damp, smoggy air from the congested highway was doing little to relieve her of the suffocating current she felt rising out of Tyler's journal. She knew he'd be furious with her and Delaine that she was in possession of something so personal of his, the hands he detested for crushing his heart now holding a piece of his soul. As much as this distressed her, she was also glad to have this pure window into Tyler from before they met, someone so known and familiar morphing back into an enticing, unexplained stranger. Petra was fascinated by what she might find, though she didn't know when she'd be ready to delve into the world of the poems, the peril of potential answers outweighing the urgency of her questions. She closed her eyes, and tried to recapture the placidity of Delaine's steadying consolation, but her frail peace was crudely punctuated by the customer's rude insinuations. If Delaine was correct, and there were no accidents, what did that snappish bottle blonde signify in Petra's existence?

Chapter 8

The following day, Petra determined to dismiss menacing thoughts of artistic plagiarism and Tyler's condemnation. She made a dessert-like creamy raspberry smoothie and prepared to take a run through the East River greenway. Petra had occasionally gone there with Jeremy, her ex-coworker, when they had aligned in one of their fleeting exercise pacts. Memories of their inside jokes, spot on impressions of officemates, and post-work goofiness tramped through her mind now, leaving regret in their wake. She had meant to stay in touch, and hadn't, except for a cursory response to his many unanswered texts. He probably hated her too, she cynically mused, just like her other friends at work, just like Tyler. Her eyes darted to his foreboding book of lost poems, and she ran out of her apartment to find the rhythmic relief of concrete steps.

*****

Pausing to catch her breath a half hour into her run, Petra bent down to tighten her shoelaces, and was startled by a light slap against her rear. Instantly regretting she had forgotten her mace spray, she defensively stood up, seeing Jeremy's round, boyish face crinkled in a mischievous grin.

"I'm glad it's really you, otherwise I was about to 'MeToo' myself right into the slammer. Though I am a gay male, so doesn't that give me the freedom to pinch a little rear and squeeze some tit?" affecting wide-eyed innocence as he exaggeratedly hovered his hand over her breast.

"Ugh," Petra disdainfully puffed, jabbing his arm away, "You are so disgusting and offensive. How I've missed you," hugging him tightly.

"Missed me, huh? Just not enough to actually call or see me, hmm?"

"I'm sorry, I've been kind of lost in my own world these days."

"I forgive you. I'm actually flattered. I mean, this bump in," employing showy air quotes, "easily qualifies as stalking."

"Busted. Seriously, I was thinking about you when I decided to come here today. Hey, why aren't you at work?"

"I needed a mental health day. Miss Melanie has been a raging bitch since you left. Paranoid City. She thinks we're all plotting to leave one by one, and steal her fucking big-name authors. She's got dipstick Penny slithering through the halls, trolling for evidence of this big coup. It's a real shit show, honey."

Pounding footprints suddenly pulsated through the ground, and they both turned as a blurred huffing runner split the air between them.

"Enough about Vis-Cunt Publishing. Let's grab some frozen yogurt, P, before we turn into *that*," nodding towards the quickly receding sprinter. Locking his arm with Petra's, he led them to the redbrick ambiance of Front Street.

After absorbing the neighborhood's mix of eighteenth century and contemporary architecture from a shaded courtyard bench, double iced espressos from Jack's Coffee swiftly gulped down, they ventured to their perpetual favorite, Big Gay Ice Cream. With a rainbow bench out front, and menu options like the Salty Pimp ice cream cone, the initial appeal to Jeremy was obvious, but he and Petra had fast discovered that the shop's frozen treats were as sublime as they were irreverent. In between dripping spoonfuls of their shared house specialty Mermaid sundae, they continued to catch up, the laughter and bantering naturally dwindling along with the indulgent contents of their Styrofoam tub. Savoring the last delectable morsel, Jeremy tilted back in his seat, fixedly studying Petra in a way that suddenly made her self-aware.

"What?" Petra posed after several protracted moments, crumpling her napkin to offset her tenseness under his microscopic watch.

"I'm sorry, I was just thinking of what eligible straights will be at the rooftop party."

"Okay, what conversation are you in? Nothing you just said makes any sense."

"Sorry. I am such a Gemini, thoughts running all over the place. The ice cream here made me think of having a "make your own sundae" bar at Clyde's Fourth of July party. He and some fellow tenants are hosting a celebration on the roof of their building because they have great views of the Macy's fireworks. I know you've been sorta laying low, but I really want you to come. I can't possibly continue my relationship with Clyde until my female bestie scopes him out, right? And there will be lots of yummy hetero guys there for you to devastate with your Kate Moss goddess-ness." Fluttering his eyelashes in emphasis, "So?"

Petra wanted to come up with a fast, believable excuse to decline, but her sugar buzzed mind and Jeremy's corny sincerity were hindering any such easy copouts. "I forgot the 4th was coming up. I guess it sounds fun. All right. Just remember, this isn't *The Bachelorette*. If I see a line of impossibly perfect guys waiting to woo me, I'm out of there, got it?"

Chapter 9

Jeremy had told her to arrive any time after seven. It was now half past six, and Petra's bedroom was a wasteland of rejected garments and unmated shoes. The sudden change of weather had thrown her, consistently overheated mugginess replaced without warning by chilly, overcast dampness. The raw, gray air lightly wafting through her window was more predictive of a Halloween gathering than a Fourth of July celebration. Turning from her closet to the knocked around clothes recuperating on her bed, Petra fished out an off the shoulder white sweater, black shimmery bra, and deep navy jeans.

Strolling out of her building, she hadn't decided how she was going to get to Clyde's Seaport district building. Proceeding towards the subway station, a vintage yellow taxi rolled out of the dusky mist like a prop from an old movie, and she instinctively raised her arm to summon the driver. His raggedy tweed hat, downturned honey brown eyes, and faint emanation of cigar smoke immediately endeared him to her, and during the fifteen-minute taxi ride, she shared her reawakening to art, the difficulty transitioning back to single life, the nervous allure of new career paths. Arriving at the tall white washed brick building, Petra gratefully handed the soothing man a generous tip, the first sound of the driver's voice mingling with an apologetic shrug of his shoulders, as he announced in a thickly Serbian accent, "Sorry no English."

A lethargic creaky elevator ushered her to the top floor, and climbing the narrow stairs to the roof, she started to hear the drone of dance music, laughter, hurried steps, and animated conversation, and wanted nothing more than to burrow back inside that mobile Serbian therapy chamber. Remembering Jeremy's pleading face catapulted her out of her hesitation, and she opened the heavy door to the night's festivities. Her first sighting was of the East River, bottomless indigo in the late day's fragile light, absorbing the ashen stillness of the sky. Seeing no familiar faces, Petra skirted the crowd, clustered in intimate groupings, and walked towards the edge of the concrete expanse, breathing in the air and watching the upriver barges that would soon be splashing pyrotechnic paintings onto the stratosphere. Hearing deliberate strides coming towards her, she turned to see Jeremy, casual in a Pink Floyd T-shirt and faded ripped jeans, beside a preppy, cleanly attractive male.

"Petra, you made it!" Jeremy's words beaming from his mouth, he enveloped her in an affectionate embrace. "Looking gorgeous, I might add. I'm liking this whole edgy artist look you've got going on. This my love, is Clyde."

Extending his hand, Clyde raptly assessed Petra with the faintest trace of sexual interest. "I'm glad to finally meet you. You are just as beautiful as I feared. I have to admit, I've been a little threatened by you. This one over here has been fairly inconsolable since you left Viscount."

"Please, don't give her a swelled head," Jeremy winked at Clyde, and then turning to Petra, "I just miss the delicious muffins and cookies you used to bring to staff meetings."

Clyde's phone then sounded, and looking at it, he gazed back at Petra contritely, "Forgive me, I have to respond to this, but we'll talk more later." Pointing to a billowy fairy-lit white canopy, "The refreshments and hors d'oeuvres are over there. Please make yourself at home."

Petra was surprised by the dichotomy between he and Jeremy. Wearing a crisp, light blue button-down shirt, impeccably creased beige cotton trousers, and russet Italian loafers, Clyde exuded quiet sophistication and culture. His voice, mannerisms, and subtle flirtation with her were all distinctly masculine. Petra laughed to herself, knowing that "refreshments and hors d'oeuvres" would more likely be described by Jeremy as booze and grub.

Seemingly able to read her mind, Jeremy mused, "Yep, I know, not a gay thing about him, other than his neatness and perfect grammar, of course. Old money, Protestant family. He's a newbie to all this."

"What do you mean?"

"He only came out a year ago." Pinching his thumb and forefinger together, "That poor boy was *this* close to suburban minivan agony with an icy deb named Paige. Two weeks before their huge Greenwich society wedding, he told his parents he was gay. Lucky for him, Episcopalians are more homo-friendly than Catholics. My father still barely talks to me."

They both inwardly sighed, simultaneously reflecting on their tense relationships with their respective fathers, depressingly resigned to years ahead of awkward or nonexistent paternal encounters.

"Okay, I am officially the world's worst party host," Jeremy laughed, attempting to recirculate the stale air given off by his words. "We both need a 'refreshment,'" he chirped with lovable mockery, guiding her to the bar area.

The linen covered table and steel ice buckets were well apportioned with designer vodka, tequila, rum, and whiskey, cellar worthy wines, assorted beers, mixers, and every trendy "hard" beverage, from cider to iced tea. "Hmmm, what do I want?" Petra posited, more to Jeremy than to herself.

Taking her cue, Jeremy grabbed a glass and began adroitly tempering different liquids into one seamless whole. "Your elixir, darling. Sauvignon Blanc topped off with tangerine hard seltzer and a splash of Rose's lime juice. This will get you sloshed the classy way. Drink up!" Grabbing a frosty Blue Moon for himself, they clinked drinks and walked towards two folding chairs tucked behind a half shriveled rose garden.

"I haven't seen anybody familiar. Do I know anyone here?"

"Probably not. I invited just a handful of people, and only you and Rianne from work."

"She's coming here tonight?" Petra asked hopefully.

"No. She's at her sister's in NJ for a BBQ. Is that okay? I want to introduce you to some people. Clyde is Mr. GQ real estate developer these days, but in college he was just another burnout with a trust fund, so he has a lot of interesting, anti-establishment friends and a few of them are here tonight," the last few words coquettishly uttered in singsong.

"What did I say? Don't turn this into Petra in Paradise." Seeing Jeremy's brow arching up cartoonishly, "Okay, every now and then I might briefly watch cheesy reality television, but I don't want to live it." In a quieter voice, self-consciously interlacing her suddenly jittery fingers, "I'm not…ready."

Playfully rubbing her chin, equally protective and mischievous, he coyly hummed, "Everything doesn't have to be about *that*, Sugar. Men and women, I meant. Smart, cool people you might enjoy getting to know. Let me show you off. I hope at least one person starts a rumor that you're my sweet sidepiece."

A soft giggle escaping her lips, "Maybe later, I just want to walk around by myself, and enjoy the view for now."

"You're the boss. I better check on the caterers; they've been high-maintenance assholes all evening." Reaching into his pocket, "Here. This is the key to Clyde's apartment—12 C. Feel free to go there if you need the bathroom, or to be alone, or if you hook up. Clean, supple Egyptian cotton sheets...."

"Ugh, just go!" Petra sat back, struggling to find stars through the thickening clouds. The city's electric beauty was especially intense at night, but she missed the homey, starlit clarity of the Massachusetts sky that had been the backdrop of so many past July 4th celebrations. The memories of multicolored flares exploding like jets of liquified jewels into the twinkling navy heavens flooded her mind, and she found herself comfortably dozing beside the dried roses.

Plump drops of scattered rain tickled her nose, moving her back to consciousness, and her phone revealed that it was half past eight. Walking back towards the fellow partygoers, she saw that the cool wetness had impelled most of them inside the candle glowing warmth of the canopy. Petra caught a glimpse of Clyde and Jeremy, swathed in smiling closeness, and not wanting to intrude on them or force conversation with faceless strangers, she meandered back to the unencumbered solitude of the East River view, now a rippling blanket of black water. The sweet pungency of marijuana soon reached her, and she followed its hypnotic trail, firmly on the outskirts of the roof, to a darkened corner where a young man lazily straddled the floor, wisps of smoke puckering above him. Hearing her approach, he shifted his head slightly, his heavy-lidded eyes barely registering acknowledgment as he turned back to stare at the other buildings near and far. Something about his shaggy hair, casual demeanor, and disinterested poise reminded her of Brady Rhodes, the first guy she had kissed, a month shy of her sweet sixteen.

"Do you mind if I sit here?" she asked, trying to sound nonchalant, even as she felt her teenage insecurity steadily resurrecting.

He shrugged in indifference, solidifying her return to adolescent misery. Without looking at her, he extended his joint. Pausing for just a second, Petra accepted it, and took a deep inhale. The mellow fog of the pot merged nicely with the numbing relaxation of her cocktail, and she unconsciously mirrored his laidback posture, wordlessly sharing the nighttime vista. The rain had ceased as quickly as it arrived, and though the cement ground was damp, neither minded.

"The fireworks are about to start!!" someone yelled shrilly from the center of the party, jarring both Petra and her unknown companion from their pleasant daze. They looked at each other, keenly for the first time, and attraction flickered over them simultaneously. He leaned in first, the sensory temptation of her tuberose scented neck intensified by the weed, initiating a kiss they both wanted. Rain started to pulse down again, and the inconvenience of the dripping onslaught only served to heighten the force of their chemical pull. Their passionate hollow was suddenly filled with thunderous crackling, the loudness distorting any sense of spatial distance. The seeming immediacy of the fireworks further sparked their mutual eagerness, and Petra felt the plunder of blindly groping hands, prodding under her sweater and pulling at her jeans. What had been unbridled and raw quickly veered into clumsy and inept. *How young is he?* Petra began to speculate.

Pulling back, Petra breathlessly spoke, "Wait a second."

"What's wrong?" her acquaintance asked, in a fragmented voice, awkwardness having seeped from his bungling hands into his vocal cords.

"You work with Clyde?"

"What? Who's Clyde?" he responded in a cloud of pot, frustrated lust, and swelling embarrassment.

"What's your connection to this party?"

"My older sister lives in this building."

"And you live in the city?"

"I'm about to this fall, when I start NYU."

"Grad school?" she asked with desperate hope.

"No, undergrad. Why? Are you in grad school?"

"No. So you're eighteen?"

"I will be in October. How old are you?"

"Wow, I'm uh, a little older than you. Anyway, I left something downstairs in my friend's apartment, I'll be right back," she lied, practically sprinting towards the door.

Clyde's key was suddenly red hot in her pocket, and she ran downstairs, not bothering to look at the fireworks. Fumbling with nerves and humiliation, she finally made it inside to Clyde's empty apartment, leaning against the door in deflated relief. Despite the lack of occupants and cool outside temperature, the thermostat seemed to be set to meat locker frozen, and she shivered as she searched for the bathroom. The tiny wash room was modern, clinical in its void of whiteness. The only adornment was a large circular mirror with a delicate white fleur-de-lis porcelain outline. Splashing water on her face, she stared into the unforgiving look-ing glass, seeing a horrified, confused stranger, much like the boy she had aban-doned on the roof. "Seventeen?" she disgustedly spat into the mirror. What was the age of consent in NY, she wondered? An NYU student of all things, he could wind up in one of Tyler's classes, she shudderingly considered. "Ugh, I have to get out of this godawful party. So much for avoiding *The Bachelorette*, now I've become Mrs. Robinson."

Coming into the hall, she was startled by the specter of Mitch Gainsley, her former Viscount protégé, leaning stolidly against the wall.

"Mitch, what are you doing here?"

"At the party or in the hallway?" minor condescension infusing his voice.

"Both."

"Jeremy is editing my latest book. I overheard him talking about the party with Rianne, he mentioned he was inviting you, so I figured I would drop by and hopefully run into you. I was really disappointed you left Viscount. How could you leave me like that?" At this, he slowly stepped closer to her, leaning one arm against Clyde's door and positioning himself so that her means of exit was blocked.

Still disturbed by the ill-advised encounter with the nameless teenager, she wasn't in the mood for any sexual innuendo, and replying as coldly matter of fact as she could muster, "It was time to move on. Well then, I'm going back up-stairs, see you later."

"But wait," pressing even nearer to her, "I didn't tell you why I'm in the hallway."

"That's okay," attempting to physically circumvent the barrier of his body. When previously seen through the rosy lens of her haven with Tyler, Mitch had been a harmless, refreshing distraction, but in the dense half-light of the cramped, hot hallway, Tyler painfully distant, he was an over-cologned, slippery shark that Petra needed to escape.

"Don't," his tone momentarily aggressive, then slipping back into schem-ing seductiveness. "I saw you come down here and I wanted to be alone with you. I miss spending time together. Just because we aren't affiliated professionally any more doesn't mean we can't still be friends." He reached toward her and began fondling the fabric of her sweater sleeve.

Moving to kiss her, she smelt liquor on his hot breath, and she pushed him away. "Stop it. You're making me uncomfortable Mitch, and now I'm leaving."

Pinning her against the wall, a malevolent sneer overtook his normally handsome countenance. "Don't act innocent with me. I saw you with that kid. You were about to fuck him within earshot of seventy-five people." Reaching under her voluminous sleeve to stroke her arm, "C'mon, it's obvious Mama wants to play tonight. Let's go back into the apartment." He then tried to kiss her while grabbing her hand and placing it against his crotch. Petra instantly yanked her hand away and kneed him in the groin.

"You fucking bitch!" he screeched, "mother fucker!" He continued yelling after her retreating figure, "Miss Perfect, acting like you have your shit together. You're nothing but a fraud, Petra."

Running the two flights to the roof, Petra grabbed her purse from under the canopy. Jeremy rushed over, his alarm heightened by her frazzled demeanor, "Hey, where have you been? Are you all right?"

"I went downstairs for a while. I have a headache. Here's the key, I'm going to head home. Thanks for having me."

"Let me walk you down at least." Not wanting to be cornered by Mitch again, she nodded in acceptance.

Attempting to diffuse his growing concern, Petra babbled unconvincingly, "Clyde seems really great. I'm sorry I didn't get to speak with him more, apologize for me. We'll get together soon though."

"Petra, are you really okay?"

Entering the stairwell, wary of another uninvited confrontation with Mitch, she feigned nonchalance. "Yes. I just need an aspirin and my bed. I mean it about the three of us hanging out, let's set something up."

"I'd like that. Even though I can tell that the three percent of Clyde that forgets he's gay definitely has a crush on you."

"Oh, stop it, I saw you two together, you're a good match." A solemn look fell over her. *Good match.* How many people had said that about her and Tyler?

"What is it P? Is there something going on besides a headache? Level with me, did something happen?"

Statutory rape, sexual assault, and self-defense threateningly melded inside her brain, and Petra wryly thought, *Fuck yeah something happened, take your pick.* Instead, she blandly replied, "Nothing really."

"Okay, I won't nag you. Oh, did you see that Mitch crashed the party?"

"Yeah, I did."

"Thanks to you leaving," kiddingly elbowing her, "I have to work with that egotistical prick. Remind me again why I like you?"

A taxi pulled up, and Petra hailed it, reaching over to hug Jeremy. He waved from the curb, watching as the cab whisked her into the uncertain drizzly night. *Fraud.* That word beat like a drum, pounding throughout every cell of her body. Mitch was a loathsome pig, and logically she recognized that she shouldn't give anything he said the slightest bit of credence, yet he had plucked a chord that rang out in discordant noise. She feared there was something counterfeit about her, snaking through everything in her life, upending her personal and professional commitments, insidious and unremitting, stealthy enough to destroy everything in its path and still remain uncaught. Would she ever be able to grab hold of the slithering fiend, face it in all of its ugliness, stripping it of its mystery and destroying it once and for all? At home, she crumpled into her sheets, her cushiony pillow on top of her head, the oblivion of sleep her only refuge from unanswerable questions.

Tyler and I are standing in front of my grandmother's house in Marion, Massachusetts, a picturesque hamlet, upwardly mobile and Americana wholesome. We're taking a Fourth of July road trip, en route to a Nantucket bed and breakfast. The house is on the way to the ferry, and I am feeling sentimental, especially since I am relocating to Chicago in a couple of weeks, to join Tyler, and of all my Northeast touchstones, this one has always held the most meaning. The pale blue Victorian house looks much the same as it always has, but the absence of my grandmother's gently expansive spirit is palpable even from the edge of the front lawn. She's been in a nursing home for a few years, fastened in the remorseless grip of dementia, and I can't bear to see her withered, boggy eyes, but at least I can revisit this house, so marked by the woman she once was.

"So, this is where adorable little Petra spent her summers?" Tyler asks as the late morning sun mercilessly beats down on us.

"Yeah, until I was eleven or twelve, and then..." I distractedly trail off.
"What?"

"We just stopped coming, I'm not sure why. I always missed it, though. It felt like a completely different world from our house in Holyoke, even though there was only a two-hour distance between them. My grandmother loved the beach, and we'd spend so much time by the water, sometimes only the two of us. It's sad,

how things you cherish just end. Grandma's been in a nursing home for a few years, and now we rent out the house. I hope the people living here appreciate how special it is."

"It looks well cared for," wrapping his sinewy arm around my sullen shoulders.

"I guess."

Peering into the uncurtained bay windows, I imagine being curled up on the couch, reading romance novels too luridly advanced for my tender age, while my grandmother hypnotically crochets, the curved hook spiraling like a vaulting gymnast in her facile hands. Then I notice the wooden bar in the corner of the living room, empty glasses calling out for the dizzying splash of liquor, and a sense of disquietude descends upon me, making me chilled despite the incessant heat of the pulsating cantaloupe sun. I know then that I need to be alone with Tyler, to find consolation pinned against his muscled skin, diversion in his anchoring touch. "Come with me," I order him, pulling him towards the backyard.

"Petra, what are you doing? How do you know these people aren't home?"

"Shhh, trust me."

I usher him past the large swimming pool, a fallen fluorescent blue sky, into the woods behind my grandmother's house. Several yards into the thicket, there is an abandoned shed in which my cousins and I used to play, innocent hours of pickup sticks, dolls, and campfire-like stories once again coming to life. The door is stuck, warped by humidity and age, and Tyler nervously pleads, "Let's get out of here, this place is creepy," but I hear only my need to avoid whatever dark recess opened when I looked into that bay window, to transcend it through him, my gate to peace, to heaven. Forcing my way into the dilapidated shack, I ignore the dust and decay, the stale, thick air. His light eclipses all. Climbing onto a forsaken wooden crate, I draw him to me, and unfasten his zipper. The second he enters me, I'm elevated and grounded. Pleasured, pacified, safe for the moment. I'm able to drive off that day, without a backward glance, at least for a while.

We arrive at the car ferry with a couple of hours to spare, and amble dreamily through the town, still emotionally enveloped by our untamed grappling in the shed. A small coffee shop beckons us with a smoky aroma twisting through its slightly opened door, riding the crest of an air-conditioned wave. Sitting down with our cappuccino slushies, I notice a Nordic looking female at a back table, fat candle blazing, deck of cards before her, and a plump middle-aged woman thanking her profusely before she canters towards the front door. Wordlessly, I communicate my curiosity to the flaxen haired girl, and she waves me over. Tyler remains seated at our table while I venture to the rear of the coffee shop. "Hi, I'm Wilma, please sit down," she states in a flat Midwestern accent. My semi-disappointment that she is not Freya from some icy, windswept Scandinavian country, directly descended from forest dwelling seers, is mitigated by the mysterious cards laid out before her. Longhaired maidens, fierce warriors, elfin creatures, stormy fortresses, and gilded swords, vibrate off the table in a magnetic siren call.

"What are those?" Celtic tarot cards, she replies, handed down from her aunt. They are frayed yet sturdy, and after she scoops them up, I shuffle them, feeling them dissolve into my palms. I return the deck to her, and she lays out three cards, my journey, past, present, and future. The first is a disembodied goddess cradling a radiant full moon, looming over a still waterway. The Moon, Wilma explains, represents hidden conflicts, subconscious emotions afraid to greet sunlight. The next card is a sinister castle, jutting out from a choppy sea, inflamed by jagged bolts of lightning. The Tower, she tells me, is a cleansing breakdown, a revelation that brings necessary chaos and ultimate transcendence. The final message is a nude female, kneeling beside a leafy stream, catching stardust in her hands, and blowing it out as a wish into the starlit sky. The Star captures hope in the face of desolation, healing after pain, the light at the end of the tunnel.

The reading unsettles me, the imagery so captivating and ethereal, but something bleak and wintry bending throughout the cards laid out before me, in this misleadingly bright summer café. Observing my dread, Wilma extends the deck to me, and tells me to pick out another card. I see a stout golden chalice, rising up from a lily pad studded pond, forever overflowing, an explosion of golden runes bursting from its wide mouth into the teal sky. The Ace of Cups, the source of purity, intimacy, infinite love. Wilma smiles, the roughness all comes to beauty, she reassures me, and I want to believe her.

The ferry ride is tranquil, Tyler and I huddling together against the rail as we take off, the hot wind and sea spray bathing us. We retire to our rented car, where I languorously fall asleep against his harboring shoulder. Unexpectedly, I am in my grandmother's living room, but she isn't there. I'm ten or eleven, and my grandfather is standing in front of the bar holding a heavy etched glass. I am reading and he leans over and kisses my forehead, wet and sloppy, I wipe it away. The strange heady fume he exhales is pungently sweet, I don't recognize it, but it makes me uneasy.

Now it is Mitch, standing in that once idyllic living room, assaulting me in a whiskey laden grasp, and my grandfather is asleep on the floor, blocking the front door, heaps of sadistic haloed moons filling every entryway, and there's no way out.

Chapter 10

Petra awoke knowing she had to revisit her grandma's house, despite her mom's misgivings about her returning. She checked rail listings on her phone, and made a reservation for a midmorning train out of Penn Station to Boston. Packing just enough clothes and toiletries for a weekend trip, she quickly dressed, took a granola bar and bottle of water, and headed for the subway. Penn Station was ensconced in its customary summer lull, but the energy seeping from the subdued flux of tourists, panhandlers, and diehard natives smoldered with latent expectation. Scuttling to her platform, fragments of her grandparents and Tyler, within and outside that old blue house, collided and liquefied into each other, leaving Petra determined and scared to arrive there. The train arrived five minutes early, and with just a smattering of fellow passengers, and whooshing jets of frigid air permeating the connected cars, Petra felt like she was embarking on a lonesome trek into polar caverns, astounding beauty or ice-covered despair awaiting her.

Reaching Boston's South Station within four hours, Petra purchased a ticket for a connecting train to Wareham Village, a ten-minute car ride from her grandmother's house in Marion. With over ninety minutes of layover time, she sauntered into a dimly lit, wood paneled tavern, for a hard black cherry cider and fried mac and cheese bites. An unkempt drunkard at the end of the bar played with an unlit cigarette, his head oscillating between falling onto the counter and gawking at Petra. More irritated than threatened, Petra finished her drink and, placing the remaining greasy treats into a wax-lined paper bag, ventured back into the damp, diesel-infused atmosphere of the station.

Strolling by a shop called *lovepop*, she mindlessly stopped and reached for the door, entering into a candy-colored vortex of paper delights. Masterful, laser cut pop up cards for all events and seasons completely invaded the small space, billowing in banners and streamers, guarding doorways and windows, seizing tables and countertops. Petra noticed the "Every day is Valentine's Day" section, inwardly wincing, and yet unable to resist closer inspection. One card in the pink and red sodden panorama seemed to lock Petra in, her gaze continually settling upon it. Two waiflike creatures, a huge scarlet heart looming like a boulder above them, threatening to crush them as they innocently cradle it, joyfully unmindful of its devastating weight. Snatching the card, Petra brought it to the cash register, not knowing if it was solely for her, or Tyler, or perhaps some specter of a man she had yet to meet, but wholly positive that the bizarre valentine had been waiting to leave that transient shop in her hands.

The connecting train ride was smooth and relatively quick, yet Petra couldn't arrive at her grandmother's house fast enough, and with each passing minute, she was getting more and more fidgety. Munching on the cold scraps of her mac and cheese appetizer as a sputtering cab carried her on the last leg of her journey, she compulsively opened and closed her new greeting card, the ever-springing oversized heart an aspiration and a lament. Her emotions were exploding and careening everywhere, and she wanted the stabilizing comfort of a loyal romantic partner. Hadn't she had such a partner in Tyler, though, and rashly thrown him away? Maybe she didn't deserve anything other than a bleak life of experiencing her sorrows and joys in isolation. The cab jerked into a sudden turn, jolting Petra into the door, the card blown out of her hand in a whirl of hot wind. She looked back wistfully at the doomed winged cupids, steadfastly sharing the encumbrance of the granite heart as they were pounded against the pavement.

Once at the house, Petra was relieved to see her mother and aunt's cars parked in the driveway. Sprinting for the door, she was prepared to let herself in, and was surprised to find it locked. She eagerly rang the doorbell and then persistently knocked, eliciting no response. She retreated to the back of the house, finding the door to the kitchen open. Half-finished glasses of iced tea sat on the counter, as well as a teak salad bowl with wilted shreds of lettuce. Calling out a tentative "hello," Petra walked through the dining room to the living room, instinctively gliding her hand against the edge of the bar, the nicked Spanish cedar menacing in its durability. Shaking away thoughts of her grandfather and his lumbering, alcohol fueled affection, she heard laughter bellowing from upstairs. Following the sound, she came to the rickety pull-down stairs that led to the attic, and climbing up, found her mother and aunt poring over a large photo album.

"Helloooo."

Calli and Chloe looked up in startlement. "Petra!" they exclaimed in unison.

Petra walked into the large attic, the smothering heat made slightly more tolerable by the vastness of the space.

"This is a wonderful surprise, honey! I was so disappointed you weren't coming!" Aunt Chloe effused as she walked over to hug her niece.

Petra peered over her aunt's shoulder, mouthing "WTF?" to her mother for pretending that Aunt Chloe's jealousies were the reason she had discouraged Petra from making the trip. Calli grimaced in innocent bewilderment, and Petra knew that her mother was not ready to surrender her fictions.

"Sweetheart, you have to look at some of these paintings we found up here," Calli excitedly suggested, trying to coax her daughter into a good mood. "A few of them were favorites of yours when you were little. See if there is anything you want to take."

The allure of her grandmother's prized art momentarily overshadowed her indignation, and she strode to the line of paintings abutting the wall. The first one was a small oil painting of a robed, long-haired woman, viewed from the back as she gazes out a large window onto a barren farm. Despite its gothic, sensual beauty, that one had always unsettled Petra, all the more now because she could relate to the subject's seclusion. Petra could actually feel the solitary teardrop dripping down the undepicted face. Rummaging through for more optimistic pieces, she found several still life and pastoral paintings that she remembered, but none with whom she wanted to share daily living space. Then, she came across something that snatched the breath directly out of her lungs.

"Oh, I don't believe this. How is this happening?" she marveled aloud, her mother and aunt rushing over to see what had spurred her amazement.

Petra was agape at the sight of her own two recent sketches, languishing here in this long-forgotten attic, suffused with dust and cobwebs, when in reality they were being newly framed by Delaine in another state. Had the train ride carried her through some time-bending wormhole or was she just losing her mind?

"Ah, you found them, those were the ones you especially loved. You would sit in the den where they hung, and just stare at them. Remember? Why do you look so upset?" Calli asked in worried confusion.

"I *don't* remember. Mom, I started sketching again, after you left, and I drew these two exact scenes that I'm seeing here. But I don't remember ever seeing them before, I thought they came from my own imagination. And this horrible woman in Delaine's store recognized them as belonging to some New England artist, but I didn't believe her. Am I going crazy? How can I not re-member?"

"You are not crazy. There was that one summer you got a concussion," Calli said, her eyes darting uneasily to the floor, rejoining Petra in a sidelong glance as she continued, "you know, from the diving accident in Grandma's pool. I guess it affected your memory."

"Yes," Aunt Chloe then interjected, wanting to ease the growing tension, "but I think it's good you remembered the drawings. Even if you didn't know where they came from, the memories were there. Grandma would be happy her art inspired you to draw again, right?"

Petra looked at the sketches, searching for answers in the charcoal strokes of another's hand that had so briefly seemed to be her own. She enviously assessed the obnoxiously florid signature in the lower right corner of both pieces. Peterson Tate. Who was this person? Petra needed to find out, but first, she had questions for her mother.

"Why did we stop coming here? We never came after I had my accident. Why?"

"Lots of reasons, I guess. Your father and I weren't getting along, you discovered boys, you wanted to spend your summers with your friends. I don't know; it wasn't one thing in particular," Calli intoned defensively.

"But we never came back at all, even for weekends or holidays," Petra persisted. "Was it because Grandpa drank? Is that why you didn't want me to come here? Bad memories?"

"What? No. Why are you saying that? Grandpa wasn't an alcoholic."

"Just a dream I had, it seemed like a memory. But I suppose I can't tell the difference lately. I still don't understand why we never once came here after my accident. Was it worse than you're saying? What really happened to me, Mom?"

"Oh, Petra," Chloe pled through nervous laughter, "stop bothering your mother about ancient summer vacation plans. Who knows what any of us were thinking about back then? Your mom and I are lucky we remember what we had for breakfast today. Speaking of which, I am starving. Wanna have pizza? I'll order a large pepperoni pie and a couple of spinach calzones."

Petra was about to continue her interrogation as Chloe descended the wobbly attic steps, but Calli spoke first. "Look, honey, I thought Aunt Chloe and I might get very emotional going through Grandma's belongings, and I didn't want to make you sad when you've had your own problems. But you are here now, and I'm glad. And please, don't let anything discourage you from drawing again. You need talent even to re-create someone else's art, right?"

Petra nodded weakly, and then noticed that her mother was holding an old, cracked Polaroid. Reaching for it, she saw herself as a carefree preadolescent, lying on a raft in her grandmother's pool as her father playfully splashed her with water. "That's weird," Petra mused aloud.

"What?"

"I don't remember ever laughing or playing with Dad. It always seemed to me he wanted a son, and grudgingly settled for a daughter."

"Petra, don't be ridiculous. I know that man is not the most demonstrative person, but he loves you. He calls or texts me at least two or three times a month to check up on you."

"He does?" Petra asked incredulously.

"Yes. He said you never respond to his messages, so he stays involved with you through me."

"Why didn't you tell me?"

"He asked me not to. He's not looking to guilt you into a relationship, Petra. He just wants to know how his little girl is doing," she explained, lovingly pinching Petra's cheek.

Calli then returned to the boxes and photo albums she had been exploring with Chloe, and Petra focused on the antique picture in her hands, sadly mesmerized by its misleading advertisement of father-daughter bliss. Her fingers traced one of the breaks in the fractured photo, until it ended at her ignorantly cheery face.

I'm sitting in our family room, watching Buffy the Vampire Slayer, *the mulled warmth of nutmeg and cinnamon undulating from the kitchen, where my mom is preparing a spiced apple crumb pie to celebrate my first-place ribbon in the junior high art fair. The front door opens, and my father is wiping his wet brow. It's late March, and as a corporate accountant, he is knee deep in financial spread sheets and tax forms, and has been blowing off steam by shooting hoops with the monosyllabic athletic punk next door. "Wow, that kid Kenny is some basketball player. He's not very tall, but he's got a great feel for the net, makes a lot of impossible shots." I'm not sure if he is directing his comments to me, or just thinking out loud, but I grab my prizewinning watercolor depiction of a majestic Ferris wheel eternally circling against the heavens, and rush over to him, excitedly squealing, "Daddy, I know Kenny is good at sports, but look at this! I won first place!" Bending down to untie his sneakers, without having turned towards me, he asks, "First place in what? The science fair, I hope?" I place my painting in front of his face, my skinny jittering body more loudly insistent than any words. "Oh right, the art thingy," then standing up and dismissing me with a pat on my head, "that's fine as a minor hobby, but there's no money in art, kiddo. You're getting older, you need to be practical if you're going to survive in this world," and he disappears into the winding staircase.*

...Tyler and I are relaxing in his parent's backyard. They invited us for the weekend, and we are savoring the last tenuous grip of Indian summer. His mother is taking art classes, and an easel is propped at the periphery of the tiled patio. Tyler has bragged to his parents about my artistic prowess, so Delaine has been encouraging me to paint. The acrylic colors are coagulating into the palette as I struggle to settle on a fitting subject, the pristine beauty of the hilly, jade landscape almost overly inspiring, flooding my mind with too many visual pleasures. Dressed for a swim party later in the day, a neighbor's homage to the gently fading summer, I am wearing a green bikini top and baggy, cut off, bleached denim shorts. I'm focusing on the blank canvas as Tyler comes up behind me, nuzzling my ear and reaching one hand into the back of my shorts. He caresses my butt, as his other hand rhythmically rubs my stomach. I involuntarily shiver against his touch, wanting him so bad, but acutely aware of his parents somewhere nearby. Just as his hand travels inside my bikini bottom, a rock tumbles lose from the impromptu sculpture Tyler has distractedly assembled earlier in the day, and I have a sudden flash of what I need to paint. Turning to kiss him, I motion Tyler back to his lounge chair, and start to let my hand transcribe the beautiful picture already alive within me.

Midway through the painting, I pause, deeming that enough of my internal vision has seeped onto the canvas to allow a preliminary viewing. I ask Tyler to come look, just as his father, Owen, emerges from the glass sliding doors. Both stare into the painting, a rough silhouette of a young boy, clasping a rock as a storm rages around him. Tyler's eyes swing back and forth from me to the canvas, his irises deep cups of cobalt, brewing tears of appreciation and wonder. Owen is the one that breaks the reverential silence. "Amazing, absolutely amazing. Was Rembrandt here while I took a shower? Petra, I had no idea you were this talented. I know you are a successful editor, but honestly, I think this is your gift. You should really pursue your art, see where it takes you. This is something too beautiful to be hidden, it needs to be shared."

Chapter 11

Petra's mom had driven her to South Station, ostensibly so they could talk, and dispel any lingering tensions, but Petra had fallen asleep almost as soon as they hit the interstate. Gently roused awake by Calli as they approached the train station, Petra reached for the red thermos of black coffee she had filled at a gas station as they left town. It was lukewarm and gritty, but nonetheless invigorating, and Petra savored each muddy sip. Hugging tightly before they separated, Petra wanted to peel through the layers of her mother's evasion, but the sky had grown ominously dark, and frozen pellets of rain began to hit the windshield.

"Mom, it looks like a hailstorm. Please be careful."

"You too, call me when you get to Penn Station, okay?" Calli urged.

"Promise," she said before blowing her mom a kiss as she walked into the station.

Settling into her uncomfortable seat in the nearly empty rear car of the train, Petra was trapped in that awful wasteland between drained body and wandering psyche. Knowing her restless mind would momentarily prevail, she dug out her phone from her roomy purse, and began researching Peterson Tate, the artist she had inadvertently impersonated. "I can't believe that bougie bitch was right," Petra scoffed, thinking about the obnoxious woman in Delaine's store who had immediately spotted the true origin of Petra's drawings. As Petra discovered in her online sleuthing, Peterson had indeed been the darling of the Northeast art scene, starting in 1986, when a caricature he painted as a Bridgeport, CT street artist created a buzz in the New England society pages. His model was the teenage daughter of a prominent Yale art historian, and the Professor was so impressed by the off-the-cuff sketch that he placed it in an "up and coming" artist's exhibit at the New Haven Art Council. Galleries that had rejected his works started clamoring to showcase his drawings, commissions rolled in, and by the summer of 1988, he was living in Martha's Vineyard, appreciated by an ever-widening pool of scholarly art enthusiasts, avant-garde rebels, and neglected soccer moms with lots of money to spend and countless hours to spend it. Then, just as violently as he crashed the art scene, he departed. His last showing was in a Maine gallery in 1990, predictably followed by a burst of "Whatever Happened To...?" articles, ultimately dwindling into bare silence, as if none of it had ever been real.

Petra deflated into her rigid, waxy seat, frustrated both that she hadn't found out more about Peterson's whereabouts and also that she had no idea why it mattered so much to find him. The real mystery was why she had lost her memories, what were the actual events surrounding her accident...if it even was an accident? Whatever Calli did or didn't know, she wasn't talking, but that's where the answers lied. Peterson Tate was nothing but a red herring, an unnecessary distraction, and Petra knew it, but she couldn't stop obsessing about him. Even the two black and white, fuzzy photos of him she found online piqued her curiosity. In both, he's looking away from the camera, permanently suspended in vibrant conversation in one, and staring into the depths of Nantucket Sound in the other. His sculpted chin and regally straight nose seemed so at odds with his puckered clothing and messy hair, and Petra couldn't help but plummet helplessly into those pictures, as if knowing his secrets could unearth her own.

Walking home from the subway, the air was still and muggy, trapped between storm fronts, and Petra once again felt her own occlusive limbo, past, future, and present murkily surrounding her. The low hanging sky became a vast museum where Peterson's spooky fairy tales floated eternally. She could see the mangled castles and gnarled, rotting forests in the gray vapor of the clouds, shadowy taunts from the elusive artist. "Who cares if I can't find him?" she chided herself. "He's got nothing to do with me. Anyway, maybe he's dead."

"Who's dead?" came a disembodied male voice.

Petra's head pivoted quickly from her aerial wanderings, seeing the familiar caffe latte-colored bricks of her building. Then, a lanky presence separated from the façade of the apartment house, and she recognized the pouty youth from her fourth of July tryst. Petra's mouth opened, but before any words arose, he spoke again.

"Don't be mad, I wanted to see you, so I got your address."

"How?" she asked in alarm. "We didn't even exchange first names," and admitting this made her face flush with shame.

"I saw you leave with that guy, and he called you Petra. When he came back to the party, I made up a stupid story about having a rescue kitten that you wanted to adopt, that you told me your address so I could bring the cat by, but I forgot it."

"He bought that?"

"Not really, but then my sister came over, she's an anesthesiologist and lives downstairs from that guy's boyfriend. I guess she gave me credibility," he shrugged, a nervous laugh leaking out from his baby pink, downturned lips.

"How long have you been waiting here? Please tell me this is the first time you've come by, that you haven't been staking out my apartment."

"Um, I haven't been here that long," he said haltingly, "I mean, my buddy, Derek, is crashing nearby, I kinda just walked by after I left him. I was only gonna wait a couple more minutes, then you showed up."

Alarm bells blared inside Petra, predatory older woman tangled with lovesick teen, one or both sliding into painful passion and eventual abandonment. But she was tired, eager to get upstairs, and this still nameless boy was now stripped of all his rooftop swagger, unsure and vulnerable, himself a rescue kitten in need of refuge.

"Okay, since you're here, you can come upstairs, just for a little while. And don't get any ideas." Throwing his hands up in surrender, they headed into the lobby, breezing past Charlie, the affable auxiliary doorman, professionally opaque as this coltish stud followed Petra obediently up the stairs.

Entering her apartment, he surveyed his new surroundings with deferential esteem.

"Wow, this is just what I expected your place to be like. Classy, artistic, homey, clean but a little messy. I love it."

Something about his uninhibited interest tore down her stony resolve to keep him at arm's length, all the more forcing her to do just that. "I still don't know your name," she stated in her most businesslike voice, trying to dampen his attentiveness and her response to it.

"Greg. Look, I get the feeling you're bothered by my age. I've always liked older girls, it's not a big deal."

"Greg, you told me you're turning eighteen in October. Well, my birthday is in early September, so for a few weeks at least, I'll be thirty while you're still only seventeen. That is *definitely* a big deal."

"Almost thirty, huh? Wow, you look really young." Walking nearer to her, "My god, you are so fucking sexy."

Swatting away his hand as he reached towards her face, Petra scolded him, "We are not doing this. You are very cute, but when we hooked up, I didn't know how young you were. This isn't right."

"Please, let me be the judge of that," he pleaded with genuine need. "I want you. I haven't been able to stop thinking about you since that night."

"No, no, no," Petra emphatically declared, his puppy dog seductiveness hurling her over a cliff. "Just go, now."

"All right, how about a compromise? Hear me out, okay?" he lovably entreated, and Petra subtly nodded in uneasy compliance. "I want to kiss, and touch, and lick every inch of you, but I'll settle for giving you a shoulder and neck rub."

"I don't think so."

"C'mon, you were carrying that big duffel bag when you came home, you look tense. Let me help. Please." Again, the unconcealed want, so naïve and yet provocative, reached inside and tugged her towards him.

"Fine, my neck is a little sore, but then you have to leave."

Petra opted for a seat at her small dinette table, rather than the couch, to keep her body from becoming too comfortably disengaged from her mental reservations. Rigidly stationed in the chair, her shoulders stiffly braced against the threat of touch, Greg lightly chuckled behind her, gently kneading her upper arms. "Boy, you are really wound up. Try to relax. Trust me, I give good massages. You'll enjoy it." He slipped down her unzipped hoodie, letting it drop onto the seat of the chair. She quivered slightly, exposed and small under his towering watch. Interpreting her body language as spoken hesitation, he softly uttered, "Shhhh," the exhalation resting on her tense skin.

It was oddly disconcerting to her, how he seesawed between juvenile diffidence and manly assurance. Petra tried to rein in her own discomfort, feeling that it somehow emboldened him, and she knew he'd be easier to resist as a fumbling minor than a confident aggressor. Loosening her upper body, she blithely responded, "Well, you're probably not as good as Madge, the German massage therapist at my gym, but whatever, knock yourself out. You've got three minutes, and that's it."

Without wasting another word, he sunk his buttery fingertips into the base of her neck, lightly at first, her head leaning back into his hands, the strength of his rubbing increasing as his fingers fanned into her shoulders. He was so much more deliberate and composed than he'd been during their previous rendezvous, and she was tempted to roughly disrobe him and take him into her bedroom.

"Not bad," she pretended, "but your time is almost up."

"Then I better step it up." Intensifying his manipulation of her taut muscles, he then let one hand travel down her arm, barely touching her damp skin, until he reached under her loose tank top, cupping her breast through the light mesh of her bra. She released a guttural whimper, entranced by his rhythmic rubbing, now underneath the skin of her bra, directly on her flesh. Mentally, she was already having sex with him, perspiring bodies blissfully knotted together, his young libido and her emotional susceptibility making them both wildly insatiable. *This is so wrong*, she thought, astonished and disgusted that she didn't care. Her leather bag, perched nearby on the table, then sprang to life with a series of beeps, and Petra hastily grabbed for it, glad to have a concrete reason to break free of Greg's intoxicating clutch. Retrieving her phone, she saw several texts from Rianne. Greg retreated into the kitchen, sighing in frustration as he filled a plastic cup with tap water.

Petra joyfully focused on the frenzied texts, losing herself in Rianne's hyperbolic world. She had become suspicious of her latest suitor, and after running his name through QuikPI, her favorite internet stalking tool, she had found that Mr. Wonderful was not a bachelor attorney living in an uptown penthouse as he claimed, but rather a mechanic residing in a Staten Island duplex with his wife Ginny and their three kids. *Ginny*, Petra thought sourly, that seemed the perfect name for a clueless, betrayed wife. Greg returned then, caressing the back of Petra's neck, but their moment was broken yet again, and Petra recoiled from his warm hands. Standing up to face him, she saw his bravado disintegrate, and she wanted to console him, but thought better of it. *I'm not his mommy or his girlfriend, time for him to leave.*

Placing a teacherly arm around him, she guided him to the front door. "You are absolutely adorable, and I admit, part of me wants to just eat you up, but it's not happening. Please, don't come back here." Looking down, his long, choppy sable hair fell sadly into his slit like chocolate eyes, and Petra lightly grazed his cheek with a brief kiss as she opened the door, and sent her lost puppy into the unpredictable city night. Leaning against the shut door, she caught her tired, disheveled image in the mirror hanging across the room, realizing that she still had a lost puppy to contend with, herself.

Chapter 12

The next morning Petra was startled awake by her trilling phone. It was lying on the floor by her bed, where she had left it charging. Too tired to reach for it, she waited for the racket to subside. She wondered if it was Rianne, calling to vent about her two-timing lover. Knowing her friend as she did, Petra wouldn't be shocked if she had confronted the lout at his house last night and ended up having sloppy sex in a minivan parked around the corner, poor gullible Ginny ignorantly reading bedtime stories to their kids while he's ferociously fucking another woman from behind. Yeah, Rianne, bless her heart, was definitely a screw up, but then again, Petra had twice almost screwed a boy more than three years shy of legal drinking age, so she wouldn't be picking up any stones to hurl at Rianne. Finally mustering the energy to reach down for her phone, she went into her voicemail, and was surprised to hear the soothing, even timbre of Delaine's voice. She calmly explained that the person installing the glass panels in the picture frames had a family emergency, causing him to fall behind on his work, and so Petra's sketches wouldn't be ready for another few weeks. She promised to keep on top of it, and wondered if Petra had gotten a chance to look at Tyler's journal.

Tyler. The mention of his name and his poetic musings made Petra feel dirty and deceitful. Abandoning herself to a horny young pothead without even knowing his name initially, letting him come into her apartment—the apartment that was until recently her home with Tyler—allowing him to stroke and fondle her, wanting to invite him for an all-night fuck fest in the bed she shared with Tyler. It was reprehensible behavior, and she hated herself for it, and yet felt herself getting wet remembering Greg's hands, insistent and gentle, exploring her body, now frustratingly wondering where those hands would've lingered and ultimately

85

settled if she'd let him stay. And to make her guilty conflict even worse, Tyler's journal was currently sequestered in the darkest, dustiest corner of her closet, fighting for space with Christmas wreaths and half burnt advent candles, Halloween skeletons and witches—not out of a lack of caring or curiosity, but because she suspected the relationship was dead, particularly after their horrendous last meeting. Bad enough he haunted her dreams, she didn't want to spend her waking hours delving inside his gentle, poetic sensibility, finding more reasons to love a man she still wasn't sure she had ever truly loved in the first place. Why add to her confusion, she reasoned. And what if she did want him back, his poems awakening new feelings or reawakening old ones, maybe he'd been so hurt that he would coldly rebuff her, cruelly laugh in her face. Better to leave him alone, Petra decided, for both of their sakes.

Falling back against her pillow, she sullenly laughed at how in a fairly short time, her own personal life had devolved into the same pulpy ridiculousness as Rianne's, lurid stories that were entertaining to quickly splash through but too dangerously shallow in which to dive. She envisioned the eroding moat in her drawing of the ruined castle, Peterson's drawing actually, its depth dangerously unknown, until you attempted to walk or jump into it. Then, in a burst, her roving thoughts coalesced, and she yelled, "QuickPI!" That was her ticket to finding out Peterson Tate's present location. "Thank you, Rianne," she cheered as she accessed the site on her phone, rapidly keying in his name. Within seconds, she had an address and phone number in Dover, Delaware. Operating on sheer instinct, she called the number, figuring that an ad-libbed untruth would play more authentically than a rehearsed one.

"Hello, Tate residence," a nectary South American voice dripped into the phone.

"Hi, is Mr. Tate at home?" Petra asked, desperately hoping he wasn't.

"Who's calling?"

Petra wanted to hang up, but impulsively continued, "I'm calling from Ri…" nervously trying to avoid blurting out Rianne's whole name, the only thing landing on her clumsy tongue, "Reversal Graphics. We've had some computer glitches, and I'm not sure if Mr. Tate wanted his order shipped to his billing address, which we have listed in Dover." There was a pause at the other end of the line, and Petra anxiously held her breath.

"Oh, well, I am not sure. Mr. Tate is currently at his summer home, so I think he would want anything sent there. Would you like the address, Miss?"

"Yes, that would be great, thank you."

Petra stared down at the address she hastily scrawled on a Japanese take-out menu—34 Starlight Way, Fenwick Island, Delaware. Repeating it out loud, the address floated off her lips, crystalizing into the distinguished artist himself, now as silvery as a twinkling sky. Scrolling through images of this magical sounding place she had never heard of, she discovered a pastel summer paradise of sun-bleached bungalows, straw hats, seafood bistros, and ice cream vendors, all under the sturdy wink of a watchful lighthouse. Just for fun, she scanned the available lodging, rustic B&B's, predictably nondescript hotel chains, worn but beachy motels, upscale inns, lending themselves to romantic weekends and laidback family holidays. Not falling into either category, even for a hypothetical trip, Petra looked at longer term options, affordable efficiency suites, well suited for extended solitary jaunts. One in particular appealed to her, a sandy beige one bedroom cottage, with a sunny front porch, walking distance from the beach. She was surprised that such a jewel was still available, the summer already in full-swing, and unexpectedly her imaginary trip became a reality. She secured a three week stay at the cottage, reserved a rental car, and began packing for her unforeseen journey. Free of both reason and hesitation, she was going to find Peterson Tate.

I'm far inside a deep, dreamless sleep when my vibrating phone hums alive against my naked thigh, and I grab it without thinking, but my body is as asleep as my mind, and I have forgotten how to answer it. The humming stops and starts again, and I see that it is Tyler calling. Tyler, I am stunned, why is he calling me in the middle of the night? Why is he calling at all? The threat of an emergency carries a flood of caffeine into my veins, and suddenly alert, I answer, my "Hello?" both frail and frantic. It's his voice, measured and kind as ever, telling me that he saw my sketches at his mother's store, how beautiful they are. "I know it's late, but I need to see you, Petra. I miss you. I have to see your face." Wherever he came from, it must have been nearby, because it seems he's at my door in a few seconds, or maybe the promise of his nearness is altering my sense of time. We are silent, just embracing and pulling back to make sure it's real and then falling into each other again, crying and laughing, feeling so much that there's nothing to say.

We move to the couch and are just cuddling, folding into each other's warmth even though the room is so stuffy. He is running his left hand hypnotically up and down my stomach, the white cotton of my baby doll pajamas retaining every corpuscle of his touch so that the fibers have become extensions of his supple fingers. All my misgivings are vanishing, and it is as though Tyler and I are not a distinct couple reuniting, but two halves of a whole, once again intact. I am now falling back asleep, but within the sweet drowsy pleasure of him, when a grating chime explodes into the lull, this time from his phone. He's chuckling as he responds, but not in the innocent, grateful way we were earlier. A hue of scorn has leached into his face and voice, and I timidly ask who he is texting. "Lexi," he coldly states. His ex-girlfriend. "Yep, she's my baby doll. Did you really think I'd ever go back to a cold destructive bitch who bails out for no reason, and then whores around? Your buddy Mitch is telling everyone you double teamed him and some fifteen-year-old at a rooftop party. You disgust me." As he leaves, he grabs something from a bag he carried in, my sketches, which he crumples with revulsion onto the floor. "You're nothing but a pathetic fraud." And now it is Mitch's haughty, lecherous face, hissing at me.

I jump out of my bed, trembling in rage and pain, cursing this nightmare version of Tyler, and wanting to throttle Mitch, real and imagined. I'm relieved it was a dream, but disappointed that Tyler hasn't actually rematerialized, even though I still don't know where we fit into each other's lives anymore, if we ever could again. But for those few delicious moments in that alternate realm, my dream self had no doubts about her relationship with Tyler, and I hate and envy her for that. I grab Advil PM from my medicine cabinet, and then have a small glass of red wine, needing to calm my jangled nerves, and hopefully have a more pleasant dream.

...Tyler and I have been living in Chicago for a few years, and we have traveled to see his brother Brent and wife Dana at their farm outside of Elmira, NY for Christmas. We are sharing a quintessentially rustic bedroom, caramel wood paneling, a moose head on the wall, handcrafted pine furniture, with all the trappings of a perfect wintry Christmas: red and white snowflake embroidered quilt, miniature fresh balsam fir tree, candy cane wreaths, painted porcelain angels, reindeer throw pillows. I have been really busy at Watermark, and am munching on one of Dana's picture-perfect gingerbread cookies as I scan my latest manuscript, a much-anticipated account of a lawyer's death penalty defense for a notorious bicoastal serial killer. It took me over a year to adjust to working for such a multinational firm, but now I am loving it, and am most likely headed to a promotion in

the new year, managing a team of junior editors. Tyler kisses the cookie out from my mouth, and mischievously grabs the manuscript from my hands.

"What are you doing?" I ask, with mock annoyance. I've been working for almost two hours straight, and his ski-burned face and thick flannel shirt are giving him an enticing mountain man quality that I'm finding hard to resist.

Playfully jiggling a bottle of thick golden fluid, he grabs the Sensual Art of Couple's Massage handbook that Brent gave us as a pre-Christmas gift. "I think we should try this. I found the massage oil in his bathroom, it's nice and almondy. Let's do it."

"It's almost dinnertime," I halfheartedly protest, craving his hands more than fried chicken and pecan pie.

"So, we can be a little late," he says, gently removing my bulky sweater and lace bra, and guiding me onto my stomach.

"I barely know Brent, and I think that book was a strange gift. From what I gathered glancing at the pictures, massage is just an excuse to have lots of bendy sex."

"Which we are going to have, my dear, right now, thanks to my pervert brother."

"What do you mean?"

"Dana is a doll, but she's a little vanilla for Brent. I think he got us this book because he wants the vicarious thrill of stroking your gorgeous body up and down."

"Okay, I'm begging you, don't say any more, I'm barely going to be able to face him at dinner now. You don't tell him about our sex life, do you? How does he know I'm not vanilla?"

Tyler leans down and suckles the back of my neck, now slippery with oil, whispering, "Even a blind man in your presence for five minutes would be turned on by you. Your voice, the sound of your laugh, the feel of your skin, the way you smell…mmm…you are very arousing." He presses into my back muscles with deeper strokes, the oil allowing his hands to move like silk against my skin. "To see you, though, every curve of your body, each angle of your face, it's like beholding an angel and a temptress. You're the only girl that makes we want to go to church and have dirty sex ten times a day." He slips off my thong underwear, and begins squeezing my buttocks, with just enough roughness to make me moan into my pillow, and forget that a houseful of people, including Tyler's parents,

Dana's parents, and Brent and Dana's three young daughters, are expecting us at the dinner table any moment.

The massaging ceases and I hear his pants and shirt plop onto the floor, and he gets on top of me, and I bite down on my finger to keep from screaming out as he presses into my lower back with his body, thrusting into me and holding on to my shoulders like I am his grounding and his life force.

"Dinnertime," Dana chirps from the hallway.

"In a minute," we breathlessly say in unison, not meaning it because we have climbed outside of time.

Afterwards we are lying side by side on the tousled bed, sheets spotted with almond oil, its beautiful nutty scent interlacing with our salty sweat and the woodsy night air coming through the open window. I look over at him, and he seems preoccupied, sad almost. "What is it?" I softly inquire.

"Being back in the city for a couple of days, it was nice, right?" he dreamily replies, staring at the ceiling.

"Yeah, I love Christmas in NY, though your ice skating was a bit rusty. Next time we come back East for Christmas, I'll get you a few refresher lessons before we leave Chicago."

Turning to face me, "I'm serious, you know I'm not happy at the University of Chicago."

"Yeah, but I thought things were better with the new department head."

"Yes, she's better than the last one, but there's just not enough funding for the research I want to do. NYU is doing a lot of exciting research, at the interface of developmental and neuro linguistics. Isaac, my old friend from Columbia told me. When you were at the Guggenheim with your mom, I met with him, and gave him my CV. He's in the philosophy department at NYU, but he knows the head of linguistics. Oh, and the best part, his sister works in the same building as Viscount Publishing. She has lunch with people from that office sometimes, and she can definitely get your résumé to the right people."

An unsettling sense of déjà vu comes over me. Like the long-ago discussion he raised about my joining him in Chicago, I'm once again completely vulnerable, naked and post-orgasmic, totally blindsided. Once again, he's making life-changing geographic and career decisions for the both of us, without any input from me. "Tyler, I'm happy in Chicago. Shouldn't you wait to see if things improve for you at work?"

"*A position is opening up at NYU this semester. I had to act now. Their spring semester starts in late January. I told my department months ago that I was thinking of taking a leave from teaching this coming semester to focus on writing a book, so they've had a back-up plan in place. We can sublet our loft until we find a buyer. I was thinking you could tell Watermark you've got a family emergency, and need to move back to NY. Isaac is teaching in Germany this spring, so we can stay in his place.*"

"*How could you not have warned me about any of this?*"

"*It all came together so quickly, there was no time.*" Tracing my mouth with his fingers, "*I'm sorry. If you don't want to move, we won't. I just believe we belong in NYC, Petra. Trust me. I want this for us.*"

Chapter 13

The windows of the red Jeep Grand Cherokee were rolled down, the quick, warm air traveling in and out of the moderately speeding car as Petra maneuvered along I-95. Having reserved a fuel efficient, economy car, she was told by the overly smiling car rental agent that the compact models were all gone, and that an SUV was available at the original small-car price. An hour into the journey, a frown clung on to her face, plastered there by invisible sonic fingers emanating from Tyler's "road trip" iTunes playlist. Bruce Springsteen, Alanis Morrisette, and Maroon 5 had overlapped into a cackling chorus until Petra snappishly silenced them, focusing instead on the robotic drones of her navigation app. The huge white cotton candy clouds rhythmically puffed over the sun, the alternating light and shadow making Petra feel like a sky-high child was engaging her in a game of peekaboo, reimbuing her with hopeful anticipation. *What will I do when I get there?* she wondered silently, *Do I go to his house? No, that's crazy. I'll settle into my cottage, wander around the town, and take it from there.*

Midway through New Jersey, Petra stopped to replenish her environmentally challenged gas guzzler, and stock up on empty, momentarily satiating fast food calories. The smell of greasy deliciousness ushering her through the crowded parking lot, she ordered a cheeseburger, waffle fries, and a chocolate milkshake, opting to eat inside her car rather than sit at one of the grimy, cramped rest stop tables. Walking back towards the SUV, she found a rusting, hippie-ish van idling in the spot beside her, an early twenties couple rummaging through the van's gaping back. The pale, waifish girl tentatively addressed her even paler, beanie capped male companion as Petra breezed past, "Trevor, I really want to spend a few days in Virginia. Why can't we?"

"I told you, babe, we don't have time," his voice tumbling out deeper and heavier than his pasty, scrawny exterior would suggest.

"Please, Trev. I haven't seen my sister for so long. We'll still have lots of time in DC with your family, even if we take a little side trip."

"Just trust me, babe. We're gonna be so happy and busy in DC, you won't want to miss even an hour there, okay partner?"

"All right," she wavered, the muffled sound of patronizing kisses circling over to Petra, choking the dripping burger into her throat.

"Ugh," Petra groaned under her breath, "Tyler, Trevor, 'trust me.' Fucking bullies."

Two spots over, a silver minivan was parked, drawing Petra's attention when its alarm chirped. A briskly walking woman, chin length chestnut hair elegantly bobbing in the wind, tramped toward the minivan, a preadolescent boy closely trailing. An exasperated and disheveled, yet obviously handsome man struggled to catch up, cradling a chubby infant and holding the squirmy hand of a bouncing toddler. The red cheeked baby smiled at her father, poking at his goateed chin, when the drill sergeant mom turned sharply to face her troops, sternly bellowing, "Michael, up front with me," the boy obediently heading to the front passenger door. Nodding imperiously to the bedraggled hubby, "Put Lola in her car seat, and sit in the back with the baby. Keep her occupied so I can drive in peace." Deferentially nodding, he swiftly arranged the two youngsters, and pausing to wipe his brow, glanced quickly at Petra, his self-conscious grin full of grim resignation and battered hopes, before entering the vehicle and closing the door, shutting himself inside his domesticated cage as it barreled him into another emasculating, sleep and sex starved day.

"Wow," Petra whistled as she leaned into the hot, cracked black leather of her car's front seat. Despite the gender flipping, the two rest stop couples were achingly similar, one half utterly dominating the other. Admittedly, her Tyler and this Trevor were more subtly domineering than the brash minivan mommy, and perhaps had innocent enough intentions, but who knew how kids and the complacent solidity of marriage might mutate Tyler and "Trev" into the overbearing alpha-wench she had just seen. Petra looked over at the newly vacant parking spot, the young husband's unhappy face still hanging over it, like a drooping awning. She felt a bizarre kinship with him, and half-wished that she could have grabbed him away for a brief second, and given him a sympathetic kiss on his

94

cheek before he was stolen back into the stony monotony of the highway and his marriage. "Partner," Petra sarcastically grumbled. *Could there be a more manipulatively misleading relationship term?* she mused. The runt of the coupling always got consumed.

*****

Two hours later, Petra pulled into the narrow driveway of her rented cottage. It was mid-afternoon, and in the radiant glow of the sun, the small home was not quite as pristine as the internet photos had indicated, but was nonetheless welcoming. Freeing the key from its electronically coded box, she gathered her bags and entered into her temporary home. It was spare and neat, with just enough beachy touches to announce that she was indeed on vacation. A high-backed wicker chair with palm tree cushions sat next to a tortoise shell end table and pewter pineapple lamp, and a large glass hurricane vase brimming with sand and seashells sat astride the eat-in kitchen table. The décor was otherwise nondescript, but very clean and well-kept, and Petra happily slumped into the wicker chair, closing her eyes for barely a second when she heard knocking at the front door. Standing on the front porch were two slightly plump older women, with closely cropped gray hair, and similarly baggy sweatshirts and Bermuda shorts. Not waiting for a prompt, the slightly taller of the two women extended her hand to Petra, and introduced herself as Bennie, and her companion as Terrie.

"Gwen, the real estate agent, told us to welcome you when you arrived," Bennie explained. "We have been coming here every summer for years, and we know all the good places: beaches, restaurants, bars, shopping, whatever you're looking for." Pointing to the nearby coral stucco hut, "We're right next store if you need us." Terrie nodded agreeably, and they turned to leave.

"Wait, I'm Petra. Thank you for coming by. Actually, I do have a question. Are there any art galleries nearby?"

"Are you an artist?" Terrie inquired with enthusiastic curiosity.

"Sort of, I'm getting back into it. I like browsing galleries for inspiration." *Inspiration to get close to Peterson*, Petra inwardly admitted.

"Well, there are several high-end ones as you travel inland, but there is a wonderful gallery right here, a mile down," Bennie relayed, her head bending south. "Sandz, with a 'z.' Darla runs it, she's always showcasing quirky, gifted artists. Definitely go there, she's got a great eye for talent. It's open Wednesday through Sunday."

"Thanks, I will definitely check it out."

"Do you have dinner plans?" Terrie asked.

"I'm kind of tired. I was thinking of just settling in, and having some soup. I brought a couple of cans with me."

"Well, that sounds perfectly awful. Our husbands are barbecuing, if you'd like to join us. It'll be much better than canned soup," Bennie flatly stated.

"Oh...huh...," Petra blurted out, "um, I haven't had good BBQ in a while, that sounds nice," shocked at the mention of husbands, clumsily trying to sidestep her obvious assumption as to their sexual orientation.

Terrie playfully nudged Bennie's side, and they both detonated in laughter.

"I'm sorry, kiddo," Bennie sputtered through uncontrolled giggling, "I just can't resist messing with newcomers. I mean c'mon, look at us, we couldn't be anything other than nuns or lesbians."

Petra laughed too, feeling instantly comfortable with her new neighbors.

"The invitation and the BBQ are real," Terrie assured her. "Please come. We'll be grilling in the back yard by 6:00 p.m. Walk over anytime."

A couple of hours later, Petra was mostly unpacked, and ready to collapse onto the soft full-sized bed occupying most of the tiny bedroom, when the sizzling aroma of charcoal briquettes beckoned her to the adjoining bungalow. Strolling into their backyard, she was greeted by an energetic sheep dog, jumping onto her, smelling and licking her flip-flopped-feet and freshly soaped hands.

"Shasta! Calm down girl," Bennie warmly chided.

"Oh, I don't mind," Petra cooed into Shasta's white fuzzy face, bending down to tickle her soft ears.

After a few minutes of playing fetch with the oversized puppy, Petra sat down at the umbrellaed stone table with Terrie, while Bennie tended to the grill. Reaching for a large pitcher, Terrie poured Petra a tall glass of something golden and minty scented. "Here, have some iced tea, the good kind," Terrie said, winking, and Petra took a deep sip of the cold drink, refreshed and buzzed at once. A short time later, Bennie and Terrie started placing down various appetizing platters: shrimp kebabs, grilled chicken, veggie burgers, corn bread and spinach salad. The drinking and eating and light conversation conveyed them into the blushing nightfall, and the three were relaxing into a balmy silence when Bennie looked at Petra, and probed, "Forgive me if I'm overstepping, but I need to ask. I take it that you're here alone. So, are you running away from or towards something?"

"Ben, don't put the poor girl on the spot." Turning contritely to Petra, "She's so damn nosy. You don't need to answer."

"Don't worry, I'm not offended. Actually, you're very perceptive. I suppose it's a little of both. I'm about to go for my final gender reassignment surgery, and my fiancé hasn't been very supportive."

"Oh," Bennie and Terrie said in unison, stunned by the admission. They were mutely struggling for an appropriate and supportive response, when Petra suddenly pointed at them in laughter.

"Gotcha, I also like to mess with newcomers."

"Oooh, you're just as bad as this one," Terrie smiled, simultaneously pinching Bennie's arm and Petra's.

"Sorry, I couldn't help it. Seriously, I've had a tough time lately, and even though I haven't seen much of this place yet, I sense that I'll get what I need while I'm here. I'd be more specific if I could, but questions and answers are all hazy for me right now."

"And all those 'Fenwick Iced Teas' you've had aren't adding any clarity, I'm sure," Terrie joked.

"Honestly, they were just what I needed. I'm going to sleep like a baby tonight."

A half hour later, Petra was showered and bath robe encircled. Not wanting to be disturbed by the loud window AC, she opened the windows, the mild incoming breeze comforting in its slightly cool stickiness. She let the robe drop to the floor, and welcomed the swirl of air on her still damp skin. Wearing only cotton underwear, she curled into the velvety white sheets of her impermanent bed, sinking inside the fleecy mattress, and yet floating on feathery clouds of fatigue and alcohol. The pensive, brooding profile of Peterson Tate broke in and out of her semi-consciousness, an acrobatic butterfly too perfect and elusive to capture. "Peterson..." vaguely rolled off her lips as she fell into a dreamless sleep.

Chapter 14

The next day, Petra was greeted by a forebodingly drab sky and a mild hangover. *Those older lesbians sure know how to party*, she commented to herself. Still half asleep, she took one of the aspirin she always carried in a small pill case, wondering just how expired it was, and washed her face with cold water. It was Thursday, and she couldn't wait to visit the Sandz gallery. Her instinct told her it would somehow bring her closer to meeting Peterson. Brushing her teeth, and walking into a light spritz of the delicately aquatic French perfume Delaine had given her last Christmas, she slipped into a yellow mesh sweater and faded khaki shorts, and headed the Jeep into the small town. It was half past nine when she arrived at the modest smattering of eateries and shops, but several summer tourists were already milling about in search of meaningful souvenirs or take out breakfasts to be enjoyed beachside.

Petra wandered over to the Sandz gallery, peering into its wide paneled windows, hoping for an indeterminate beacon, some sign that would justify and explain her quest to find Peterson Tate. What she saw was a rather small, unlit space, devoid of activity. The pieces that she could make out in the obscuring shade were mostly deconstructed modern art configurations, amalgams of twisted metals, geometric shapes, cellophane, and haphazard paint. One sculpture looked like it might even contain popcorn and shredded argyle socks. *'Quirky' is an understatement*, Petra reflected. Finding nothing even slightly reminiscent of the warped medieval exquisiteness of Peterson's art, her eyes fell on the small sign listing the gallery's hours. It wouldn't be open for almost ninety minutes, so she meandered along the sidewalk, browsing in store windows and people watching, wondering if she'd even recognize Peterson if she did manage to bump into him. A door opened suddenly, two young girls bursting through with matching braided bracelets and jumbo sized pink slushy beverages, and Petra looked up to see a tiny café simply called Coffee.

The café was dimly lit, with just two tables, and a fairly large display case of baked goods. A desultory ceiling fan was doing little to cool the room, which appeared to be empty of customers and workers. Petra was about to walk out, when a demanding voice summoned her from the periphery.

"Hey, do me a favor," a kerchief covered head rising up from behind the display case spoke, "Open the door, and place the rock there in front of it, so it stays open. This place is hot as balls."

Given the raspiness and crude insistence of the voice, Petra was expecting to see a chain smoking, sun and time wrinkled hag, a true townie born, raised, and about to die in some dingy trailer. Instead, it was a pretty teenaged girl with long silky jet-black hair and a porcelain complexion, her china doll appearance at odds with her hard affect. The girl scowled at her with authoritative irritation, quickly prompting Petra towards the door. Propping the rock as instructed, Petra returned to the counter, the girl showing no vestige of thankfulness. "So, what do you want?" she unenthusiastically mustered.

"A cappuccino?" Petra asked without conviction, actually scared of this youngster who seemed like the even bitchier younger sister of the sketching museum bitch in NY.

"Broken, no foam." Rolling her eyes toward the ceiling, and imperatively strumming her fingers against the plexiglass display, she then cast a downturned gaze at Petra, challenging her to ask for something else.

"Okay…ummm," Petra stuttered, "j-j-just give me a black regular coffee, medium." Nervously scanning the display case, "And a blueberry muffin, please."

Frowning at the supreme inconvenience of pouring coffee, the girl practically glowered at Petra as she proceeded to shove the blueberry muffin in a bag. Petra uncomfortably looked away, noticing a butter dish on the back counter. She thought of her mother, lovingly preparing sumptuous fat laden breakfasts, and even of Tyler, and his romantic morning feasts in bed. Suddenly, she had enough of this girl's arrogance, and needed to challenge both her discourtesy and that of the disdainful faux artist from the museum.

"Stop." The girl froze, more out of shocked contempt than fear of reprisal, as her emerging sneer proved. "Look, Missy, save me the attitude. Put the muffin in the microwave, heat it up for *exactly* twenty-two seconds, then slice it in half, and butter it, generously. Do that, and maybe I'll leave you a fucking tip."

The sullen devil of a girl didn't dissolve into an angelic Disney princess, but she lost a trace of her angry bluster, and silently obeyed Petra's instructions. Handing her the coffee and the buttered muffin, she tiredly explained, "My dick boyfriend just broke up with me in a text, and meanwhile I am going to Dartmouth University, in the middle of bumfuck New Hampshire, just to be near him. He's a sophomore there. I could've gone to Columbia University. Fucking asshole. That's why I'm being a bitch, or at least, more of a bitch than usual."

"Don't feel too bad. Guys in NYC can be assholes too." Petra took a twenty-dollar bill from her purse, and left it on the display case. With still more than an hour to go until the gallery opened, Petra took her breakfast and sat on a nearby bench. The somnolent creaminess of the muffin diluted the jolt of the coffee, and she closed her eyes, drifting into a rosy daydream world.

The sky is still overcast when I close my eyes, but then I feel sun beams dancing across my face, their emergent heat penetrating my skin. This town is surrounded by water, and the smell of salt, taffy, and sunscreen wraps around everything like a perfumed snake. I am starting to become relaxed and at ease here, like I belong, at least for a time. A shadow pushes out the light covering me, and a strangely familiar man is grinning down at me. "You dropped this," as he hands me the paper bag holding the crumbs of the muffin. Instantly, I know it is Peterson. But how can this be? It's as if he stepped directly out from the old photographs of him, the past now ageless in the present. He sits beside me on the bench, steadily looking ahead, never facing me. "I wish you hadn't come here, Petra," he says after a few minutes. How does he know my name? I don't ask, but he answers. "I've always known you, but you don't know me. Find your home, and go there." And then, without moving away, he is gone.

"Well, that was creepy," Petra said aloud as she opened her eyes. Ignoring the advice of the ghostlike Peterson, she rose from the bench, and seeing that it was now past eleven, she headed back to Sandz. It was empty when she entered, except for the tanned, curly-haired woman standing on a step ladder, hanging an intricate curtain of beads from a white rod attached to a pedestal. Petra thought of offering her assistance, but the woman's every expression and movement suggested untouchable capability. Disembarking from the ladder, the sylphlike woman stepped back into her sandals and wheeled the art piece to the gallery's center, just beneath a skylight. The sunlight seeping down intersected with the rays from the front windows, electrifying the beaded sculpture, the pieces of glass and shell becoming lightning streaks of diamonds.

"That is so gorgeous. I've never seen anything like it."

"I know, this is one of my favorite pieces that I've ever shown. The artist, Opal May, is near ninety years old, and she's the most innovative, energetic person I know. She's got a boyfriend more than twenty years younger than her, smokes pot every day, flirts with everyone. Absolutely precious." Turning to Petra, "I'm Darla. What brings you here today?"

"I'm Petra. Bennie and Terrie recommended your gallery. I rented the place next door to them."

"Welcome to our little community, Petra," her words smiling. "You couldn't ask for nicer neighbors. So, are you just browsing?"

"Sort of. Art has always been my love, and now I'm trying to see if I want it to be my career."

"Well, that sounds exciting. If you're still here next Sunday, I'm hosting an exhibit of Opal's work. You should meet her. We're using the space next door, the last tenants just left, so it's empty." Her phone began vibrating, and she quickly offered, "Have a look around and tell me if you need anything," walking away to answer the call.

Petra then returned to the front of the gallery, reexamining the pieces she had peered at earlier in the day. Admittedly, the canvases and sculptures seemed less random and misshapen in the ambient brightness emanating from the light fixtures as well as from Darla herself, but none of the pieces aside from the crystal drapery seized Petra's attention. A freckled, gangly high school aged girl then gushed through the front door, motioning to acknowledge lateness and regret, and immediately set herself up at a small table in the corner. Still talking on the phone, Darla grabbed a portfolio from a shelf, and placed it before the girl, who began flipping through it. Petra continued to circle around the gallery, finally arriving at an oil painting, tucked into the recess of a back exit, almost too large for the restrictive space. It depicted a sprawling farm, stereotypically replete with red barn, grazing cattle, and spinning weather vane. The picture was so stylistically out of sync with every other piece of art in the gallery, so thoroughly out of place, and yet the only one that seemed to truly belong there, like it had always hung on the wall, the anchor to all the other floating guests. Petra stood immobile before it, refraining from the urge to touch it, when she noticed a dilapidated silo in the corner of the painting, tilting out of the frame, apparently disintegrating into the lush rural landscape. It gripped her as so recognizable, and she was coming into full perception when Darla materialized beside her.

"You have great taste. This is my other favorite piece. Only, this one isn't for sale."

"It's not?" Petra asked, only half-turning from the painting.

"No, a family friend painted it. I only display it here because it's so beautiful. It deserves to be hanging in a gallery." Suddenly, Peterson's presence was incredibly palpable, and Petra knew he was the family friend behind the painting.

"Do you have any other works by this artist?"

"No, he doesn't really paint anymore."

"That's too bad. You know, my grandmother was an avid art collector, and something about this piece reminds me of an artist she liked, I think his last name was Tate."

Darla's head abruptly swiveled from the painting to Petra, and her previous openness condensed into guarded suspicion. "Doesn't ring a bell. Anyway, I have a conference call to prepare for. Thanks for coming by."

Petra took one last look at the painting, and then exited into the now bleakly sunny day. She was almost to her car when urgent footfalls sounded behind her. Turning in alarm, she saw the young girl from the gallery.

Pausing for a moment to catch her breath, the girl introduced herself. "I'm Eve, Darla's granddaughter. I heard you guys talking. I know where you can find him."

"Peterson Tate?"

"Yes. Don't be insulted by my grandmother lying to you. He's very private, and she's protective of him."

"So why are you helping me?"

Shrugging her shoulders, "I don't know. Uncle Pete has seemed a little lost lately. You obviously like art. I just think he could use a friend who shares the same interests. I kind of feel like part of his bad mood is 'cause he doesn't paint anymore. Maybe you can help him with that. He hangs out a lot at Holt's

Landing. It's a state park not far from here. He likes to read there, sometimes goes crabbing. Check it out, but don't say I sent you." Eve then hurried back towards the gallery, and Petra got into her car, a broad expectant grin veiling her face.

I am sitting in a nondescript sports bar, a bowl of pretzels and a perspiring mug of beer in front of me, both untouched. The place is crowded, huddles of strangers I have no interest in meeting, and I'd like to leave but I don't know how I got here and I have no place to go. I go to the bathroom, just so I can look in the mirror and regain some sense of location, physical and emotional, but my reflection in the mottled, smoky mirror only disorients me more. When I return to my barstool, the frazzled husband from the New Jersey rest stop has landed on my seat, sipping from the beer I left behind. "I hope you don't mind; I was thirsty." He offers no explanation for his arrival, and I ask for none, but sit on the vacant stool beside him. Peter, he says simply. I suppose that is his name, which I find amusing, since Petra is the feminine version. I study his profile as he gazes through the pretzel bowl, into some private place I am not allowed to see, but yet I know I've been there, that I am there right now, with him, both of us wandering and afraid. He looks even sadder and more boyishly vulnerable than when I first saw him, and I want to bury him in my arms, drowning out his despair and mine, if only for a little while.

"My wife, she's not a bad person," he says, perhaps continuing a conversation we are already engaged in subliminally. "She had a vision of her future and I allowed her to fit me into it. We're living her dream, not ours, definitely not mine."

"What do you want?" I ask him, hoping his answer applies to me as well.

"Hmmm. Right now? Just quiet. I stopped listening to myself so long ago, I forgot what I sound like."

A hush descends on the bar, everyone's attention drawn to a special news report breaking through the hockey game on TV. On the screen is the waiflike girl I saw standing behind the hippie van at the rest stop, a banner beneath her smiling photo saying that her remains have been found in a Maryland ravine. The video cuts to her mother, pleading with the public to help find justice for her murdered daughter Petra. "Her name is Petra?" I nearly shriek, but no one looks away from the television screen. The wan face of her boyfriend comes next, a person of interest in Petra's demise, now himself missing. I reach for Peter's hand, feeling myself being sucked into the misery of the television broadcast, but he is no longer there, and I wonder if he ever was. I run out to the parking lot, and now I am somehow inside of the idyllic farm painting by Peterson. I keep running, but always end up back in front of the burnt-out silo. Peterson steps out from its toppling shadow, and I ask him what happened to Peter. He holds my face in his hands, and says, "My name is also like yours, but we aren't the same." Then he disappears just as the silo is about to crash upon me.

Chapter 15

It was Friday morning, and Petra awoke hungry and realizing she still hadn't purchased any groceries. Grumbling out of bed, she rummaged through the cabinets, hoping to find at least instant coffee or a not too stale granola bar. Nothing, not even an empty gum wrapper. She still had the two dented cans of soup she'd traveled with, but was craving a real breakfast. She heard her phone, and walked back into the bedroom, smiling when she saw that Terrie had texted. "Good morning. Don't know if you're an early riser, or if you have breakfast plans, but Bennie is making French toast, and we have fresh fruit and coffee if you want to join us. Pajamas and morning grumpiness are allowed. Just drop in if you want." Petra brushed her teeth, pulled on a long-sleeved T-shirt over her sleep tank, and kept on her pastel pajama bottoms. Slipping into her black Croc ballet slippers, she headed next door.

Terrie answered the door, and smiled broadly upon seeing Petra's sleep wrinkled face. "Wow, that was quick! You must be hungry. So glad to see you again! Did you ever get to the gallery?" Terrie led her to a small olive-green couch, and noticing Petra's slight nod, responded, "Darla is great, isn't she?"

Petra hesitated in answering, her face registering her faraway mind, remembering how Darla's initial friendliness fled at the mention of Peterson, and the subsequent intervention of Eve. *Holt's Landing, I have to get there.*

"What's wrong? Didn't you get to meet Darla? Did she upset you?" Terrie asked with noticeable concern.

"No, not at all. Amazing gallery, glad you guys recommended it. I was just thinking about the exhibit Darla mentioned, next weekend. Opal, you know her?"

"Opal, she's something, all right," Terrie recollected, now completely disengaged from her previous apprehension. "Yeah, Bennie and I will probably go. You should too. Just to warn you, Opal can be a little racy. She's libel to tell dirty jokes and pinch your butt. Political correctness is meaningless to her, but she's so lovable and talented that no one really gets offended. She refers to me and Bennie as her Cute Chubby Dykes, and we honestly think it's adorable. Her last showing two years ago coincided with her eighty-fifth birthday, and she made her grand entrance wearing a flesh toned mesh dress with eighty-five strategically placed shells. You have to meet her, Petra, it's a Fenwick Island rite of passage. You'll leave here with an off color but priceless nickname, courtesy of Opal."

Bennie called out just then, unseen from the kitchen. "Hi Petra, so glad you came. Terr, come here for a sec, help me grab the plates."

"Let me help," Petra said as she started to rise from the doughy soft couch.

"No, no," Terrie gently insisted, "you stay here and relax," turning quickly towards the kitchen.

Petra slumped into the plush cushions, gazing around the bungalow. It had a less open layout than hers, and was a bit more spacious, with a dining area that appeared to lead into the kitchen. There were several homey touches absent from her cottage, like embroidered pillows and crocheted throws, and she wondered if Bennie and Terrie had brought them, habitually carrying homelike snugness into even the most dingy and wayward motel rooms. She was lulled by the playful antics filtering into the living room, and began thinking of her plans for the day. She wanted to go to Holt's Landing, as Darla's granddaughter had suggested, but the strange visions she had been having of Peterson were making her edgy. Plus, she was actually enjoying the romantic anticipation of meeting Peterson, and she didn't want that deliciously ripe longing to degenerate into frustrated disappointment, whether she never found him or actually did, only to discover reality much less compelling than fantasy.

"Come into the dining room, Petra, it's ready," Bennie called out. She and Terrie emerged from the kitchen, carrying platters of cinnamon French toast, seared Canadian bacon, honeydew, peaches, and plums. An urn of coffee already rested on the table, as well as orange juice and banana nut bread. "Please, help yourself."

"Wow, this looks delicious. Thanks for inviting me."

"We're just glad you could come. Bennie and I love to cook, and we always have extra, so our door is open to you whenever you want."

Petra took a healthy portion of everything, and sipped the pleasantly robust coffee as she waited for Bennie and Terrie to fill their plates. "I was thinking of doing a little exploring today. Do you have any suggestions?"

"Well, it's supposed to be really hot and muggy, but sunny, so if you like the beach, this would be the perfect day for swimming and sunbathing," Bennie suggested. "There are some beautiful sandy areas right here, overlooking Indian River Bay."

"She can do that anytime, Ben. Personally, I think you should check out Seashore State Park. It's about twenty minutes away, and right on the Atlantic. Lots of powdery sand, a couple of restaurants, a bit touristy, but not as bad as the Jersey shore. Still, a little more exciting than staying right here. You might even meet a hunky surfer."

"That's true. You're too cute not to be seen. If you do go, have lunch at the Big Chill Beach Club. The crab cake sandwich and the Seaside Martini, you'll think you died and went to heaven."

"Okay, you sold me, though I don't know how hungry I'll be after eating all of this," and Petra tunneled into her brimming plate.

*****

An hour later, Petra was on her way to Seashore State Park, wearing a purple bikini and flowy white linen sundress. The traffic was light, and she looked forward to long, unhurried hours of sun basking, trashy romance novels, and fried sea food, the pounding surf and screeching sea gulls a pervasive white noise lullaby. The beach was relatively uncrowded when she arrived, and she set her large towel not far from the incoming tide, the sand refreshingly wet at her feet, the ebbing edges of the waves tickling her skin. She meditated upon her two sunscreen options, the wise protection of waterproof SPF 30 vs. the tropical sexiness of SPF 8 oil. Ghostly pallor blanketed her body like a February snowfall, so she opted for the oil, relegating the higher SPF to her face. As she was struggling to coat her back, a semi-familiar voice called out, "Let me." Standing before her was the young girl from Coffee, her angry, dark attractiveness at odds with the blinding sun. Observing Petra's startled hesitation, she knelt down and grabbed the oil from her, rubbing it into her back. "I was a clit the other day," she said, and Petra could sense the apology hiding within the girl's crass explanation.

"I get it, your ex-boyfriend sounds like an immature bastard."

"He is. Fucker. Anyway, screw him." Covering the last exposed part of Petra's back, she tossed the sunscreen onto Petra's blanket, and sat down on the sand next to her. "I'm Star."

"Oh, you..." Petra began, preempted by the girl's dismissive head shake.

"Don't. I've heard it all before. I know I seem more like an Elvira. My grandmother was a Woodstock hippie, and she wanted to name my mother Morningstar Glory. She got pressured into choosing a more regular name, Gloria Jane, which my mom has always hated. So, she decided that if she ever had a daughter, she'd give her the name she was supposed to have."

"I think Star is a beautiful name," Petra said, thinking of Peterson's address, repeating *34 Starlight Way* silently.

"So, what's your name?"

"Petra."

"Not exactly Heather or Kelly, so you probably got ragged on too as a kid."

"Sometimes. I used to pretend my name was Debbie or Jen, just to blend in. Someone I was close to made me really appreciate my name, though. Now...," sighing self-consciously, "never mind."

"Ex-boyfriend?"

"Yeah," Petra barely murmured, peering into the water, the golden sun kindling its surface.

"Asshole?"

"Not really...well, maybe once in a while. Hmmm, if anything, I'm probably the bigger asshole." Turning to face Star, "So, are you from here?"

"Connecticut originally. Now Dover. My mom and stepdad have had a summer place here for the past few years, but I've been coming to Fenwick since I was a little kid. My great aunt lives here year-round. That's actually how my mom and her husband decided to get a place of their own."

"You're staying with them?"

"No, they aren't both here steadily, so I'm hanging out at my aunt's place." Shifting her eyes towards the limitless ocean, she continued as if talking only to herself. "I'm not that close with my mom anymore, and I fucking can't stand my step...the guy she's married to."

Suddenly, Petra thought of her stepfather Beau, and his exaggerated Southern politeness, and she started to laugh.

"What the fuck is so funny?"

"I'm sorry. I wasn't laughing at you. It's just, I have a stepdad too, and he's really nice, but I hate his guts most of the time, and there's no legitimate cause."

"That's nice for you, but I definitely have a reason."

"Shit, I didn't mean to bring up something uncomfortable. He's never…?"

"Molested me?" Star assumed, and Petra involuntarily shivered. "No, I would've castrated the prick if he tried that. Forget it, I'm not wasting my day off talking about him." She removed her black tank and camouflage cargo pants, revealing a black bikini and pierced naval, and spreading out her towel, laid down next to Petra. "I'm going to listen to my music and try to fall asleep. Wake me up if I look like I'm getting burnt." She inserted her AirPods, and soon drifted off.

Petra studied her sleeping form for a few minutes, feeling some intangible yet definite connection with this complicated girl. Even in repose, she conveyed defensive alertness, simmering with subtle danger, as if warning that she could awake at any moment and spring into attack. But there was also something poignant and vulnerable about her, the whisper of a once innocent girl forced into oblivion. She wasn't even sure if she liked Star, but her enigmatic presence was welcome nonetheless. Petra was still consumed with the contradictory needs of stalling and pursuing contact with Peterson, and at least now she had a temporary companion who also seemed to be wrestling against time. Her trancelike focus on Star was broken by a beach ball landing near her feet, and quickly scurrying footsteps eager for its retrieval. A laughing little girl scooped up the ball, a blur of curly dark hair and creamy freckled skin. Petra watched the carefree youngster return to the comforting harbor of Mommy and Daddy, and she, too, closed her eyes and fell asleep under the blazing watch of the sun.

I'm still on the beach, but the air is different now, sultry and oozing in that way it only gets near the equator. Bali, that's where I am. Tyler is beside me, sleeping soundly against our velvety beach blanket, and this is our honeymoon I realize. We always dreamed of going to Bali, and now here we are, finally. My eyes dance over his muscled skin, wet beads glimmering against a dark honey tan. I return to my body, and see a pronounced bump under my very modest tankini bathing suit. I touch my distended and hard belly, gasping in shock, but then in happiness. I'm pregnant! So what if I can't wear sexy lingerie and skimpy dresses on my honeymoon, we're having a baby! Why had I been so afraid of committing to him in marriage? I've never felt more sublimely at peace than I do right now.

A beautiful red headed child runs over to me, plopping herself against me, nestling into my chest. It's the little girl from the Bluebird Café, who thought I was her mother, that awful day with Tyler and the shell necklaces, after we had broken up. Why is this little girl here in Bali? Please, don't let this be a dream! I need to stay here, with him, with the promise of our baby. "Dani!" a woman is calling out; it must be the child's mother. "You kinda resemble my wife," Dani's father had said when he collected her from me that day, and I am expecting to see a version of myself now. "There you are! Never run away from me again!" The voice is more harsh than loving, and it is not my twin standing before me, but the bossy minivan wife from the rest stop parking lot. She turns her superior gaze from her daughter to me, and grabbing the child away, roughly yanks up my bathing suit. A beach ball rolls out, and she cruelly laughs at me and my now flat stomach, kicking the ball as she victoriously marches off with her daughter.

"Fucking bitch!" Petra bellowed suddenly.

"Huh?" Star asked groggily, removing her AirPods as she slowly sat up.

"Oh, nothing," Petra replied, reflexively touching her stomach and rubbing her eyes, hesitant to open them for fear that her dream monsters had reached through into daylight.

"I'm hungover and I need some food. Wanna grab something," Star sleepily stated rather than asked.

Petra fully opened her eyes, and seeing that the sky was now slumping towards them with opaque grayness, she agreed to a meal break. "Sure. I was told the Big Chill Beach Club is great."

Groaning in revolt, and suddenly fully reawakened, Star shot her an exasperated look, "Pet, don't be such a fucking tourist. You're with a local, crawl out from Zagat's ass, and experience the real Fenwick. Seriously, if I came to visit you in NY, I'd be totally ticked off if you took me to the stinking Hard Rock Café and Tavern on the Green."

"How do you know I'm from NY?"

Impatiently answering, "In Coffee, you said NYC guys are assholes too.

I just assumed. Please, lighten up woman, I'm not stalking you." She pulled on her clothes and grabbed her towel, waiting irritably for Petra to follow suit. "Hello? Let's get moving."

Stalking, Petra thought unpleasantly. *Isn't that what I'm doing, searching for some mysterious artist who's probably just a self-important has-been?* Her face flushed in shame, certain Star would soon sniff out her pathetic reason for being on Fenwick Island. Suddenly cognizant of her annoyance, Petra scrambled to collect her belongings, and followed after Star, treading in her sandy imprints.

After a brief ride in Petra's jeep, they wound up on a remote side street, seedy compared to the wholesome coastal hangouts she had so far viewed. A scruffy older man sat on a stool propped against a steel gated shop, dragging intently on a cigarette butt he had probably salvaged from the sidewalk. As they walked past him, Star pulled down her tank and bikini top, briefly flashing a small but perfectly formed breast. Petra was slightly aghast, but the old man betrayed no response. "Hi Gus," Star teasingly breathed, then turning to Petra, "Poor guy, his brain is permanently fried. Too many acid trips."

"ECT," Petra mumbled sadly.

"What?"

"Shock therapy. Or a lobotomy. Something ungodly was done to him."

"Shit, I thought *I* was dark. You need a drink and a joint." Reaching into her pocket, she pulled out a small, plastic bag filled with dull green weed. "For later. If you haven't totally pissed me off by then."

Star then stopped in front of a small luncheonette, layers of ancient grease parasitically clinging on to the windows. Recognizing the barely disguised disgust on Petra's face, Star chuckled, and said, "Don't worry, no one's died from eating here." She opened the door, waving Petra inside. A dust caked vent was loudly droning linty stale air into the cramped interior, and Petra imagined dead rats inside the shaft, their decay permeating the damp atmosphere like a swarm of invisible bees. A strung-out looking couple was slumped over a table in the back, and an overweight, sweating cook was frying something on the steaming grill behind the linoleum countertop. Sitting upon a creaky swiveling stool, Star motioned for Petra to sit beside her.

"This place might look sketchy, but you won't find better burgers and fries anywhere, right Lenny?"

"You know it, BB," the cook said without turning around.

"BB?" asked Petra.

"Baby Bitch," explained Star, somewhat proudly. "You're not a new age, vegan, 'save the whales,' Peace Corp pussy, are you?" she asked, lightheartedly sneering at Petra.

"Yeah, and I also make my own soap, wear only hemp clothing, and live in a solar paneled house with a windmill. I take it you're more the drinking baby goat's blood, voodoo, Santeria type?"

"Ooooh—K, I'll stop making fun of you." Exaggeratedly whispering, "I'm actually not the terrible bitch I pretend to be."

The day ended up being so much different than I thought it would. I'm back in my bungalow now, and light rain is pattering against the windows. The ceiling fan is nimbly dropping fresh pockets of cool air upon me, and I am halfway into sleep, where the mind alternates between deep insight and cloudy misperception. Lunch in that greasy dive was actually delicious. Apparently, lard is the secret to sumptuous French fries, and I don't even want to know what hidden ingredient made the plump, juicy burger singularly delectable. We entered that place as tentative acquaintances and left almost like sisters, well, sisters that just met, if that makes any sense. The vodka lemonades abetted the fatty delights in breaking the ice, the alcohol supplied by the tarnished flask Star whittled out of her ripped black knapsack.

I relate to her vacillating moods, the fluid trapeze flying her between bravado and insecurity, the latent traumas we may or may not be aware of. I wonder if she is better or worse off than me for having her first relationship and aspirational crisis now, in the embryonic period before college, rather than at the near thirty benchmark. No impossibly perfect supermoms making her feel inadequate. Minivan bitch hasn't reared her smug head in Star's dreams yet. But I am grateful that I had those halcyon college and post-graduation years, even if my happiness was only a mirage, or perhaps a borrowed reality from a fantasy version of myself.

We left Lenny's greasy spoon, and Star walked us around back, to the garbage strewn alley. She adeptly rolled a joint, and we stood there, in the damp pre-thunderstorm stagnancy, the herbal, intoxicating vapor of the pot blunting the menace of the putrid, darkening alleyway. The laughter induced by the vodka was now forgotten, and the pot was making us both quiet and moody, even sad, but in a pleasant way, passing the melancholy between us as if it too were a joint. I don't know how long we stood there, and the details of the ride to her aunt's house, where I dropped her off, are foggy, but she told me when we arrived that she'd be back in Dover for a week, and as she walked into her aunt's perfectly quaint home, I felt like I was saying goodbye to some part of myself that I had only just discovered and might never find again.

How long did I stay sitting in the car after she walked into the house? I don't know, but somehow, I am back in the car, and all the lights in her aunt's house are off, so it must be late. Am I dreaming, or have I actually driven back here? A strong hand grips me from the back seat, and I'm terrified, but I don't scream. I turn, and it is Peterson, devilishly smiling at me. He's not the young Peterson from my imaginings, but an older and even more handsome one, the romantic Hollywood version that would be cast to play him in a movie. His hair is angel white, long and pulled back in a pony tail, and the years have chiseled his features into a marble perfection of maturity. I stare at him, wordless, trying to figure out why I wanted to see him, and afraid I'll find out. He picks up my hand, gently enfolding it like a vulnerable newborn, but his eyes bore into me ferociously, and I feel protected and assaulted.

"I'm glad you're here," he says finally.

"But I thought you wanted me to leave. Isn't that what you've been telling me?" I ask, hoping he'll deny it, admitting that he's always missed me, even before we met.

"Yes, because you have no place here, child." He lightly touches my chin, with the innocent fondness of an uncle, and I feel disappointed and rejected, and I'm about to ask him to get out so that I can leave, go anywhere that he is not, when his contemplation of me again becomes devouring, and his hushed words illicitly blow into my ear, "But I am only a man."

Chapter 16

Petra had forgotten to shut her bedroom drapes the night before, and the mid-morning sun crashed through the windows, wrenching her out of sleep. Terrie had given her a box of Earl Gray tea and some leftover banana bread, and after what seemed like the most hellish wait, the floral ceramic kettle boiled, and Petra took her tea and banana bread onto the front patio. She was glad to be wearing her thick bathrobe, because despite the sun, the air had that chilly and clean emptiness that sometimes snuck in after a summer storm. She tightly clasped the mug of tea, wanting its warmth to spread into her, a further barrier between herself and the early morning coldness. Finishing the banana bread, her phone vibrated in her robe pocket, and she saw a text from her mother. Calli had attached a picture of herself, doing yoga in her Zen garden, and Petra knew it was a postcard announcing "Wish you were here." She had told her mother where she was, but hadn't mentioned the length of her trip or the reason behind it, and she still wasn't ready to share anything else, so instead double clicked her love of the picture and eagerly got dressed for her day at Holt's Landing.

She sensed that she would run into Peterson, or at least desperately hoped she would, and dressed accordingly, wanting to look attractive but not cheaply provocative. The man was a complete mystery to her, yet she was certain that his tastes were more vintage Playboy than raunchy Hustler, so she chose her fifties style white halter bathing suit, pink cropped open weave sweater, and white cotton shorts. Standing before the floor length mirror inside the bedroom closet, she viewed herself through Peterson's imaginary eyes, and a sizzle of enticement ran through her, knowing this stranger would somehow sense her as something be-yond a stranger, just as she had with him, those old newspaper clippings of him seductively new and familiar. Before leaving, she sat down with her journal, hoping that the act of committing her butterflies to the page would still their fluttering. Holding the pen, she felt so many words and feelings rushing into her brain, competing for expression, but all she could manage to write was *Peterson. Today.*

Reaching Holt's Landing, she headed for the crabbing pier, as Darla's granddaughter, Eve, had suggested. Three men were currently there, and none were of the right age or general appearance to be Peterson. Mildly discouraged, Petra walked to a sandy area adjacent to the pier, and settled into the beach chair she had borrowed from Bennie and Terrie. Putting on the large sunglasses she had gotten from her office Secret Santa last Christmas, she grinned wistfully, knowing as soon as she had opened the gift that they were from Jeremy, his proud, silly smile a dead giveaway, and also that he must have pressed Tyler into helping him pick out the gift. She had seen the exact sunglasses in a boutique window one day the previous November, when she and Tyler were hurrying to catch a Thanksgiving Day train to Westchester County. They were barely going to make it in time for turkey with his family, but Petra saw the Jackie Onassis-like sunglasses peeking outside from their plastic pedestal, and she stopped for a few seconds, arrested by the fanciful feeling that they wanted to escape with her into the windy holiday chaos of the city. "C'mon, Petra, we're late" Tyler had said, not hinting that the glasses had registered upon him. *He noticed so much*, Petra mused, *so why didn't he see that something was wrong with me, with us?*

A tiny white and gray sandpiper then appeared beside her, repeatedly nipping its adorably small beak into the sand, searching for food or unknown treasure. Its wobbly determination caused Petra to reenter the landscape around her, and she became humbled by the vast spectacular beauty of the almost cloudless sky pouring its abundant blueness into the sun speckled Indian River Bay. She had brought a sketch pad and pencil with her, and began drawing the stunning natural view. Her eyes returned to the pier, a group of teenagers now appearing there, but still no sign of her slippery artist. She began adding the wooden lines of the pier to her sketch, and with the coil of impatience and suspense twisting through her mind and heart, the pier emerging on the pad seemed to Petra a mythic reptile, savagely biting into the pristine bay.

She attempted to distract herself with a paperback novel, a shallow, sanitized hybrid of mystery and romance, sure to have a satisfyingly dull Hallmark ending. The mood of the book was light and sugary, but she couldn't escape into it, every word of romance or intrigue weaving into an off-page sentence that was as clear and big as skywriting, *Where is Peterson?* She dumped the book into the sand, and drooped sulkily into her chair, closing her eyes, needing the splashes of heat and sound to numb the sensation of want growing within her. She had fallen asleep briefly, when a barking whistle emanated from a nearby volleyball game. Absent-mindedly she looked up at the pier, now sprinkled with several more people than earlier, indistinguishable in the glaring white sunlight. There was one man by himself at the beginning of the pier. Removing her sunglasses, she squinted against the sun-light to better examine the solitary figure, and found no discernible net or pole, noth-ing to indicate that he was crabbing or fishing. He just seemed to be embedded into the planks of the pier, staring inertly into the water, a sculpture keeping watch behind stony eyes. She retrieved her sketch pad, and quickly added the lone man to her sketch, the lines of his figure overtaking the rest of the view, on paper and in life.

"It's him," she suddenly said aloud, looking back and forth between the distant man and her drawing, reminded of the old photo she had found of Peterson brooding into Nantucket Sound. She pulled on her shorts and began trudging to the pier, running through various excuses for approaching him, all seeming too foolish or unoriginal for such a potentially extraordinary encounter. She had almost reached him, and still had no clue what to say, when he suddenly turned around, his look heavy with a question that seemed to be there even before he saw her. Within milliseconds, she catalogued every visible inch of him. It was definitely Peterson, but he was thinner than she had imagined. His former mess of inky hair was now short cropped and rippled with gray, and his sharp facial features were exaggerated by the leanness of age. But the overall effect was of an extremely at-tractive, strong man, middle aged but with palpable traces of youthful ripeness.

The will to speak to him, to break into his world, overrode her reticence to speak, so she began, "Do you mind if I sit here?" Pointing to where she had been stationed, an instantaneous fabrication slid comfortably off her lips, "Some creep was bothering me, and I just wanted to get away from him." He nodded, and then returned his eyes to the water. She shyly sat down, wondering what he was so silently pondering, and if she'd ever get to hear his voice. Her right hand began nervously tapping her pencil against the pier, and he turned briefly towards her, looking only at her hand. It was then that Petra consciously realized she had brought her pencil and sketch pad, and she returned to the drawing, grateful for a security blanket in which to bury herself.

"Is that me?" he asked a short time later, peering into the sketch, his words sounding resonant and exposed.

"Yeah, from where I was sitting, you were the closest person on the pier."

"Well, even if it was only because of proximity, it's nice to be part of any artistic inspiration these days."

"What do you mean?" Petra asked, hoping not to betray any foreknowledge of his artistic past.

Ignoring the question, he finally looked back at her, a dim smile easing onto his face. "So, did we fool him?"

"What?"

"Your unwanted admirer. You think he figured we're here together, and gave up his pursuit?"

"Oh," making a pretense of scanning the surroundings, "I don't see him, thankfully." Willing herself to stand up, she politely continued, "But I've had enough sun anyway, so I'll go back for my chair now and leave. It was nice meeting you."

"But we didn't really meet." He peered up at her with intent for the first time since she had strolled over to him, and her words and breath got locked inside her throat. Still boring into her, "I'm Pete. And you are?"

"Petra," she replied after an almost too long silence, her name now sounding foreign and fake to her own ears.

"That's lovely. The female form of my name," smiling provocatively at her.

His slightly haughty flirtation annoyed her, arousing unpleasant memories of Mitch Gainsley, and she retorted, "Actually, you have the male form of *my* name." She remembered Tyler's beautiful card from long ago, looping together the ancient origin of her name and their relationship, a poetic figure eight that was supposed to wrap them inside eternity. She looked down, the sight of her fidgety feet doing little to quell her unease.

Standing up, his sudden nearness summoning her to face him, he clasped her hand inside both of his, an electrical zap bouncing between them, as he said warmly, "It's nice to meet you, Petra. I'm ready to leave too. Let me escort you out, so that 'creep' stays away."

She nodded in agreement, and they walked silently toward the parking lot after gathering up her belongings. Without asking, Peterson had taken the chair from her, his ease masking its bulkiness. Nearing her car, Petra wondered if this was it for them, a gentlemanly escort and a polite goodbye. She didn't even know what she had expected or hoped for, but a cordial, brief exchange wasn't enough. Sagging under her disappointment, they arrived at the jeep.

"You're from Tennessee?" he asked with surprise, resting the chair against the rear of the car.

"Huh?"

"Your plates, they're from Tennessee," he explained, with a hint of suspicion.

"Oh, I rented this car. I'm from New York," embarrassed that she'd been so distracted lately she hadn't even noticed the plates, the gracefully coiling "Tennessee" branded against a mountainous landscape. She blushed, convinced he could flush out the true source of her distraction: *him.*

Instead, he seemed to relax out of his misgivings, and inquired, "The city?"

"Yes, I've lived there on and off since college."

"Yeah, I didn't get a Syracuse or Buffalo vibe from you."

"Thank you, I think. I know it's elitist, but I've always felt that I'm more of a true New Yorker than someone living their entire life in some humdrum hamlet near Canada that nobody has ever heard of." He said nothing, appearing to study her like an exhibit in a museum, or maybe like an exotic animal in the zoo she thought, enticing but safely caged. Sighing in chagrin, "Sorry, that sounded mean."

"Don't apologize. I agree. It takes someone special to thrive in a big city, and when you hear New York, in film, music, or casual conversation, you think Manhattan."

"Have you ever been?"

"Yes, somewhat frequently over the years, less often now. I lived there for a few months when I was much younger. Chelsea."

"That's a great area, very artistic."

"Mm hmm," shifting on his feet uncomfortably, "Uh, your sketch is really good. Are you an artist?"

"Maybe, I'm still trying to figure that out. Well, thanks for walking me to my car." She wanted to suggest they go somewhere, but couldn't make herself ask, thinking that any eagerness she showed would clue him in to her agenda.

"No problem, take care." He pointed to the chair, silently asking if she needed help, turning away when she nodded in denial. Petra watched him for a few steps before glumly stowing the beach chair in the back of the jeep, annoyed with herself for being so nervous and letting an opportunity to speak further with him slip by. Also vexing was that she still couldn't understand why learning about him was so important to her. "It's a smokescreen, Petra," she counseled herself as she settled inside her car, "a way to avoid self-examination. This is a pathetic soap opera fantasy that some dashing older artist is going to magically transform your life. Stop being an idiot." Closing her eyes, she was soon startled by tapping on her window; seeing Peterson, she quickly opened her door.

"Didn't mean to alarm you. Umm, this will probably sound strange, but I was just wondering if you wanted to take a ride with me? I have some fishing equipment in my car that I borrowed from a friend, and I was going to drop it off at his house. It's a pretty scenic drive, and since you aren't from here, I thought you'd enjoy it."

Petra stared back at him in silence, wondering if she should pinch herself. Had he actually come back to invite her to spend more time with him? Was she dreaming?

"It's okay, I'm sorry. You've already had one weirdo bothering you today, and for all you know, I could be another one. Enjoy your stay here."

"No, I'm sorry. I think I was in the sun too long, makes me tired. I would love to go for a ride."

"Really? Great, my car is just over there," pointing towards the next row of automobiles.

They walked in silence as before, but now Petra was feeling less anxious. Seeing glimmers of his own uncertainty made him less intimidating, more human. He wasn't some larger than life, swashbuckling figure from a classic novel, he was a flesh and blood man, surely with his own unglamorous idiosyncrasies. And more than ever, she needed to know more.

Arriving at a spotless and sleek white Mercedes coupe, Peterson announced "This is me."

"Nice car."

"It's my wife's. She's into status symbols. She borrowed my old pick-up truck because she's moving into a new office."

"She works nearby?" Petra asked, straining to sound nonchalant even though the mention of a wife disturbed her more than she wanted it to.

"About an hour and a half away, near our house. Our vacation home is here in Fenwick."

He opened the car door for her, and lightly grazed her arm as she settled into the beige passenger seat, the hot supple leather searing her less than her own heated thoughts. *Great, I came all this way to meet a married man.*

Perceptively gauging her apprehension, he explained, "My wife is getting back into her career, and she's barely been here this summer. And even when we're both in the same place, we're not. But I am married." He turned away from Petra then, staring blankly out the unbearably clean windshield. "Maybe it was inappropriate or forward of me to ask you to come on this ride, but honestly, I just wanted some company, and I thought you'd like to go sightseeing."

"Yeah, I'm glad you asked me. I've been meaning to drive around more, and I'm happy to do it with someone who knows what they're doing." *Oh, no. Did I just say that? Welcome to Penthouse Forum. Horny young traveler seduces older man.*

"All right, good. My friend's house is in Bethany Beach. It's about ten minutes away, but I'm going to take the back roads. It'll take a bit longer, but the view is prettier, if you're not in a rush."

"No, I'm not."

They drove through town, passing Coffee, and Petra smiled wistfully, thinking of Star and wondering if she'd ever see that lovely and awful girl again. Leaving behind the cluster of familiar shops, they soon came to a lighthouse, pearly white in the late afternoon brightness. Peterson pulled the car over, turning to Petra. "You've seen this already, right?"

"Yes, when I first arrived, but I was in such a hurry to get to my cottage, I didn't really stop to notice how beautiful it is."

He then navigated the car into the driveway of an adjacent house, the innocent hominess of the white clapboard and red shudders an antidote to the strange mix of curiosity and fear bubbling within Petra, finally close to this man her imagination had been circling intimately.

"What is this?"

"The keeper's house. It's vacant now, but open for tours on the weekend." Turning the car off, he looked at Petra with eagerness. "Come with me, I want to show you something." He led her to the locked metal fence encircling the lighthouse.

"It looks closed."

"It is," and Peterson winked playfully at her. He pulled out a wallet from his shorts pocket, and dug out a key. "I was on the restoration committee for a few years, and they gave me this." He quickly unlocked the gate, and encircled Petra's waist as he walked her around the lighthouse.

"What are we doing here? Is there an alarm or security system?"

"Relax, this isn't NYC, and we aren't robbing a bank."

He then knelt down before the lighthouse, and motioned for Petra to come next to him. She rested her knees on the dried grass, feeling the peppery heat of his arm fusing into hers, panicked that he would kiss her, and bothered that he might not. He reached up his hand, and began tracing the surface of one of the white bricks. Petra studied his profile as he became entranced in this rhythmic touch, and she wanted desperately to enter this private space with him. He took her hand then, gliding his index finger over hers, a silent invitation for her to carry on his tracing. She felt a ridge embedded into the brick, and followed its familiar curve, seeing it by touch more clearly than she had ever seen anything with her eyes.

"It's a heart," she said after a few prolonged seconds. "But it feels so sad."

He turned briskly to her, a look of wonder that dissolved into a mournful grin. "The lighthouse was built in 1858, and no one really knows the actual story of the heart. But I always felt like I did." Petra's eyes widened with anticipation, and he turned back to the lighthouse. "I think a traveling mason showed up one day, looking for work. He was quiet and somber, and nobody liked him, but they were desperate to finish building the lighthouse, so he was hired. The last day of work, the mason was seen kneeling at the base of the lighthouse. He was crying, so no one approached, and they all went to eat lunch. When they came back, he was gone, and the next day, he never came to get paid. A few days later, some kids playing on the beach found his boots lying on the sand, and inside one of them was a picture of a young woman. The other builders went back to the area where he had been kneeling, and saw the heart carved into one of the bricks. The woman was his wife, she drowned, and he built the lighthouse for her, to find her way back to shore. When he finally realized she wasn't ever coming back, he walked into the ocean, so *he* could find *her*."

We didn't say anything for a while after he finished his story. It was so utterly beautiful in its tragedy, and it reminded me of the raft-bound lovers I had sketched while in Jamaica with Tyler, drifting into certain doom, sealed inside their love. The ride to his friend's home in Bethany Beach was picturesque, lots of winding, shaded tree-lined streets dipping back and forth from sunny ocean vistas. When we arrived at the house, a gated gray ultramodern oceanfront mansion, I nearly gasped, the still bright sky with subtle hints of pink dusk illuminating its exterior into a mountain of silver. The side garage door was opened, and Peterson left his borrowed fishing equipment there, walking me to the back of the home, the vast patio seemingly diving into the ocean. Occupying center stage was a kidney shaped pool, a lightly trickling waterfall gently lapping at its surface, the dark tiling making it more like a twilit lagoon than a late afternoon swimming pool. A wooden gazebo in the far corner was flickering with electric candles, and we perched on its circular bench, the briny air tickling our bare skin in gentle, teasing gusts. It felt so natural sitting with him, this unfamiliar person, in some other stranger's home. Maybe it was the timeless crashing of the surf, or the days I had spent studying him, or even a genuine connection between us, known by us both, even if yet unspoken.

On the way back, we said very little, other than mentioning the magnificent scenery. We were lazily listening to the radio when a Pink Floyd song came on, "Breathe." We both reached for the volume control, shyly smiling at each other when our fingers briefly rested side by side. He told me that a Pink Floyd cover band is playing this Sunday at a nearby "redneck biker bar." Selbyville is the town, it sounds generic and tame enough, but he says the bar is in a sketchy area, attracts a rough crowd, and that I shouldn't go alone. I tease him, "this isn't NYC," echoing his earlier words, but he is insistent. He is cancelling his own plans so that we can go together. This makes me happy, but also guilt-ridden. Ours wasn't an innocent meeting. I researched him, orchestrated our "bump-in," manipulated fate. He might not be producing any more art, but his artist's eyes are surely still alert, stealthily observing and distinguishing designs and patterns, artificial and natural, man-made and organic. He'll figure it out, and see that I'm a fraud. And then what? Whatever regard or interest he has for me will be smothered by revulsion.

Fraud, again that horrible slur Mitch threw at me. I hope the poison of Mitch doesn't follow me into sleep. It was a mostly satisfying day, and that's all I need to know right now.

...Tyler has his laptop in bed. For weeks, he's been working on a research grant application. As dedicated as he is to his career, he has always made time for us, until now. I feel both intrusive and invisible as I slide under the sheets next to him, not sure if his sudden impatient shifting is in response to or in spite of my presence. There have been no half awake, playfully ridiculous nighttime conversations, no shared meals, not even an absentminded caress or an honest kiss. I've never seen him this preoccupied and stressed, and I want to support him, but he dismisses

all my efforts, apologizing for "being a jerk," without bothering to look up from his array of papers, books, and electronic devices. Now I've shut my eyes and rolled myself inside the comforter, my barrier against his disregard, when I feel his arm crossing over my body, rolling me onto my back. I think he mutters "Okay?" and then he is on top of me, the heat from his body as cold and hard as an icicle. He finishes, and collapses onto his side of the bed, the other side of the world.

The next morning, I try to act normal, but I feel awkward around him, like I've just spent the night with someone whose first name I don't even know. I probably babble as we are drinking coffee, him rushing through his as I barely taste mine. There is a Jeff Buckley retrospective this coming weekend at an arts center in Brooklyn, and I am dying to go. "I know you are slammed right now, honey, but I would love for you to come with me. Members from his band will be performing his music, his poetry will be displayed, and the best part..." He interrupts me, "You go, that's your thing, not mine. I'll probably be working all weekend, but if I do get a free moment, I'm going to watch March Madness at Kilgannon's with some guys from work. Sorry babe. See ya later." And I am pacified with an absent kiss atop my head as he heads out the door.

... "This guy was a fucking genius," Mitch says as he reads one of Jeff's profound and melancholic poems. "What a waste of talent, drowning at thirty. Hey, how old are you?" I'm barely listening to anything Mitch is saying because I am still angry that I am here at the Jeff Buckley tribute with him instead of Tyler. I recently finished editing Mitch's latest book, and after all the meals and massages he has gifted me, I figured I owed him this much. Normally, I enjoy his company, but tonight he is annoying me. He's a huge Jeff Buckley fan like me, so I asked him to come, no big deal, but maybe he thinks this is a date.

"Stop staring at my tits!" I want to scream at him, but then again, I am wearing a very low-cut sheer sweater, my not-so-subtle fuck you to Tyler for choosing college basketball with the Linguistic department misfits over a night out with me. I once sat through a lisping professor's bone-dry three-hour lecture about sub-Saharan language development because it was important to Tyler, and he couldn't come to enjoy this night with me? "Why isn't your boyfriend here tonight?" Mitch purrs annoyingly into my ear, and I want to strangle him. I look at Jeffy's beatific, artfully carved face staring down from a poster, and I want to wish him back into existence, this pure, sensitive, innocent man, now forever lost. But even he, so angelically epic in death, could probably be an asshole too.

126

Chapter 17

Kat's Nip was the name of the bar, and it rested at the end of a dilapidated string of stores, all with questionable wares and patrons. Straggly lost souls, weather beaten by life, milled about, entering and vacating grubby places like EZ Check Cash, Big Bubba's Smoke Shop, Tiny's Tattoo Emporium, and Massage Mania. The unpaved parking lot of the bar was filled with motorcycles, some idling noisily, amid scattered clusters of grizzled bearded faces, scuffed leather boots, and bandana shrouded heads. From her earliest college days at Columbia, when she and her friends would gamely explore their new home, Petra had felt at ease in even the scuzziest of NYC neighborhoods, grateful to experience people and smells and sounds that her fairly cloistered suburban background had limited to remote abstractions in movies and TV shows. Yet here at this biker bar, she felt even more discomfort than she had when dining with Star at the grimy lunch spot. It was as though the wide open, beachy clean sights held an unforgiving spotlight, exposing this claustrophobic, threatening underbelly.

They entered the wood paneled tavern after Peterson handed a pock-marked, stocky bouncer type the ten-dollar cover charge for them both. The air in-side was heavy with nicotine, stale sweat, and spilt beer, and Petra held back the urge to obnoxiously cough and fan her face, lest some leather clad biker chick put a cigarette out on her face.

"So much for no smoking indoors," Petra furtively whispered to Peterson.

"That's probably the least serious of the laws being broken here tonight," and as he uttered the last few words, Petra sensed a sensual undercurrent, but it flickered off as quickly as it emerged. "The band is really great. I saw them in Maryland last year. They're starting to develop a pretty big following within the central East Coast. Though I'd say from the looks of things, this crowd tonight is mostly local."

"I don't get it. Why a biker bar? I never associated Pink Floyd with the Hell's Angel crowd."

Peterson smirked, and leaned into her ear, her neck prickling where his voice vibrated off her skin. "See the girl with the tambourine, standing next to the other band members?"

Petra gazed towards the back of the bar, seeing a tall, slender young girl with big doe eyed beauty and thick light brown hair cascading down her back, her flared jeans and off the shoulder white peasant blouse ripped out of 1969 Haight Ashbury hippie-dom. "Yeah."

"Now look behind the bar. That's the owner. You do the math."

Petra's gaze fell on a potbellied older man, with an ill-fitting T-shirt and a pug nose, staring at the tambourine temptress with undisguised lust, his meaty hands practically quivering as he toweled off a beer mug. "Ewwww. That poor girl. I'd rather die than have that letch touch me." She instinctively entwined her arms, feeling suddenly bare in her delicate cardigan.

"She's the one calling the shots, trust me. Old Harry is just along for the ride. I'm sure she's going to grab his drunken flabby ass and…"

"Stop it! Look, I *don't* want to hear anymore. You obviously don't have a daughter," and Petra's combative tone surprised even herself. *Where is this coming from? Why am I being so hard on him? He was nice enough to escort me to this hellhole.*

Pausing before he spoke, "No, I don't." He seemed taken aback and wounded, and Petra further regretted her ill-chosen words.

"Pete…" she began in apology before he interrupted her.

"Hey, you are right about him being vile." Pointing towards the back of the bar, "Why don't you grab a table, there seem to be a couple of free ones, and I'll get us drinks. What would you like?"

"Seven and seven. No wait, a scotch sour. Oh hell, just get me a Bud light, not on tap, in a bottle."

Peterson went to the crowded bar, and Petra observed him ordering their drinks from a well-groomed, bespectacled young man that looked even more out of place with this rough and tumble crowd than she and Peterson did. She felt overwhelmed with sorrow and fear for all three, herself and these two men, in reality just oversized little children infiltrating a perilous, adults only playground. *This is a mistake. What am I hoping to gain here? I should have left him alone that day on the pier, where we were both lonely but still safe.* She found her way to a table in the corner, unlit and seemingly abandoned. Slumping against the hard chair, she wondered if she should call for a car and escape from Peterson, never to look back. He was still at the bar, and she glanced around, searching for a nearby exit.

"Hi Little Lady," came a hoarse, decrepit voice. Petra turned back to see the owner gaping down at her, even more disgustingly lustful up close. "On vacation? I never seen you round here before." His eyes slithered around her face and body, his gaze as invasive and rough as actual fingers pushing into her skin.

She said nothing, just looked at him with contempt, which seemed to excite him further. "What's wrong darlin? I just came to make sure you're having a good time. What can Harry do to make that happen?"

"You really want to know?" and then motioning him to bend in closer, she said breathily, "Get the fuck out of my sight."

"Why, you little bitch. I have a mind to...."

"Harry, is there a problem here?" Peterson placed his double whiskey and Petra's beer on the table, and smiled tauntingly at the man, moving within a hair's breadth of him. "I certainly hope you haven't troubled my niece."

Harry backed a step away, fury giving way to bitter resignation, "No problem here, Mr. P. Enjoy." He sneered briefly at Petra, spitting under his breath as he walked towards the band, "Niece, my ass."

"Nice guy. You're friends with him?"

"No, but I've been coming here since I got the summer house. I had a motorcycle until last year, and I used to ride out to this place when I needed a break."

"A break from what? Your beach vacation home? Sounds a little spoiled." She pinched his arm lightly so he'd know she was teasing, not wanting to be rude to him a second time in the same night.

"I don't know. Perfection maybe, or the illusion of it. This place, the whole area, it doesn't pretend to be something it's not. It's horrible and it doesn't hide that." He took a long sip of his whiskey then, and Petra stared at her beer, sensing that they both were thinking of all the ways they were hiding things, especially from themselves.

Picking up her Bud Light, Petra wanted to cut them both loose of the inner tumult brewing between them, and lightly asked, "So I suppose for the rest of the night I have to call you Uncle Pete?"

"Sorry about that. It's just, small towns, big gossip."

A lilting laugh rose above the crowded noisiness of the bar, and Petra's eyes were directed towards the band, the girl with the tambourine locked in amused conversation with Harry, touching his shoulder and tossing her head back.

"I'm gonna be sick," Petra announced, unable to pull her view away from the disturbing scene. As Harry reached up to touch the girl's face, a shuddering coldness rippled throughout Petra's body, and she visibly winced.

"That old pervert really bothers you," Peterson observed.

"Hmmm, I know," Petra said dreamily, "and I'm not sure why, beyond the obvious 'ick' factor."

Placing a protective arm around her, he reassured her, "The music is going to start soon. Forget everything else."

When I entered this raunchy bar with Peterson, I felt so out of place and nervous. Now a couple of hours later, I am subdued, unbound, almost satisfied, like I have just had a hot stone massage, a steaming cup of honey rich herbal tea, and a valium. The music is one reason...he was right, I just needed to absorb the sound, to let it buzz into my mind and body, to block out the noise, especially my own...but he is part of it too. We are caught in this comforting web of platonic introduction and mutual intoxication, ease and captivation growing with every moment. Of all the things I shared with Tyler, music wasn't one of them, and I am so happy to be here with Peterson, the songs echoing within and through us both, his close by sensory experience mingling inside of mine.

The band started their set with "Another Brick in the Wall," and they were better than I expected. They segued into "Money," trying to soften the potentially unreceptive crowd with radio friendly offerings. No one was throwing tomatoes or booing, but the chattering hadn't ceased, and I felt bad for the musicians, so lovingly rapt in a musical gift that was only being partially opened. Then, the keyboard player began playing the woeful, otherworldly chords of "Great Gig in the Sky." The compelling quietness of those sounds slowly began to cling on to the competing din, until the girl stepped forward to the mic, her silvery tambourine laid to rest somewhere. Her head tilted back towards the water damaged ceiling,

her body unnaturally still, as if she were searching for heaven in the damp stains
and peeling paint. A spectral wail began to echo from the microphone, her delicate
voice penetrating through the smoky, stagnant air, and hypnotizing everyone into
awed silence. The song ended after a few minutes, but its chilling pulse seemed to
reverberate long after she sung the last note. For the rest of the set, no one spoke
or moved.

*****

The bar was now nearly empty, and Petra's head rested against Peterson's shoulder. Her half-closed eyes took in the corner of the room where the band had assembled, now vacant, no vestige of person or instrument. She breathed in the scent of his shirt, breezy mountain air with hints of earthy wet skin, and wondered if the band's performance had been a shared and intimate hallucination.

Peterson gently rubbed her arm, and said, "Hey we need to go. We're practically the only ones here."

"Did I fall asleep?" she asked groggily.

"For a little bit. I didn't want to disturb you. But that bartender looks like he's sixteen and late for curfew."

His phone lit up, and he absentmindedly grabbed it. Petra was roused by the sight of a smiling baby, wearing a pink hat and with improbably knowing eyes, reminiscent of his.

"Who is that?"

"My granddaughter. Seven months old."

"She's precious."

"Mmm hmmm," seeming farther and farther away with every second.

"She's your first one?

"Yeah, too bad I'll probably never see her in person," he said with grim acquiescence, his eyes probing inside and past his phone.

"Why would you say that?"

"My daughter-in law sends me pictures and updates, but I don't have a relationship with my son, never really did, and it's just gotten worse since..." he trailed off, looking adrift like he had when she first spied him from afar at the crabbing pier.

"Since what?"

131

Looking directly at her now, "He was always much closer to my wife. With me, uh, I don't know, we just never connected."

"How old is he?"

"Probably about your age. He'll be thirty soon."

My exact age. She felt uncomfortable all of a sudden, his words dragging up some specter of a buried feeling or experience, and she wanted to get far from that psychic sinkhole. "Well," she began haltingly, "maybe you and your wife could both visit him, she could bring you two together?"

He looked away, staring into his now almost flat club soda and lime, sardonically smiling, "That's not going to happen."

He then stood up, and reached out to her. Arm in arm, they walked quietly to the Mercedes, its crisp white exterior frail and ghostlike underneath the settling mist. He opened the passenger door for her, and they stood there rooted by a twin pulsation to be as close as possible to one another. He pulled her towards him, and they clasped on to each other tightly. She felt blissful inside his rugged embrace, yet a tear glided down her cheek, from a primitive lens that saw things much deeper and sooner than her burnt chocolate eyes. He then slowly pulled away and ushered her into her seat, his attentiveness as warm and dewy as a kiss.

Once he settled inside the car, he distractedly shrugged, staring out into the parking lot, a depressed void in the wake of the now disappeared motorcycles. "My wife wouldn't have come with me tonight, even if she was here. And even if she had, well, it wouldn't have been as good as it was being with you. Shit," he sighed, "I'm sorry. I shouldn't have said that."

"Not to your niece, anyway."

"What? Oh right, my niece. Funny."

"I'm glad we got to go together too. It's nice sharing something meaningful with a kindred spirit."

He seemed surprised by her comment, "You really think so? What makes you feel we're alike, other than our obviously good taste in music?"

Petra felt all the blood in her body rush to her cheeks, and she was afraid her secret knowledge of him was about to explode out of her veins. Attempting to regain her composure, she coyly queried, "C'mon, Pink Floyd, isn't that enough? How many seventies babies were conceived based solely on Dark Side of the Moon?" *Oh no, again I'm making overtly sexual remarks.*

"Even some born in the nineties, I would think," he whispered, lightly tapping two fingers against her collarbone, then ever so faintly sliding down the warm slope of her chest. Pausing his fingers to meet her gaze, he smiled faintly, and drifted back into his seat, turning the car on and taking her home.

I can't fall asleep. My tired body is still awake within my beautiful evening with Peterson. The music was transcendent and healing, even more achingly beautiful in contrast with the smutty environs. And Peterson...wow. Even when I was a bit prickly to him, or shamelessly flirting, he was never anything but a perfect gentleman. That makes me think even more highly of him, but I'm not sure I want him to stay polite and respectful. In his car, when he reached over to touch me, I felt that sublime hum of nervousness and sexuality encircling and moving between both of us. I'm glad that nothing happened though. Too messy. He's married, much older than me, we met under false pretenses, my personal and professional life is in chaos, I'm having an early midlife crisis. This could only end badly. What's the point? No reason to see him again.

Oh, fuck common sense and propriety. I WANT to see him, I need to. Yes, I engineered our meeting, but the attraction, the rapport, the sexual tension...that's all organic. No one person or event could manufacture this connection we have. Okay, we both have our issues, but who doesn't? The marriage. That gives me pause. But if he's not happy, he's not happy. Don't we all have a right to be happy?? Maybe we'll keep things innocent, I'll try to anyway, but if things go another way... well, some things can't be stopped, no matter how hard you try.

We are good for each other, at least for right now. Darla's granddaughter encouraged me to reach out to him, said he needed to reclaim his art. I think it's already happening. Tonight, when we sat in his car in front of my bungalow, he asked me if I was still sketching, if I did any painting. He wants to paint again, said it's always been a hobby, but didn't admit that he was once a professional artist. What is he hiding? Why is he omitting certain truths? Never mind, glass houses, and all that. He said we could spend some time Monday morning sightseeing for artistic stimulation, and then go to his friend's gallery to paint. "There's a small workshop adjoining the gallery. She's closed on Monday and Tuesday, it'll be nice and quiet, we can paint there, together." Together, it sounded so appealing when he said it. Of course, I knew he was talking about Sandz and Darla, but I said nothing. I'm thrilled to share this creative rebirth with him, but Darla, she could be a problem. I'm going to have to confess I knew who he was before I arrived in town. Somehow, I have to tell him this before Opal's show, which he also mentioned attending with me. Darla was suspicious of me and if she's sees us together, who knows what she'll say. But what do I say?

Let me not think of that now. I'll see him on Monday. He told me he's planning a day of exploration for us. I wonder where he'll take me? He didn't mention getting together tomorrow, didn't even ask me if I had plans. Hmmm. Sunday. Maybe he's just tired, or needs to do things around the house. Church? No, I doubt that. He has friends here, maybe he's having a nice dinner with close friends. That's probably it. Or, his wife might be in for a visit tomorrow.

Peterson's wife. Why does this annoy me? I have no right to be annoyed, but I am. I feel jealous of this woman I've never met, whose husband I am lusting after, and yet in my mind, she's the meddlesome bitch infringing on my turf. "Even some born in the nineties, I would think." The way he said it, how he touched my skin as he said it, it was sensual and delicately suggestive, and yet I can't help but think, is that how his son, my same age, was conceived, Peterson and this irksome wife person, writhing in sync with the heavenly chords of Pink Floyd? Stop it, Petra! What does she look like? I see a reserved patrician type, Grace Kelly beautiful when young, now pleasant and matronly, no suggestion of past sensuality. The only thing they share is lack of common ground. They are roommates at best, ill-suited companions. Whatever. We're just spending time together, no need to dwell any further upon his homelife. Monday, our Monday, is almost here.

Chapter 18

Petra had overslept. It was just past 8:30, and Peterson was due to arrive at a quarter to 9. "Shit!!" she yelled as she rushed to the bathroom. The air from the previous night had been fairly cool, so she had slept with her bedroom windows open, but humidity and heat had crept in with the rising sun, affixing her t-shirt and panties to her damp skin. Stepping into the shower just long enough to wash away the clinging dead air, she brushed her teeth, and vainly attempted to subdue her wet hair, stubbornly mired in an awkward growing out phase. She was fumbling into shorts and a cropped camisole when a knock came at her front door. "Ugh, figures he'd be punctual. Coming!!" She opened the door, and Peterson was immaculately casual in aviator sunglasses, a Calvin Klein baseball cap, and beige shorts. He removed his sunglasses and leaned down to kiss her cheek, and she felt him lightly inhaling her citrusy cleanness. His eyes then darted over her exposed midriff and legs, elongated by the barely there shorts.

She felt uncomfortably aware of herself, and explained, "You didn't tell me where we were going. Am I not dressed appropriately?"

"No. I mean yes. Trust me, you're fine. You're…lovely."

Lovely. He said it with an almost solemn air, more of a tribute than a come on or a casual compliment. "Thank you." He had slid his sunglasses back into place, and Petra wondered what truths might drip out of those espresso eyes if he ever let down his guard.

"So, you're ready?"

Petra nodded and grabbed a large canvas tote bag, brimming with assorted items in anticipation of their day, everything from sneakers and insect repellent to voluminous hoodie and delicate lacy sweater. Following him outside after locking up, she was surprised to see an old pickup truck in place of the Mercedes, dents and rust unabashedly scattered over the dull blue exterior. Realizing he had probably spent the day before with his wife, most likely coming back to reclaim her car and her husband, Petra felt an unwelcome tinge of jealousy prickling at her, and she observed, "You got your truck back?" her insecure annoyance holding on to every word.

"Yeah, I missed this beat up thing. Glad to have her back."

She hoped he was referring only to the truck and not his wife, and ascended into the passenger side, Peterson protectively hoisting her up. Petra willfully dismissed her bitter pangs as he walked around to the other door of the vehicle. Wherever the missus was, whatever her claim to him, he was here now with Petra, and that would have to be enough.

"How do you feel about dessert for breakfast?" he questioned her as he turned the ignition of the truck, its engine stubbornly springing into life.

"I... like... it," her response sounding deliberately slow and seductive, even though it was her stifled jealousy tangling the words as they rose up in her throat.

"Wonderful. Dessert you shall have."

He animatedly pointed out places of interest as they drove, and Petra could tell he actually enjoyed seeing his familiar locale through new eyes, and getting to introduce her to its charms, obvious and hidden. Throughout the ride he was supremely considerate, modulating the inside temperature to her liking, lowering the windows at her request, even though he appeared uncomfortably caught in the relentless eddy of soggy air. Making sharp turns, he'd buffet her softly with his arm, a quiet reflex that seemed to exist outside of his conscious awareness. He reminded her so much of Tyler, gentlemanly and durable, present but reserved, and this made her covet and fear him. Was it wise to be entering into something impregnated with seeds of familiarity? Wasn't the comfortable pleasantness only masking ultimate peril? A veritable stranger with a tortured, foggy artistic past, and a wife. She should be running, she wanted to run, just not as much as she didn't.

"Here we are," he announced, his voice breaking through her distracted wanderings. "I think you'll like it."

They were in a fairly large parking lot, crowded with airy jeeps and SUVs, and Petra was surprised, having anticipated an out of the way pastry shop, all sugary romantic seclusion. "Where are we?"

"Well, this is actually a Viking themed golf and waterpark. Pretty cheesy, I know. But there's a boardwalk area, where you'll find the best funnel cakes in the world. Come."

Wading through the ocean of families and young couples, many exuberantly soaked from splashing rafts and serpentine slides, Petra looked at nearby passing faces, wondering if she and Peterson appeared to belong there, together, as much as the others did to her. As they approached the small shack selling funnel cakes, Peterson took her hand, almost casually without looking at her, and she tried not to let on how much she liked this small but concrete intimacy. He ordered two deluxe funnel cakes, which she watched in stomach rumbling fascination being placed into large Styrofoam bowls with extravagant drizzles of chocolate syrup, powdered sugar, and a thickly gleaming strawberry puree. A barely perceptible nod from Peterson led to the server finishing off the treats with healthy dollops of barely whipped cream. Armed with a stack of napkins, spoons, and forks, the two gingerly carried their dripping bowls to a nearby table. Peterson was about to dig into the indulgent breakfast when he paused, fork sagging into the gooey fragments while his focus shifted to Petra. His mouth appeared to want to break into a smile that his intense, appraising eyes weren't ready to allow. Nervously, Petra pretended not to register his suddenly sharpened attentions, and shoveled into her sugary diversion.

The dense deliciousness of the funnel cake sundae momentarily disengaged her from self-consciousness, and she practically moaned, "Yum, this is beyond…," needing another forkful before she could retrieve more words. "Mmmm."

He reached over then to wipe away a tiny bead of chocolate clinging to her lip, and she was pulled back into the sphere of his appraisal, the same provocatively complex expression mutely screaming from every inch of his face.

"Thanks," awkwardly using her own napkin to retouch the corner of her mouth now vacant of his brief touch. "Why aren't you eating yours?"

"I will. I'm just savoring," raising his eyebrows slightly, "this."

Looking down, Petra finally dared to ask, "Why are you looking at me like that?"

"I'm sorry. I haven't been here in a while. Mostly I avoid the touristy places. But I used to love coming to this boardwalk, my first few summers here. All the stereotypical vacationers, the cheap souvenirs and junk food, the post cards and garish stuffed animals." He took a deep breath as he scanned the surroundings, then closed his eyes, and continued to speak as if he were straddling dream and waking life. "Escape. I could sit here and escape into all of this banal vacation stuff, and feel like I was the same as them, passing through but *home* somewhere else. I suppose as the years have gone on, I became too fixed in place for even a pretend escape. But you gave me an excuse to come back here, and I'm thankful for that. I haven't felt hopeful in a long time, and I'm sensing it again. I don't know why exactly, but I feel like you're a part of it somehow." He opened his eyes again, a featherlight grin finding its way onto his lips, and he began wordlessly delving into his funnel cake.

He finished quickly, as Petra unhurriedly scooped through her half full bowl, her appetite now dimmed by Peterson's vacillating concentration. It un-nerved her when he fixated upon her, his wordless gaze as noisily disruptive as a troupe of tone-deaf youngsters banging on steel drums. Then, when he inevitably looked elsewhere, she felt passed over and let down, deflated. Seeing him now, satiated by the funnel cake, and contentedly people watching, he appeared smug and self-satisfied to her, and she wanted to scream "Screw you!" for teasing her, for dangling his attention only to take it away. She might have started the whole thing, but he was the one playing games now, and she resented him for it, even hated him.

Facing her with a broadening smile, "Well, we should get going now. I have something else in mind for us." Maybe she imagined it, but she detected a subtle emphasis when he said *for us*, and she couldn't help but forget that she had started to despise him.

Soon, his truck was rattling onto a highway ramp, and though she des-perately wanted to know where they were going, she asked nothing, just sat back in her seat, and allowed the fast-moving road to lull her. The pickup was surely decades older than Petra, equipped with a cassette tape player that miraculously still worked. Peterson had popped in a tape, and Joni Mitchell's plaintive voice was filling the space around them, her somber rendering of "Woodstock" trans-forming the brilliantly blue sky into an ocean of forgotten teardrops. Petra noticed a sign for Ocean City, and then couldn't resist asking, "Ocean City. That's Mary-land. Is that where we're going?"

"Yes. I hope that's okay. It's not that far."

"No, it's fine. I'm just surprised. I assumed we were staying in Delaware, but I'm happy to take a ride," softly adding, "I trust you." She blushed slightly, embarrassed that it was basically true, despite her very reasonable misgivings. She was in a battered pickup with a married man she hardly knew, and yet felt strangely at ease, mostly distressed at the thought of *not* being with him.

Before long, they had arrived at a large amusement park, the parking lot vaster and more crowded than the one in Fenwick earlier that day. "I know, it's another amusement park, but I have my reasons, you'll see," he assured her. After a fairly long hike, they arrived at the gate, and Peterson paid for their tickets. Their hands fluttered into each other as they walked into the park, and they became clasped together, neither of them sure if it was accidental or intentional, mutual or one-sided.

"We can stay here as long as you want, but I really brought you here for one thing."

"Oh?" Petra purred inwardly, imagining a darkened tunnel of love ride, where his fingers would travel inside her shorts and exquisitely meld into her.

Winking at her, his pace quickened, until they were standing before an immense Ferris wheel, pearly white spokes and blue domed cabins promising sky-bound paradise. It extended almost one hundred fifty feet into the stratosphere, and Petra absorbed its grandeur with bittersweet awe, remembering the pastel Ferris wheel she had painted as a child, admired by everyone except her own father.

Picking up on her inner tension, Peterson gently asked, "What is it? If you're uncomfortable about heights, we can go on another ride or just walk around. Whatever you want, Petra."

She didn't recall him having said her name since their initial introduction, and the sound of it rolling so effortlessly off his tongue vibrated within her, an electric ribbon unfurling around them, insulating them from the boisterous crowd. "No, I love Ferris wheels. Let's go on."

Petra entered the cabin first, and was caught off guard when Peterson sat next to rather than across from her. "I don't love heights," he whispered in way of explanation, but Petra suspected it was a ruse to stay close to her.

The wheel began its ascension, gaining speed as they swirled around, pausing with them at the apex of its climb. "It's breathtaking, isn't it?" he marveled, without a trace of discomfort at the present altitude. "If you look behind us, you can see the Assateague seashore, and to the north is Fenwick Island. You can't match this view. I wouldn't want you to leave your vacation without seeing it."

The mention of her leaving dulled her pulse, and she looked into the vast sunniness for energizing relief. "It is gorgeous. I wish we could stay here forever," and she knelt back against him, his hand resting on her upper thigh, subtly swaying against her skin in quiet assent.

After the Ferris wheel, they bounded off to other attractions within the park, seamlessly inhabiting the same interests. They were drawn to all things child-like and sweet, the carousel, cotton candy, and slowly careening bumper cars, es-chewing the aggressive velocity of the rollercoasters and shooting games. Yawning contagiously at the same moment, they laughed, and headed for his truck, drinking soda through neon twisty straws.

"That was so much fun, thank you," Petra expressed as they settled into the truck.

"The day's not over yet, kiddo."

Starting the car, the Joni Mitchell tape began playing again, but Petra ejected it without asking, not wanting anything to dim the buoyancy of their day together. She flipped through the staticky stations of the archaic radio until she heard the innocuous pop of ABBA, the plain, mindless beat of "Dancing Queen" in keeping with the candy-coated fun of the preceding hours.

"Do you like Greek food?"

"Yeah," she said as she slurped up the last of her cherry cola, "but I'm not really hungry."

"Oh, you will be. I've fed you nothing but empty sugar calories all day. You're gonna crash, doll." There was something paternalistic about his words, which both reassured and irked her. They had imbibed the same junk all day, and yet he distanced himself from any potential ill effects, as if he were the strong, impenetrable caretaker to her vulnerable child. Is that how he saw her, she pon-dered, a wayward urchin in need of protection? Up until recently, she was confi-dent and capable, a force of nature, honed by the grittiness of the Big Apple, her femininity wrapped in strength. She had not shared with him any of her recent travails, but had the enervating tumult of the previous weeks unwittingly an-nounced itself, attached leech-like to her even in this new environment? She chafed at the thought of being seen as a stray kitten, didn't want patronizing in-dulgence or pitying care. Yet still, a small but insistent part of her desired to be fathered by him, so similar in age and bearing to her own dad, but with the artistic, sensitive side he had always lacked. This aching for fatherly pampering felt per-verse given her ever-deepening physical attraction to Peterson, and she winced in shame, reaching for the radio's volume knob to drown out all vestiges of her Freudian nightmare.

"So?" he asked in impatience.

"Huh?" Petra responded, summoned back from her distracted outer space.

"You didn't hear me? Where have you been?" Shutting off the radio in mild exasperation, he said, "I ran through the signature dishes at this Greek café. You didn't get any of that?"

Ignoring the interrogatory comments, she said, "I could really go for Greek food. What do you recommend I get?" choosing to submit to his presumptuous comfort after all.

"Well, I'm thinking something relatively healthy and substantial after all the guilty pleasures today. Their chicken souvlaki wraps are delicious, very fresh."

"Perfect." And she temptingly wished there would be one more guilty pleasure on the menu.

*****

They ate the Greek wraps inside of the pickup, and they were every bit as satisfying as Peterson had promised. Back in Fenwick as it was approaching late afternoon, Petra assumed their day was drawing to a close. She wasn't tired though, and wanting to spend more time with Peterson, thought of inviting him to her bungalow, but she didn't trust herself to be alone with him. Cutting herself off at the pass, "Thanks for all the surprises today. I couldn't have planned anything more fun."

"Oh, do you have to go now?" he asked in obvious disappointment.

"Why? There's something else?"

"If you want there to be." He said it so cryptically that goosebumps stippled her skin. "I mentioned it to you the other day. Painting at my friend's gallery? If you're not still interested, it's okay." She could tell by his sadly expectant tone that it would be anything but okay, and that made her heart jump out of her chest.

"Oh yes, I remember now. Sounds like fun."

"Good. I picked up some new paint and brushes the other day. The workshop is all set up."

When they arrived at Sandz, it was closed as expected, and Petra was relieved that there was no sign of Darla and her accusatory attitude. Entering the workshop through the back door, Petra immediately walked over to two easels, standing back-to-back, their vacant canvases waiting to be filled with color. She figured he must have prepared the room for them, and a jolt of pleasure ran through her, further indication that this man she was fascinated by also seemed to have a genuine interest in her. She meandered to a nearby table scattered with oil and acrylic paints, brushes and palettes, picking up a blue handled brush and fondling its soft hairs, anxious to produce something richly evocative that would solidify their growing connection, and prove to him that she was right, that they were truly kindred souls. He watched her intently, his hand moving to his upper lip, gliding his finger slowly back and forth along the curve of his mouth in much the same way as she toyed with the bristles of the brush. Locking eyes with him, she abruptly dropped the brush, nervous chatter spewing out. "You know, I've dabbled some in painting, but not for a while. I've always felt more comfortable sketching, so don't expect a masterpiece," Petra warned, self-deprecation arising from her fevered fantasies of their naked bodies smeared with paint.

"Talent is talent, and from what I saw at the pier, you have it. It'll come through in any medium."

"Thank you. That means a lot, coming from *you*," and she inwardly gasped as soon as the words were out, knowing that she had slipped. She wasn't supposed to know he was an artist, and she fumbled for the fake but believable explanation she would need to get out of this potential disaster.

His whole demeanor changed, and his eyes narrowed as he looked at her, the admiring warmth of a few seconds ago iced over by gravelly defensiveness. "Coming from *me*?" He opened his mouth to say more, but pierced her with silence instead, waiting for her to explain.

Think fast, Petra, come on, say something. Deflect and charm, you've got this. "What are you getting so cranky about? That story you told me, about the mason and the heart etched into the brick. What you said was so touchingly imaginative, dark and profound, haunting and romantic. If that isn't art, I don't know what is. You said it yourself just now, talent is talent. I saw how creative you are just from that beautiful story."

He looked at her in silence, his expression unreadable, frozen somewhere between apprehension and curiosity. She was about to grab her purse and flee when approval once again flooded over him, his features resettling into easygoing contentment. "That means a lot, coming from *you*," and he walked over to her, picking up the cast-off brush and teasingly whisking it against the tip of her nose.

142

Phew, that was close. I know I have to be honest with him, but I wasn't ready today. Oh, I really, really hope he doesn't hate me when he finds out I came here just to meet him. But seriously, shouldn't he be flattered? It is sort of a compliment. Or maybe it's crazy, just a step away from peeping in his window or boiling his pet rabbit, and I'm just biding time before I get served a restraining order. No, this isn't some pathetic, unrequited fantasy. It might have started out in a stalkerish way, but there is something here between us, we both feel it. Yes. Something comes alive in me being with him, and I think it's the same for him. Our paintings today prove that.

Almost in a waking dream, I began placing fragments of our beautiful day at the amusement park onto the canvas. The concession stands and rides, families and prize booths, emerged in technicolor detail, their sunniness beaming out from the lines of paint. Slowly though, vestiges of Peterson's past artistic essence seeped into my brushstrokes, my bright vista pervaded by the creepy, sinister beauty of his old sketches. A lost, frightened child became the unplanned focus of my rendering, her plaintive, desperate eyes searching in vain for her parents, gripping a teddy bear for courage that remained as distant and elusive as the indifferent crowd milling around her. Her stark, steel gray image, though tiny, seemed to yank the cheery, carnival brightness into blank oblivion. Then I noticed him, standing before his canvas as if he too were in some sort of animated daze, responding to a siren call that had somehow burrowed inside his painting hand. I carefully walked over to his side, not wanting to intrude, but unable to squelch my desire to see his creation, if it reflected me in a way that it couldn't rationally, but yet needed to.

And then I saw it, everything and nothing I was expecting. A couple sat alone, holding hands in a fishing boat, on a sunlit placid lake, their unseen eyes peering into the distance, yet I could see and feel every emotion on their hidden faces. Dark clouds were clustering in the distance, the incoming wind was crackling with lightning that had yet to strike, and they were as mad with fear as they were with love. It reminded me so much of my sketch of the couple on the insignificant raft, in the middle of the ocean, their love just as fierce as the danger circling them. Of course, Peterson had never actually seen that drawing of mine, but somehow, he felt it.

It's like we are morphing into each other, or maybe blending into one. At least for now.

143

Chapter 19

Petra was in the middle of a mid-morning, pre-wakeup dream, smiling into her pillow, her bed a puffy float in a sumptuous, tropical resort pool, when her phone unwelcomely drew her into wakefulness.

"Mom, I know your Zen garden is amazing, and I will visit soon, but please, let me sleep," she stammered, willfully opting for more rest. The phone chimed again, and now Petra shrieked in exasperation, "I love you, Mom, but you are a real freaking pain in my ass sometimes." Retrieving her messages, she was stunned to see they were from Peterson. They had left off that he had to meet with contractors regarding renovations on his house, and that perhaps they would have dinner together or go to a late-night jazz club. She read his texts with increasing excitement.

"My contractor bailed on me. Actually, I'm happy, I'd much rather look at your face than his. Are you feeling energetic? There's this reservoir nearby, with a really great running path.

It might be fun if you're up for it. I'd like to leave within the hour. Sorry for the short notice, no worries if you can't make it."

"Forget what I said, you have to come with me. I want us both there, today. Break other plans if you have them. I'll be by to pick you up in an hour. Don't let me sit crying alone in my dented pickup truck. That's a country song cliché, and I hate country music."

It was sappy and corny, and she loved it. All her laziness lifted, and she practically vaulted out of bed, quickly stripping off her sleep shirt and heading into the shower, when she heard a knock at her door. *Shit, he can't be here already.* "Who is it?" she called out, trying to sound unannoyed.

"Terrie. I have some cinnamon apple tea and a fried egg sandwich for you. Want me to leave it out here?"

Petra wrapped herself in a towel, and ran to the door, actually eager to see Terrie's cherubic face again. "Terrr-ieee," she drawled out slowly, "thank you so much," accepting the red thermos and foil wrapped sandwich.

"Oh no," seeing her towel, "I've obviously bothered you. We hate being the stereotypical nosy neighbors, but we were concerned. We haven't really seen you around the past couple of days, and just wanted to make sure you were all right."

"That's really kind of you both, but you don't have to worry. Everything's been fine." Her face brightened as she spoke the last word, its sweet, secret understatement dripping over her like slowly oozing honey.

"I'm about to date myself, but you are certainly one smitten kitten. Who is he?"

Whatever was happening between her and Peterson, it had to stay between the two of them, and their need for discretion eclipsed her teenaged swooning. "No, nothing like that. Not even close. I've found an artistic mentor, and I think I might really make art my career."

"Oh, well that's wonderful, Petra," sounding slightly unconvinced but respecting her desire for nondisclosure. "Ben and I are always looking to acquire art. Hopefully we can be among your first patrons. Well, enjoy the breakfast, and I promise, no more pop-ins from us, but you can swing by whenever you like."

Petra sat at the dinette table, sipping the tea and taking tiny bites of the sandwich, its buttery deliciousness not enough to overcome her sudden preoccupation. She was slightly guilty that she had held back the truth from Terrie, but mostly frustrated that she was brimming over with confused anticipation about Peterson, with absolutely no one to discuss him. She desperately wanted a sounding board, to dissect every nuance of their time together, to search out veiled hints of his feelings, to debate future possibilities for them. Would they remain flirtatious but detached acquaintances, or would they capitulate to base desires and have a heated, tumultuous affair? Or maybe there was something more there, a sublime domesticated happiness unexpectedly but unavoidably beckoning them. Inconvenient, inappropriate, but undeniable. Years from now, little league games, church potlucks, bake sales, and dance recitals would make respectable what was once illicit, and they would be like any other long-standing couple, well-regarded, reliable, natural.

You don't even know him, Petra, and now you're baking cupcakes to-gether for the PTA? She needed another voice besides her own to make sense of this thing developing between them, but who could she talk to about a married man, apparently hiding from his past identity, an absentee father, and old enough to *be* her father? Her mother would be horrified, and would likely speed towards Delaware on a mission to rescue her fragile, lost daughter and castrate the "philandering pig." Rianne would probably conflate her checkered relationships with Petra's, wanting to commiserate over their shared romantic doom, a *Thelma and Louise* plunge off a cliff the likely end of that dialogue. And Jeremy, wonderfully vulgar Jeremy, he would have a pragmatic and spicy perspective, like "You're finally back on the market after monogamy hell, get yours, screw the fuck out of him, then climb into your car and get climbing on somebody else." They were all well-meaning in their way, but none could help her with this, if there even was any help out there, or something real to help with.

A spam call came in then, and she realized that Peterson was due in less than fifteen minutes. Throwing the rest of the sandwich into the refrigerator, she showered and brushed her teeth in record time, pulled on lightweight, fitted heather gray jogging pants and gathered together a slouchy, sleeveless pale pink T-shirt into a knot at her upper waist. Athletic-sexy, that was her go-to casual look when she wanted to impress without seeming like she was trying too hard. Her mind was operating at full tilt, and she didn't want her appearance to reflect that same labored intensity. Taking a final look in the mirror after she laced up her sneakers, she grabbed her tote bag and the thermos, and waited on the front stoop for Peterson.

Within moments, he pulled up, and though he seemed about to exit the truck and escort her to her seat, she rose up immediately, and bounded inside the vehicle, leery that a suspicious Terrie and Bennie might burst out their door and catch on to what was really going on beneath the surface with her supposed "mentor."

"Wow, someone's in a hurry to get going. You like going for a run that much? Or maybe you just couldn't wait to see me?" He said it playfully, but it was partially true, and it left her momentarily devoid of speech.

A faint sound like "hmmph" escaped her lips, and she tried to sidestep her discomfort by extending him her thermos, silently offering him a taste. When he politely nodded no, she persisted, "It's really delicious, apple cinnamon. Here, smell." She held it under his nose, even though it was now several degrees past lukewarm, and not giving off any steam.

A captivated, faraway look came over his face as she withdrew the thermos, and he turned to her, his dark brown eyes quietly smoldering. "The only scent I picked up is you. Lavender, faint vanilla. It's pretty."

She reflexively smelled the back of her hand, remembering the body lotion she had quickly slathered on after her rushed shower. Lavender Crème, Crabtree and Evelyn, a gift from Tyler at Easter. She thought of the cute basket he had assembled for her, chocolate bunny, pastel candy, a stuffed floppy eared rabbit, bubble bath and the lotion. Now, she was wearing that innocently gifted lotion on a clandestine outing with another man, married no less. What the hell was she doing? She stared down at the tattered floormat, hoping for an answer.

"Hey, did I upset you?"

"No, not at all." His look of self-conscious concern distracted her from her own worries, and she loosened back into carefree nonchalance. "So, tell me more about this reservoir we're going to. Is it a long running path?"

He seemed relieved that she was still focused on their outing, and he shifted the truck into gear. "The Newark Reservoir Trail. It's almost two miles once around, beautiful lake, surrounded by woods. Usually very quiet. I go there throughout the year. I'm glad you agreed to come."

Soon, they were on the highway, heading north, and she wondered how far they were traveling. It seemed he was always taking her out of town, and she didn't know if she should be insulted or flattered. Was she no more than a dirty secret, a shameless harlot his upstanding, spotless wife needed to be shielded from? Or maybe she was somehow already precious to him, and he didn't want to expose her to small town gossip, didn't want anything or anyone to tarnish something so special and tentative, so perfectly their own. Petra's phone suddenly announced an incoming text, and she smiled knowingly to herself, a tiny laugh spilling out, seeing her mom in a lotus pose, meditating in her ever-ubiquitous Zen garden.

"Funny text?" he asked.

"Not really, it's my mom, posing once again in her backyard like she's in a Better Homes and Garden article. I was actually expecting…" and she stopped herself from saying anything else. She was feeling insecure with him again, unsure of the depth of his interest in her, and didn't want to tell him how his earlier texts had jolted her from morning surliness into giddy enthusiasm, merely at the prospect of an unexpected outing together.

"What?"

"I don't know, I lost my train of thought. Tea is great, but I need caffeine in the morning. Umm, you said this place is nearby? How much further is it?"

"I sort of fibbed. Nearby is a relative term. It's almost two hours away. I'm sorry. I really wanted you to come with me, and I didn't want to give you any excuse to say no. When my day got freed up, I knew I wanted to do something special with you." His attention then shifted entirely to the road, and Petra was too awestruck and happy to say much of anything for the rest of the ride.

*****

The reservoir was smaller than Petra expected, but in some way even more spectacular, its pristine blue sparkle condensed and potent. They made their way to the paved running path, and as she was breathing in the tranquil beauty of the scene, Peterson sighed in annoyance.

"What's wrong?"

"Like I said, this place is never crowded. Except for today, apparently."

Petra then took note of the trail before them, clusters of people, some in groups, some alone, scattered across the path, but not oppressively crowded together as Peterson seemed to perceive. "I've never been here before, but it doesn't look that jam-packed to me. We should be able to have a good run." She sensed there was something deeper lurking beneath his veneer of annoyance, but she was too captivated by the natural splendor to press him, and was looking forward to the release of a run to soothe her own unease.

"Yeah, I suppose. You ready?"

Petra nodded, and they set off on the running path. Foot traffic did become fairly heavy, complicated by bicyclists, rollerbladers, and strollers, but they managed to maintain a brisk pace. The sun was relentlessly pulsing, and before long, they were both heavy with perspiration. Still shy of the halfway mark, Petra was ready to take a break, but glancing over at Peterson, absorbed in his running and seemingly unaware of the tiredness spoken in her body language, she chose not to interrupt him. When a teenager on a skateboard practically crashed into her, almost causing her to fall against the pavement, Peterson snapped out of his workout fugue, and promptly tended to Petra, glowering after the unapologetic skateboarder's receding figure.

"Are you all right? That little shit is lucky I don't kick his scrawny ass."

"I'm fine, really, but if it's okay, I'd like to rest for a couple of seconds."

"Of course." He put his arm around her shoulder, and led her to a bench sitting beside a mossy brick building housing the restrooms. They stared out at the reservoir, and his hand lightly moved across the back of hers. It felt unconscious to Petra, the instinctive, habitual language that develops in a relationship after time. Suddenly, she shuddered in spite of the blazing heat, cold from the memory of that same instantaneous rapport with Tyler. *Look how that turned out.*

"Hmmm?" Peterson questioned. "How what turned out? Is that what you said?"

"Nothing. I didn't mean to say that out loud. I was just thinking about a book I was reading, trying to remember where I left off."

"You sounded a little annoyed, so I'm thinking it's not a fun, 'laze on the beach' type of book."

"No, more like *The Bell Jar.*"

"Yikes, suicidal themed book by suicidal author. Come on, I know exactly what you need." He stood up, and motioned her to follow. For a few yards they continued to proceed along the running path, now walking slowly, arms casually entwined, though it felt more than casual to her. "Here," he suddenly announced, and pointed at the woods on the periphery of the path. Petra saw only dense greenery, and instinctively scratched her skin, anticipating rough branches, ticks, and mosquitoes waiting to attack. Addressing her unspoken concerns, "There's actually a clearing right past here." A boisterous foursome passed by just then, apparently having stepped out of a beer or clothing commercial. They were carefree, tan, young, and beautiful, greedily drinking in the sun, the lake, and each other. Peterson made a show of furtively whispering in Petra's ear as they noisily scuttled by, "It's a beautiful wooded trail. Most people don't know it exists." He put his finger up to her lips to ensure their silence, and ushered her into the wooded hush.

Within a few steps, they had entered another world, the curtain of shrubbery expanding into a verdant walkway, lush and private. Their footfalls were absorbed into the soft, grassy dirt, the sounds of invisible forest life reverberating in the trees and brush. Everything else already seemed lightyears away, the reservoir and every other place converging into one distant and immaterial unknown. They walked side by side for a while, the sun pleasingly dimmer under the blanket of trees, solitary nature encircling them, knitting them together. They came to a massive old tree, proudly standing upon its knotty, warped trunk, jeeringly impervious to snow and wind, rain and heat. Petra reached into a hollowed-out notch in the stem of the tree, waiting for some forest hobbit to grab her into a dark, ghostlit world straight out of *Grimm's Fairytales*. Instead, a warm flesh and blood hand descended into the small of her back, naked beneath her knotted shirt.

"Beautiful," Peterson murmured, and whether he was referring to the tree or to her, she wanted to collapse into the moment with him, for however long a moment could exist before it carried too many burdens from the future.

"This is what I wanted today," he continued after several beautifully silent minutes, gently rubbing her lower back, her head resting against his shoulder, as they marveled at the grand tree. "The last few times I was here, there was hardly anybody else, not on the running path, not by the water or in the woods. I got lost in this sensation that I was the only person left on the earth. It was surreal. The sense of death made everything else come alive. I felt the life force of the water and the trees. My footsteps, and the scurrying animals, the wind, leaves dropping, all the sounds vibrated together and intensified one another. It was like an LSD trip but so much better because it was organic. I was hoping to step into that world with you today. I needed to."

They turned to face each other. A plump lady bug suddenly appeared on her wrist, its faint tickle riveting away her mesmerized gaze. "Oh, a lady bug, I love them."

"Me too." He led them into a sitting position at the base of the tree, the red beetle stubbornly clinging on to Petra's sun-kissed, lavender scented skin. He carefully wove his finger in a circle upon her skin, the lady bug at the center, until she sprouted her wings and flew away. "Let's stay here for a bit." They shut off their phones, and everything was still, even the sun seemed bolted in place, like it might not ever set again. It could've been ten seconds or ten hours for all she knew, just her and Peterson, leaning against the knowing tree.

*****

The drive back to Fenwick was traffic laden and hot, the pickup's air conditioner having an off day, and seemingly everyone on the eastern seaboard driving to the same place. Petra dozed on and off, partially hiding in real and pretend sleep. Sitting in the woods together, their physical closeness in the quiet solitude an exquisitely abstract foreplay, she had felt emotionally naked with him, and still, they hadn't crossed over into any physical expression of that unguardedness, not even a chaste kiss on the lips. Maybe they shouldn't, and never would, and the messiness of denying it or surrendering to it was driving her crazy. She snuck a sideways peek at him, hoping to study him unnoticed, maybe catch him in the same throes of emotional questioning. He was looking impassively at the roadway, and she felt like hitting him for mirroring none of her own angst. Then a smile snuck onto his face, totally disarming her.

Sensing her wakefulness, he turned towards her, and spoke, "Good, you're up. I was thinking we might enjoy a swim."

"Yeah, I'd like that. But I don't have a bathing suit with me."

"Not a problem," he answered cryptically.

Not a problem, she repeated silently. What did that mean, she wondered? Was he going to take her to his house, and perhaps suggest she borrow one of his wife's bathing suits? *No, he wouldn't do that, too disrespectful of both me and the wife.* Maybe he was taking her to a secluded pond or lake, where they could swim naked under the descending starlight? She felt her skin flush, imagining his trim figure totally unclad, all his lean muscularity and sensual strength unmasked and free. *You sound like one of Mom's cheap romance novels, get a grip.* She noticed that they were passing the final Fenwick Island exit, and she wondered where he was taking her. Soon after they exited the highway, she started having flashes of recognition, knowing she had been on these roads before, but still confused. Then, they pulled in front of the immense home where he had previously driven her, their first day together.

"This is your friend's house, right? Where we dropped off your fishing equipment?"

"Yes. He has a magnificent pool, overlooking the ocean, remember?"

"Of course, it was breathtaking. Is he home now?"

"No, but we go way back, and he lets me come here whenever I want. Let's go."

He walked around to her side, and lifted her out of the pickup. "Are you sure this is okay?" Petra questioned, swept up in a perfect storm of anxiety and expectancy.

"Yes," he said impatiently. Then softening, "He's overhauling his security system, so there are no cameras right now. No one is going to see anything. We can do whatever we want to."

It was late afternoon, and the air was full of hot sunshine, the pool looming before them like a refreshing drink. Peterson casually slipped out of his sneakers and removed his shirt, and Petra nervously wondered if he'd remove his shorts as well, already deciding that she would follow his lead. She unlaced her own sneakers and remembering that she had slipped on modest boy-short under-wear that now faraway morning, she loosened the drawstring of her pants and let them drop to the ground. He showed no reaction as he unzipped his shorts, now standing relaxed before her in boxers. His easygoing demeanor was causing her pulse to quicken, but she unknotted her T-shirt and lifted it over her head, affecting a confident calm that she wished she actually felt. Her bra was flimsy and plunging, much more revealing than the bathing suit top she had on when they first met, and she already felt naked.

He moved closer to her then, and held her waist, gliding his fingers gen-tly upward until they reached her mid-back, where he artfully unfastened her bra. "We wouldn't want it to get wet," he teased, then sliding the straps off her shoul-ders, her arms giving no resistance as it dropped down. He made no pretense of pretending not to stare, his eyes widening in awestruck appreciation. He ran his fingers along the side of her breast, then looked straight into her eyes, and said only, "Beautiful." His reverent admiration emboldened her, and she removed her underwear, then pulling down his, briefly touching his exposed private skin before looking upon him. Every assumption she had made about his virility was quickly confirmed, and they stepped back from each other ever so slightly, taking in every detail of each other that their frenzied minds would allow. He grabbed her hand, and led her to the pool, stepping into the cool water side by side.

It was a salt water pool, the smell of saline so potent and raw that Petra felt she was in the ocean, and she started lazily swimming towards the deep end. Peterson followed, his strong strokes vibrating through the water behind her, tin-gling her already electrified skin. When she reached the far end of the pool, he was right behind her, swimming her towards a tanning ledge. They sat there, facing each other for several long seconds, lower bodies submerged in the water, a dull heat driving away the liquid coolness. She laid back, her head resting on a ma-rooned pink float, closing her eyes to the glow of the sun and their growing attrac-tion. His breath was suddenly heavy against her neck, licking the saltiness of the water clinging to her skin, and the sensation of being lapped up took her outside of herself, into him. He then kissed her, and it was rough and impatient, catching her by surprise, and biting into every nerve of her body. His hand cupped her breast, pressing deeply into its wet fullness, pinching her nipple, then it was his mouth there, insistent and greedy, sucking and biting. She grabbed on to his hair, fixing him against her chest, wanting him even closer to her. Brief but heavy moans escaped from them, seamlessly fusing into the ambient sounds, as natural and primal as the ocean itself. And then it was suddenly over, him pulling away from her chest, and abandoning her on the tanning ledge, at the edge of a cliff.

He stared off into the depths of the pool, and Petra waited nervously for him to offer an explanation for his abrupt detachment, finally unable to stand another second of ambiguous silence. "What is it?" she asked, and he said nothing. "Please, tell me what just happened."

"You really want to know?" he replied, still not looking at her. He let the question hang there for several excruciating moments, finally turning towards her. "Okay, I'll be blunt. What I'm feeling right now, with you, I want to fuck you, long and hard, soft and slow, and never stop. And it's not just sex. I want to eat ice cream cones with you, talk about new books, maybe go fucking skydiving, and this scares me."

"I know you're married, you're not free, I get that."

"Yeah, but it's more complicated than I've discussed, and I don't want to get into it now. Believe me, there are so many days I want only to be free; I just don't see it happening."

"Look, I'm only here for a short time. Why can't we just enjoy each other now?"

"Why?" and he sighed, looking away from Petra, seeming to ask himself more than her. "I envy you. So many things are just beginning in your life, and they've mostly ended for me."

"Oh, wait, please tell me you're okay. You're not sick, are you?"

He laughed sardonically, "Physically, no. This is existential death I'm talking about. I've been drifting, for a long time now, but being around you, it's like I'm tapping into your promise, your future, and it's inspired me, and I don't want to start something here that will leave me worse off than I was."

"Why does it have to be bad if we get closer? Can't it have a happy ending?"

"Does anything ever?"

Does anything ever? That question lingered for her, as if he were repeating it inside her head. She had no satisfactory answer, the preceding months of her

154

life bearing witness to his grim outlook. She followed his line of sight into the pool, murky liquid hardening into impenetrable stone.

He drove me home, neither of us saying a word, and when I got out of the truck, all he said was "I'm sorry." I couldn't bear to look back at him, even knowing that I'll probably never see him again. I walked into my cottage in a depressed fog, which seethed into anger. "I'm sorry," well you should be, asshole. Where the fuck does he get off? I yelled into the sofa. The nerve of him, taking me to go skinny dipping, in the world's most romantic oceanside pool, getting me so loosened up and turned on, and then tossing me aside? Yes, he's married, but he knew that going in. Okay, he's scared...but so am I, fucker, and I was willing to go for it.

I finally got exhausted from fighting with him by myself, and sulked into bed. As I struggled to fall asleep, the anger dissipated, and I fell back into black sadness. How could I be this distraught over someone I just met? I know enough pop psychology to reason that I am simply projecting the disappointment and frustrated desires of my recent weeks onto him. Years' worth of repressions and denials finally caught up to me, pulverizing my personal and professional life, and I've taken all that angst and dumped it onto Peterson, as if being loved, or even just fucked by him, could fix me. Then, when his attentions faltered, I reexperienced the pain of my preexisting trauma, Peterson being no more than a smokescreen. Oh, fuck it, I'm annoying myself with this Psych 101 bullshit. Whatever my issues, he disarmed me, he let me get comfortable, he made himself enticing and available, only to kick me to the curb. Screw him. Hope he rots with Star's awful ex. How is she? Wow, I miss that girl. I could use her twisted and sarcastic darkness now.

...It's finally morning, after a hellish sleep, and I feel hungover even though I haven't had any alcohol. I have over a week remaining of my vacation rental, but I want to leave, now. What is there for me to go back to, though? I see my forlorn apartment in NYC, gathering dust on top of the dinginess left behind by Tyler's absence and my unexpected unemployment, and I know I don't want to be there either. I am trapped, relegated to hell wherever I go, because I can't escape myself. Shit, I guess I'll just hideout at Terrie and Bennie's for the remainder of my stay here, getting fat and drunk on buttered muffins, cheeseburgers, and spiked iced teas. Not the getaway I had planned. Who am I kidding? It was doomed from the start. I've been unraveling for a while, and I glommed on to Peterson, hoping

he could be my touchstone. Stupid. It's obvious we are both drowning, and pooling together our misery is not the answer. So, what is the answer then? I still can't dissolve this burning knot I feel inside me whenever I think of how utterly amazing it felt to be near him, naked in that salt water pool, our own private ocean. I'm going to try to fall asleep again. Maybe I'll wake up somewhere, someone else…

I can't believe what's happened since I last wrote in this journal. Shasta found her way into my backyard, where I was drinking an improperly early, vodka-laced hard seltzer and wishing I had a cigarette. I welcomed her panting, playful distraction, and was momentarily lost in her carefree world of ball chasing and barking. My phone started ringing, and I thought I was hallucinating when I saw that he was calling. I had given up on hearing from him after that day from hell yesterday, wandering through the dismal fallout of his rejection, bound inside my bathrobe and melancholy. I had stared at my phone, waiting for a text or call that never came. Waking up that next day, I was hardening into anger, determined not to let the bastard ruin another second for me, but still lacking the energy to do anything other than take a shower. So, there I was, annoyed but listless, petting Shasta, when he called. For all of two seconds, I contemplated not picking up, but of course I did.

I didn't even say hello, just waited for him to start talking. I don't remember exactly what he said, I was zoning in and out, dizzy with relief that he called, annoyance with myself that I had become so dependent on him, and fright that I would be rejected again. The call didn't last long, but it ended with me agreeing to meet him in town. When I pulled up, purposefully late, he was standing beside his pickup truck, looking tense and disappointed, and I felt vindicated that I wasn't alone in my frazzled frustration. He motioned me to a nearby spot, and then we walked together, not really talking. He took me into a cheery seeming shop, its red and white awning like a big peppermint candy, and I instantly felt more at ease.

"Seaside Country Store," he announced as we entered, "one of my favorite places to unwind. I always feel like a kid again when I come here." The store incongruously smelled of pine needles and gingersnaps, as if we had stepped out of August beachiness into ski lodge quaintness. I immediately saw past the well-stocked shelves of everyday necessities, towards the back. He smiled warmly, and we walked there together, into the sentimental heart of the shop. Mounds of fudge and candied confections filled a high case, appealing in all their unfussy lack of

*sophistication. "You'll never want pretentious crap like Godiva again," and I be-
lieved him. There were several Christmas displays, as if yuletide was more a perennial
state of mind than a fleeting season on the calendar. I picked up a dragonfly ornament, delicate green and purple glass, and felt like crying, remembering my grandmother and the garden shovel she cherished, etched with dragonflies. We picked
out some fudge, and then wandered around the store separately. I found a rag doll,
in a Christmas plaid dress, with smiling sad button eyes, and I wondered if I'd ever
have a child to give such a sweet gift, her small eager hands tearing apart all her
carefully wrapped presents. His hand rested on my shoulder then, and we exited
and got into his truck, leaving my car and Christmas behind us.*

*Soon, we were at a marina, renting a jet boat. He was so comfortable
at the helm, and I felt safe and excited, to be out on the water with him, alone,
and free for the moment of questions neither one of us was prepared to address.
We managed to maintain a safe distance on the relatively narrow boat, getting
reacclimated to each other, but avoiding any prolonged closeness that might
again trigger things between us. He stopped the boat when we were a good distance from the shore, and we covered ourselves in spray sunscreen he brandished
from his knapsack, luckily not requiring us to apply lotion to each other's backs,
even though all I wanted was to feel his warm hands enclosing me. He pulled
out two small construction paper pads and felt tip pens from his bag, and wordlessly we began drawing. I remembered the rag doll, her innocent nostalgia tempered by vain regrets and fragile hopes, and began translating her tattered lines
onto the paper. The drawing seeped out from the pen, disembodied from me, as
if the pen itself and not my hand was driving the sketch. Looking at the finished
rendering, I was surprised to discover the doll now more ragged than before,
broken, stripped of its folksy charm, a little girl in profile, crying over her shattered gift.*

*That forlorn child grabbed me out from the softly rocking, sun-soaked
boat, down into whatever depths she inhabited. Maybe she and the doll were lost
fragments from my past, myself or the child torn from my belly, interrupted, cut
short. "Riveting." He broke into my silent space, and I was relieved for the intrusion. "I could live in that drawing forever, so much beauty where there should-
n't be." I wanted him even more right then, and for a second, I could actually
feel his inner dialogue, unspoken sentiments pushing him towards and away from
me. I glanced at his sketch then, a couple running blithely on the beach. Maybe*

we could be that couple, even for a short time, not running away from or towards anything, just captured inside of a beautifully fleeting moment. Suddenly, I was lifted up, and thrown into the cold, calm water, him splashing in right after. We didn't stay in long, just enough time to have the dizzying sensation of drowning and flying at once.

Chapter 20

"I'm not sure this qualifies as breakfast, but it is delicious," Petra spoke through mouthfuls of sticky bread pudding, sitting at Bennie and Terrie's dining table, cramped with serving platters, juice glasses, and coffee mugs.

"True, but that's what vacations are for, and I think that…" Terrie began.

"I disagree," chimed in Bennie playfully. "This is most definitely an appropriate breakfast food. Milk, eggs, butter, cinnamon bread. All genuine morning staples."

"Sure, and the toffee sauce and ice cream are just like cornflakes and milk, but hey, I'm not complaining. Thanks for whipping this up, hon," Terrie said as she winked at her longtime partner.

"Yeah, this really is amazing, Bennie," Petra said, scraping up the last of the thick syrup from her plate. "Did you make this toffee sauce? It's delicious."

"Yes, I did, but it's a family secret. Even Terrie doesn't know what's in it." She began clearing the table, and exited into the kitchen, the sound of water rushing from the faucet.

"Like that old cow can keep any secrets from me," Terrie whispered to Petra. "Pear brandy and blackstrap molasses, those are the prized ingredients."

Petra laughed, and then became quiet, musing internally before she spoke. "It must be nice."

"What?"

"Knowing someone so well. Closeness and space. Even with everything bare, you allow the other the sense of holding something of their own. Together in solitude."

"Oh honey, don't romanticize us. You got all that poetic sentimentalism from toffee sauce? Please, we are far from perfect. Sometimes we annoy the crap out of each other, a lot of the time actually. But there's no one else I'd rather have pissing me off, if that counts for something."

"It does."

Bennie came in then, "I'm going to take Shasta out for a walk." Turning to Terrie, "T, you mind cleaning up the rest of the dishes? I'll be back soon. Petra, stay as long as you like."

Terrie cleared the rest of the table, assisted by Petra, and they both walked into the kitchen. Petra started to rinse off the plates in the sink, when Terrie motioned her to stop.

"I'll finish that later. Tell me about him."

Petra's heart dropped in her chest. *What does she know?* "Him?"

"Whoever this guy was that you left behind in NY. It's obvious there's someone."

"Oh." She was momentarily relieved she hadn't been outed as an unabashed homewrecker, but then Tyler's face emerged before her, disappointed and dour, evaporating her relief. "Yes, there was. For a long time, we were like one person. I don't know if that stopped being true at some point, or maybe it never was. Perhaps we were always holding something back from each other, from ourselves."

"Well, then you are doing the right thing, getting some distance, and taking this trip."

"Really?"

"Yes. You're probably starting to learn things about yourself, and until you are at home in your own skin, you can't build a real home with someone else."

"You know, I've thought similar things since the breakup, but my own voice has sounded muddled to me lately. Hearing you say it really helps. Thank you."

"I'm glad, sweetheart." Walking over to the sink and adding suds and water to the basin, "So, are you going to tell me more about this 'art mentor?'"

"He's really been encouraging me, helping me to believe in my talent, reinspiring me. I do feel like I'm getting reacquainted with myself, maybe discovering who I really am. It feels good."

"You're beaming. Is this merely artistic joy?"

"We are totally platonic."

"If you say so. What's his name? If he's a Fenwick regular, maybe I know him."

Petra stalled by returning to the dining room to clear the table of any remaining clutter. Coming back with a gravy boat, cold toffee sauce spackled onto its surface, she calmly uttered, "Pete," putting the delicate porcelain dish on the counter before her trembling hand betrayed her covert attraction.

"Pete? Tall, thin, tanned silver fox Pete?"

"Not the way I would describe him, but yes, I suppose," Petra demurred, wanting to add so many forbidden adjectives to that description, all of them agonizingly caught in her throat.

"The Pete I'm thinking of helps Darla out at the Sandz gallery sometimes, setting up her displays, but I didn't know he was particularly artistic. He never indicated that, I just know him as Darla's friend."

"Painting I guess is a lifelong hobby of his," Petra explained, repeating Peterson's own misleadingly vague description of his creative bent.

"Hmmm." Nodding her head pensively, "Honey, he is married, I believe. He told you, right?" and Petra knew Terrie was being protective rather than judgmental.

"Yes, right away. I'm telling you this is strictly a teacher-pupil thing. That's it. I'll show you the drawings and paintings I've been doing."

"We'd love to see them."

"You definitely will. Anyway, he's been so generous with his time and art supplies. I wanted to thank him, so I was thinking of cooking dinner for him, tonight." Terrie's head pivoted suspiciously as Petra said those last words, causing her to quickly add, "And his wife of course. Oh, and you and Bennie too. The more the merrier." Grinning with beauty pageant fakeness, all she could think was, *I love you and Bennie, but please, please be busy tonight.*

"That sounds terrific, but Ben and I are going to a drive-in movie theater a few towns over to see *Smokey and the Bandit.* I always did have a thing for Burt Reynolds."

"Really?"

"Honey, not every lesbian grows up lusting after Judy Garland. I had my share of male heartthrobs, still do. Hell, why do you think I call Pete the silver fox?"

Petra laughed, feeling increasingly at ease, even if Terrie was just pretending to buy her mentorship alibi. "You and Bennie are great cooks. What should I make for dinner?"

"Go in the shed, in the back. There's a freezer there. Ben and I went crazy at this farmer's market, plus we found this organic butcher and a gourmet grocery store. We overbought, so take whatever you want. That goes for the pantry, seasonings, anything you think you need."

*****

Petra had been cooking for a couple of hours, the small bungalow filled with the warm, melting aroma of herbs and Italian olive oil. The living room air conditioner did little to cool the heat filled kitchen, so she had stripped down to a sports bra and Tyler's paisley boxers.

"I'll just finish frying up these pork chops, and then get dressed," she announced to the fragrant, steamy air. "What should I wear? Do I have anything prim? This is just a friendly dinner." *I hope it won't be*, she silently thought, her desire too forbidden for even the empty kitchen. Putting the last pork chop on a platter she had borrowed from Bennie and Terrie, she was startled by the hiccupping throttle of Peterson's pickup. "Shit!! He's almost a half hour early." She was about to run into her room and throw on some clothes when he knocked on the door, and then proceeded to walk in.

"Sorry, there was a huge wasp out here, and I'm allergic," he said as he slammed shut the front door.

"You're early."

"I see that," he said as he scanned her scarcely clad figure, "but I can't say that I'm sorry."

"Cute. Make yourself comfortable, I'm gonna get dressed."

"No," he said forcefully, then immediately embarrassed by his presumption. "I just mean, I don't…you are perfect just as you are now. As long as you're comfortable, stay that way."

She looked down at her bare feet, and realized that even shrouded in a burqa, her nerves would still jangle in his presence. Her near naked unease at least felt more honest. "Okay. Is that a wine satchel?" She pointed to the black leather carry case around his shoulder.

"Yes. I brought Pinot Noir and a chianti."

"Two bottles, huh? You planning to take advantage of me?"

"I thought if we got drunk enough, we could take advantage of each other, without any guilt." He said it with a jesting smile, but his eyes were un-jokingly opaque.

162

Willfully ignoring his comment, she walked over to the stove, and began ladling a thick gravy into an ornate pewter terrine she'd found buried in one of the cabinets, an out of place relic in this utilitarian coastal abode.

"What is that? It looks incredible," he inquired, leaning against her as he peered over her shoulder.

"Sherry cream gravy with mushrooms, for the pork chops. There's also roasted potatoes and an asparagus frittata keeping warm in the oven. We can eat now or later, whatever you want," she babbled tensely, taking extra long to transfer the gravy into the serving bowl because she wanted an excuse to avoid being under his gaze, her vulnerable wanting making her feel too exposed. "I made a salad too, arugula, with strawberries and..."

"Shh," he interrupted, "that can wait. You know, these are sublime," and he cupped his hands under her breasts, smoothing the soft nylon of her bra, then moving his fingers down to her rear, "but your ass, it drives me crazy." He pressed into her butt, first with his hands, and then with his body. She felt him hardening against her, and then he began slipping off the boxers, when the timer on the oven sounded.

"That stupid thing, it's not calibrated right. I set it to go off an hour ago, and it never did." She turned around to face him then, and he looked as tentatively aroused as she felt.

"I'm sorry. I didn't come here for that. You've cooked a beautiful meal, and we should enjoy it."

Petra was thrown, relieved that they still hadn't seriously transgressed any moral lines, but frustrated and confused by all his mixed signals. "Why don't we start with some wine and the salad?" she offered, trying to find comfort in the trappings of a normal meal in the decidedly irregular circumstances. "I don't want the arugula to wilt."

"Yeah, we wouldn't want *that* to wilt." He cast his eyes down at his crotch then, arching his eyebrows dramatically when he looked back at her, and they both laughed heartily, grateful for a break in the erotic tension.

She scooped the salad into their plates as he opened the Pinot Noir, using a Swiss army knife he dug out of his back pocket. They sat opposite each other at the small table, and he raised his glass for a toast. "Here's to two people who probably never should have met, but always needed to."

They each sipped the peppery wine, and she wanted to compliment him on the simplistically profound toast, but the only communication that emerged was her foot, inching towards his leg, running softly up and down his denim clad calf. He picked up a small box, wrapped in newspaper with black ribbon spun around it. It had been lying on the table, unnoticed by her, and a bemused smile lit up her face as he presented it.

"You got this for me?" she cooed happily. His eyes darted around the room, artfully miming *Who else?* to which she chuckled shyly, and began unwrapping the gift. Her eyes focused on one word in the tiny black newsprint, *rock*, and she wondered if that was intentional, did he know that was the root of their names? Maybe it was a happy accident, or perhaps just a cruel reminder, the cold hand of fate warning her that the devastation she had unleashed upon Tyler was waiting in the wings for her. Her fingers became paralyzed around the small package, its unknown contents as deadly and enticing as delicious poison.

"You can open it before Christmas."

"Sorry, I'm just surprised." She quickly unwrapped it, and saw a cardboard box with a sticker emblem advertising the Seaside Country Store. Fondly recalling their quiet time there days earlier, she removed the lid, and saw the exquisitely fragile dragonfly ornament she had affectionately admired. "Oh my gosh, I can't believe you got this for me."

"Well, I noticed how much it moved you, and I wanted you to have it. Whatever happens here, or doesn't, I've loved spending time with you, and I wanted to be a part of whatever memory that ornament stirred up in you."

"Thank you, Peterson, I'll always cherish it."

"What?" and he said it so harshly that she felt the word smash into her.

"I said I'll cherish it, not just the ornament, but also this time with you."

"You called me Peterson." His voice was barely recognizable to her, so cold she felt her perspiring skin becoming icy-numb.

"Oh, I...I ...did?"

"I introduced myself as Pete. I haven't gone by my full name in decades."

Oh shit. Do I lie? How am I getting out of this? "Well, I heard it somewhere, if not from you, maybe when we were at Kat's Nip. That pig owner probably called you that," she said without conviction.

"Cut the shit, Petra. I told you, no one around here knows me by that name. Not even my wife calls me Peterson."

His wife. The other times she had been mentioned, it had seemed the missus was the interloper, and Petra the one rightfully at his side. Now his tone was re-buking, making the allusion an insulting comparison, Petra the devious villain ver-sus his sanctified, blameless wife. "I don't know, maybe I saw your license or a credit card," struggling to get the words out, and feeling faint under the glare of his inquisition.

"Peter, they all say Peter. I could understand if you just assumed Pete was short for Peter, but Peterson? That's a stretch. Stop lying to me. How do you know my real name?"

"It's going to sound stupid, and honestly, I don't know how to explain it."

"Try."

She took a deep breath, and began. "My grandmother, the reason I love dragonflies, we were very close, and she passed away. Recently I was at her house cleaning out her things with my mother, and she owned two of your sketches, which I found in her attic. Up until recently, I had no memory of them, something to do with partial amnesia after a diving accident when I was a kid. Almost a month ago, I had woken up one morning, inspired to draw. I re-created the images from your sketches, not realizing they hadn't come from me until I saw the sketches at my grandmother's. Forgotten memories of your work somehow filtered up from my subconscious. I was confused and scared, and I know it sounds irrational, but I had to find you. So, I did. I looked you up and found out you were living in Delaware." She closed her eyes, somewhat relieved that the truth was out, but ter-rified of his reaction.

"That doesn't sound irrational, it *is* irrational. That is one fucked-up story. I would accuse you of making it up, but it's so pathetic and absurd, I think it must be true. You have this *Twilight Zone* experience, and then what? You decide to meet me? What was that supposed to accomplish? And investigating me? Engi-neering a run-in? Did you stake me out, follow me?" His alarm suddenly increased, and he was briefly silent, before he said, "Oh my god, you know my address. You really have been stalking me, haven't you? You knew my wife visited last week before I even told you, right? You've been acting guileless and innocently capti-vated this whole time, just reeling me in. What the fuck are you planning? You think I'm wealthy, you want to blackmail me, is that it, Petra? Is that really your name, or did you pick something similar to mine to increase the intrigue, make yourself more irresistible to me?"

His anger was reaching a fever pitch, and Petra was so startled she began to shake with uncontrolled sobs. "No, I swear. I don't know where you are getting this idea from. I'm sorry if I invaded your privacy. I was never looking to extort you. I do have your address, and I accidentally learned you like to go crabbing, but I have never passed by your house, not even once. I know nothing of your wife besides what you told me, and I would never intrude into your life any more than I already have. I'm sorry, I am, please believe me, I'm not here to harm you. I just..." and her cries overtook her, making unintelligible all other sounds from her mouth.

He looked at her with scornful curiosity and apprehensive concern, and she turned away, her eyes landing upon the dragonfly, its glass form obnoxiously intact, taunting her with the broken shards of her grandmother's comforting presence and Peterson's once affectionate regard. "I know this is making me sound like a lunatic," she continued quietly, "but I'm not. My grandmother was very special to me, her home, her artwork, it was my haven. My mom told me I used to stare at your sketches, lost in them for hours. I'm at a crossroads right now, personally and career wise, and I don't know what else to say. I just felt that if I found you, I could maybe get back in touch with what made me love art in the first place. To find *myself*. And you have helped me. Drawing and painting alongside you, it's been wonderful. I wasn't pretending to be captivated."

He sat back in his chair, his anger tangled within a confused muddle of exhaustion, pity, and reluctant desire. Distractedly squeezing the bridge of his nose, he stared into his untouched salad, then suddenly stood up, and headed to the door. He spoke with his back turned to her, "This is all too weird for me. Please don't contact me again. Take care, Petra." The door seemed to open and shut simultaneously, and Petra collapsed in heaving sobs, the pain of that moment traveling through time to gather up every hurt and humiliation she had ever suffered, embalming her inside of them, an insect ensnared forever inside once-molten amber.

I must have cried for an hour, immobilized by embarrassment and frustration. I was annoyed at myself, at my circumstances, and yes, at him. I understood his initial shock, but we'd spent enough time together, shared...well, something... I can't pinpoint or describe it, but it was there...and he should have given me the benefit of the doubt, not just run away, again. I was feeling irritated and keyed up, and remembered seeing a crumpled pack of red Marlboros in the shed when I had gathered food for our ill-fated meal. Dumping all the uneaten food into the refrigerator, I then walked into Bennie and Terrie's yard, barefoot and still in my sports bra and boxers. In the shed, I found one lone cigarette slumbering next to a rusted lighter. I walked outside, and leaned against the dull metal of the shed, surprisingly cool in the early evening humid air. I lit the cigarette, and it was stale and bitter, but I took long, uncomfortable drags anyway, the misery of the cigarette blunting my own. "Nasty habit," I heard from a distance, and I saw Peterson standing by the back of the cottage. He walked over to me slowly, and flicked the cigarette out of my hand, crushing it under his shoe.

I've never seen a human face so indecipherable. He struck me as a black hole right then, and I was frightened and intimidated, wanting to hide, but too scared to flee. I remembered a grade school art instructor showing us the nature of black, how it was not the absence of color. A puddle of so many brights, red, burnt brown, blue, and yellow, swirling together in our childish fingers, melding into an unlit abyss. The void I was seeing on his face wasn't a blankness, it was every emotion, every feeling, mixing together, overpowering and drowning out, until it was all individually exhausted, subsumed into one impenetrable density. I felt vindicated and emboldened then, and moving purely on instinct, I undressed, letting my bra and underwear find a home in the dried grass. He turned me around, and I could hear the unzipping of his pants as he pushed the front of my body into the shed. The cold of the metal and the warmth of his skin both tore into me, just as he did, aggressive and rough. He was unconcerned for my comfort, but I could feel that he had no care for his own either. The air was buggy and stifling, and mustiness emanated from the nearby trash cans, but it was natural and somehow right, even ideal. Something basic and instinctive was lifting us out of ourselves, into each other, and back to preexistence—to timelessness.

We went back to my bungalow, and he stayed all night. Whatever we had tapped into by having sex, we were now both insatiable for it, and it seemed that no more than a few minutes could elapse before we were entwined again, on the couch, in the backyard, in the shower, and finally in my bed. At some point before dawn, we collapsed, and it wasn't until late morning when sunlight brazenly burst into my sleep that I realized the night before hadn't been a dream, his crumpled clothes lying next to my bed. He came into the bedroom then, smiling. "We never got to eat dinner, but I just had some of the frittata and potatoes. Your talents are limitless." He sat next to me and lightly stroked my naked breast, then tracing my face with his finger as if he were transcribing me onto a sketchpad. Leaning down, he kissed me, the only sweet and gentle aspect of our sexual encounter, and yet not altogether out of place. "I want to go to Opal's show with you tonight," he said, still dreamily running his fingers over my cheek, "but I think it's better if we meet there. People are going to talk anyway, seeing us together at all, but I want to minimize the gossip."

He left, and I lingered in bed for a while, sore and satiated, physically and emotionally. I had been dreading Opal's art show, knowing that Darla's suspicions of me and her granddaughter's interventions would expose my machinations to meet Peterson, but now, all secrets are out, and I want to be there with him. I still have miles to go before I unravel the disorder of the past months, and who knows how far back the roots of my chaos stretch. But for right now, unhealthy or ill-advised as this affair may be, I crave his presence...him.

Having been domesticated for so long, I forgot how deliciously unfiltered no strings attached sex can be. The intimacy of a steady relationship can definitely sweeten sex, but it can also weigh it down, filling it with responsibilities and expectations, holding it hostage with manipulation and complacency. What happened last night was not making love, it wasn't soft or romantic. He fucked me, and it's what I needed him to do. Throughout our relationship, Tyler and I definitely did more than our share of hedonistic screwing, but it was always tempered by the manicured lawn, Connecticut home, and picture-perfect children looming ahead of us. In the back of my mind, no matter how raunchy we could be, I always envisioned old Petra and Tyler, drinking hot toddies in our rocking chairs, wrapped in matching quilts, great grandkids at our feet. There's no future with Peterson, we barely have a past, we just have now, however long it lasts, most likely not beyond my stay here. I'm leaving in a week and I can't take this whatever we have with me, but I can simply enjoy it. I don't need or even want him to be perfect. We don't have to learn how to compromise and adapt. For now, we can just be.

Chapter 21

Sunday arrived, the day of Opal's show, and Petra was more excited than she'd been in a long time. She felt as if it was a debut not just of this eccentric artist's new work, but also of herself, breaking free from her past and stepping into a new life, of which Peterson was an indefinite but integral part; if not the endpoint, then at least the initial catalyst. Only one garment she had brought seemed appropriate for this evening, her fitted white silk slip, more lingerie than clothing, its pale satiny brevity capturing the embryonic confidence of the moment. She slipped it over her barest bra and underwear, but even they seemed obtrusive and bulky under the sheerness of the slip, so she removed them, the dress now an extension of her skin. Pulling on her silvery, pearl accented kitten heels, she felt both virginal and worldly, and headed into the breezy late summer evening, a whispery shawl billowing out behind her.

She had noticed Peterson's truck parked in the small lot across the street from the gallery, and was tantalized at the prospect of being with him in a crowd of people, the deliciousness of their sex a beautiful, naughty secret they could pass wordlessly between them, the other patrons merely clueless extras in their exclusive erotic play. Petra entered into the large space adjoining Sandz, where Darla had arranged the showing, and she removed her shawl, immediately overcome by the mingled heat of all the various bodies in the room, none of them Peterson. She recognized no one, and mostly everyone seemed to know each other, animated groupings seamlessly merging and disbanding.

Suddenly, she felt garishly out of place, much younger and in much less clothes than anyone else. Conversations were abundant and noisy, but she imagined a collective hush covering the room, eyes and comments directed towards her, the big city harlot looking to corrupt one of their own. No one in particular was looking at her, though, and she headed to the small buffet and refreshment table in the rear of the room, hoping a high fat canapé and a drink would allay her fearful imaginings. *Where is Peterson?* she desperately asked herself as she listlessly scanned the food and beverage options.

"Petra, so happy you could make it," bellowed a voice that was strangely foreign and yet familiar. She turned to see Peterson, looking at her with a starched formality that she hadn't seen even when they were strangers. "I've told Opal all about you, and I showed her the paintings you've been doing."

Petra then noticed the short, white-haired woman standing next to him, radiant in a floor length red beaded gown with a plunging neckline. Her asymmetric and large expressive features indicated that her face had likely never been touched by conventional prettiness even in her youth, but the lack of classical beauty made her obvious appeal even more striking.

"Hi, I'm Opal. It's a pleasure to meet you. Thanks for coming. From what I've seen, you've got some raw talent, Sweet Cheeks. Keep with it."

Sweet Cheeks? Petra was about to express mild consternation at the objectifying handle, when she recalled what Bennie and Terrie had told her about Opal's legendary knack for bestowing irreverent and endearing nicknames, so she smiled instead, "Thank you, I'm eager to look around, and see the full exhibit. I was truly mesmerized by your piece with the hanging beads."

"Yeah, a few days of tantric sex in Tahiti inspired that one. Well, I've gotta mingle now, lovely to see such a young, unfamiliar beauty among all these tired, old faces." She gave Petra a quick peck on the lips then, while pinching her derrière. "Like I said, Sweet Cheeks." She winked playfully, then pulling Peterson down towards her for a clandestine whisper, "Glad you didn't bring wifey tonight, 'cause I don't think this one's wearing any underwear, you lucky devil."

Peterson gave her a jovially disapproving smile, and the diminutive but larger than life octogenarian evaporated back into her adoring crowd. He was about to say something to Petra when Darla rose up in front of them, smugly contemptuous. "I see you found him after all." Turning to Peterson, "You know, she came in here, snooping for information about you. I knew I didn't trust her. She's probably a reporter, or..."

Putting his hands up, "That's enough, Darla. I appreciate your concern, but Petra has told me everything. I know why she's here, but you don't have to."

170

Darla's face drooped into wounded astonishment, and Peterson said nothing to pacify her, but placed his arm on her shoulder and looked at her with something that from Petra's view resembled arrogant pity. Darla, though, seemed to read something else in his expression, and she immediately regained her willowy composure, alerting them about the server headed their way with a tray of champagne filled flutes, then gracefully exiting back into the crowd.

Sipping their drinks, Petra exhaled in relief, "Phew. I'm glad that's over with. There's something scary about that woman. What exactly is your relationship with her? You seem like more than friends."

"Yes, we are, but not in the way you're implying. We've known each other way longer than we've both been coming to Fenwick. But—"

"I don't have to know," borrowing his own words.

"Smart girl. Now, let's have a look around, shall we?"

They began taking in all of Opal's eclectic pieces: calm, palliating watercolor paintings, unabashed nude sculptures, and sea glass wind-chimes, tributaries to a vast ocean of multicolored blown glass. The vases and turtles and perfume bottles seemed delicately enflamed under the recessed ceiling lights. All were so different, and yet subtly nuanced by the artist's brazen sensuality and affection for life. An air of surreal awareness swept over Petra as she studied one of the sea turtles, its mottled shell of violet and jade a fragment of some faraway world she might've once visited.

"You know, the dragonfly I got for you, it's one of Opal's." Peterson stated it so matter of fact, as if Petra had openly voiced her sense of kinship with the turtle before her, and he was just corroborating her spoken sentiments. She looked at him with flustered awe, but he once again had shifted into his crafted persona for the night, Petra's emotionally detached, ever-professional art mentor. "There are a few pieces over there I think we should look at, Opal chose to work with some different materials than what we've seen so far," and his paternal arm guided her to the opposite corner of the room.

Cohabitating on a deceptively endless white Formica table, several bizarrely attractive odds and ends seemingly cried out for rescue: horrid but priceless cast-offs from an otherworldly garage sale. Shiny and bent coins formed a reclining statue, like a brilliantly decaying body melting back into the earth. Perched on chipped wooden stands were several unframed, paint splattered canvases, with protrusions of plastic doll parts, bottle caps, and bent metal panels. They were encased by white chicken wire, burst apart in spots and stretching out in long de-sired freedom, a twisted wreckage coupled with diaphanous rebirth. "It's like my life story, everywhere I've been, where I might go," Petra blurted out, and Peterson nodded soberly, seeming to understand her fully, perhaps even more than she did herself. Standing in the middle of the grouping was a piece so tonally different from the others, it struck Petra as a "palette" cleanser, a refreshing sorbet meant to wipe away the acrid taste of the gruesome creations. It was a cavernous glass bowl, cerulean blue, several one-winged, fleshy angels precariously sitting on the rim, perennially in danger of drowning inside its fathomless depths or maybe on the cusp of finding liberty in the sky. She could swear they had the same face as the cherub on the card Tyler had given her, first declaring his love. *These could be that cherub's brood of fallen angels, doomed forever or reclaimed by heaven, de-pending on where the wind takes them.*

Seeing the blue fragility of the dish reflected upon her face, Peterson gen-tly asked, "What is it?"

"Oh nothing," she lied, "I was just thinking how creative Opal is. It hum-bles me, I could never be a true artist like her."

"Nonsense," and then bending down to whisper in her ear, "You are more talented than me and Opal combined. You are a great artist, right now. You just need to accept that. Bring to life what you've already created."

"Petra! So, were we right? Opal is a trip, isn't she?" Petra turned to see Bennie, smiling broadly, and flanked by Terrie. "Well, hon, did Opal christen you with a new name?"

"Sweet Cheeks," Peterson chimed in with obvious amusement.

"Perfect. I like it, bawdy but cute," Terrie offered, then addressing Peter-son, "So, did you like the dinner?"

"Oh, yes," Petra answered. "Everything turned out great." Feeling she needed to explain why they knew about the dinner, she added, "Pete, they were kind enough to provide all the groceries for our...for the meal."

"Well, you two seem chummy. You answer each other's questions now?" Bennie asked, her blasé tone masking deeper underpinnings.

Terrie poked Bennie's arm, and rambled on somewhat apologetically, "Petra has become our adopted daughter, we can be overprotective, but it's all in fun. She told us how you've been encouraging her to paint. I think that's wonderful. Maybe *you'll* have a showing here next summer, sweetheart."

Opal came over then, placing her arm around Terrie, "So, Mr. Pudge, you've already got me dead and buried, replaced with this hot young thing?"

"Oh, you crotchety broad, you'll probably outlive us all," Terrie responded. "Hey, I thought I was Cute Chubby Dyke?"

"Well, you're even fatter and more butch than you were last summer, so I thought Mr. Pudge was fitting. Come on, I want you and Bennie to open up your wallets, and buy some stuff. I need funding for my next vacation." As Bennie and Terrie obediently walked away, Opal winked at Petra and Peterson conspiratorially, dramatically turning away with a magician's flourish.

"What's that about?" Petra asked. "It's like she wanted us to be alone."

"Probably. Opal's never been a fan of Lori."

Lori, Petra repeated inside her head. *That must be his wife.* She hadn't pictured a Lori, maybe an Abigail or Prudence, something classic and reserved, not anything youthfully casual and nickname sounding like Lori.

"Hello, did you hear me?" Peterson was gazing at her with expectation.

"I'm sorry, what?"

"I'll take that as a 'yes'. Wait here," and he shuffled off towards Darla, who seemed to be ignoring the couple chatting with her in favor of studying Petra and Peterson. Petra watched as he pulled Darla aside, and they briefly talked, with Darla grabbing something from a pocket in her flowy skirt and hesitatingly handing it to him. He returned shortly, and Petra saw Darla shake her chignoned head in disapproval, feeling her glare upon her even when they turned towards the back exit. He ushered her into the back alley, and went to the rear door of Sandz, using the key to enter. She preceded him inside, to the workshop where they had spent contented hours painting together. He turned on the lights, barely above a flickering dim, and pointed her towards two paintings in sleek black frames leaning against the wall. She picked them up, seeing her portrait of the lost child in the amusement park and his of the lovestruck couple in the fishing boat.

"They came out beautiful. They're so different, but I feel like they're perfect companion pieces. I love them, Peterson." Looking up at him in embarrassed alarm, "Oh, I'm sorry. Pete."

"For a long time, I've hidden from that name, from what it represented. Now, I like the way it sounds when you say it."

Her face and neck became hot, and she handed him the paintings, reflexively drawing her hand to her upper chest, fingers fidgeting against her damp skin as she suddenly became conscious of the close, confining air. "These should be hung together. Which one of us is keeping them?" Her eyes crept inside of his painting, fearfully hoping for an impossible answer.

"I want you to have them. There's something else I want for myself." He then placed the paintings back on the floor, and stared at her, his eyes burning ice cold.

"What?"

"I need to taste you, right now." He said it with such force, leaning her abruptly against the wall, and then kneeling down and roughly scrunching up her slip. The ferocity of his explorations, voraciously searching her with his tongue while intently kneading her backside, made even this act of pleasuring her more about his cravings, and this fully ignited a savage prehistoric flame, ever smoldering within her DNA. When she climaxed, she let out a screaming moan that reverberated like an ancestral chorus within the walls of the tiny workshop. He kissed her inner thigh, then moved his mouth to her finger, wetting it and inviting her to glide it against his lip. Petra let out a gratified, deep body sigh as he then rearranged and smoothed her slip.

"Time to go." All at once, he morphed back into rigid propriety, as if she were a lackadaisical student keeping him from his next class. He picked up the paintings, and escorted her outside.

"Where are you parked?" he asked, and she pointed, so as to avoid having to speak, sure that her voice would sound thin and helium like.

Arriving at her car, he placed the framed pictures carefully against the back of her seat, and wished her a safe ride home, as he quickly got into his truck and rumbled into the descending summer sun.

"What the fuck?" she asked aloud. *This guy might be the most passionate, unexpectedly romantic guy I've ever met, and then he pulls this shit. Always these disappearing acts and patronizing dismissals.* She wanted to hate him, and then she felt the satisfied wetness between her legs seeping into the car seat, and she smiled in spite of herself, knowing she still had to have more of him despite his maddeningly hot and cold behavior. *Guys aren't the only ones led by their crotch.* She drove home, her mind so foggy with orgasm and insecurity, that she made several wrong turns, and kept getting lost. Finally, she found her way back to the bungalow, and remained in the rental car for several minutes, the fragrant and hot night air soothing her through the open window. A vehicle slowly pulled up behind her, its lights shutting off and then footsteps, deliberate and strong, coming towards her. She didn't even bother to turn around or look in her rearview mirror, knowing already who it was.

"Hey," he said, with blithe disregard for any confusion his earlier departure might have engendered in her. He kissed her briefly, seductively tasting her cherry lip gloss on his mouth as he withdrew. "If you're not sick of me yet, there's one other place I'd like to take you tonight."

Before she offered him an answer, the high beams of an oncoming car blinded them both.

"Shit, it's probably Bennie and Terrie, you should leave before they see you."

"You know, right now I don't care." They stared into each other, lost together in some other place. When Terrie and Bennie strode to Petra's car, she and Peterson were barely able to pull away from wherever they both had gone, only reluctantly turning towards the pair when Bennie's loud "Ahem" shot through the muggy stillness.

"Pete, what are you doing here this late?" Bennie firmly questioned.

"Oh shush," Terrie demanded, "it's barely past eight." She walked over to Pete and lightly grasped his arm, "I told you..." then bending her head towards Bennie, "overly maternal with our gal. Pay her no mind."

Seemingly unfazed by Bennie's indicting tone, Peterson said, "Just needed to ask Petra something. Goodnight Ben, Terrie." Petra nodded with a reassuring smile, and the women retreated into their house. "Alone again, just how I like it," Peterson's words breathing into her neck. "Leave your car, come with me."

For most of the short ride, she kept her eyes closed, wanting to prolong her sense of a dreamy surprise unfolding. The truck halted, the engine purring asleep, as she beheld the angelic luminescence of the lighthouse.

They walked towards it arm in arm, Peterson then deftly unlocking the gate as he did that lifetime of days before. Once on the other side of the meshed metal, he spoke in a solemn whisper, "When we came here that first day, I felt something that I can't explain, even to myself. I just wanted to come back here with you, because I feel like this will always be our place." They kissed and then he unfurled a blanket she hadn't even noticed he was holding. She laid down beside the white brick with its melancholy heart, and he was right next to her, lost and found just like she was, within that stony etching of emotion. This time, the sex was calm and hauntingly fragile, having the circular substance of something beginning and ending.

This was such a strange night. Once again, in his presence, in his absence, I am drawn up in a crazy maelstrom, expectant, let down, angered, pleasured, mystified, afraid, relieved, exultant, and back and forth again. The lighthouse was everything it should and shouldn't be. Peaceful, promising, heartbreakingly deep. We made plans for the next day, breakfast at the Yacht Club in Bethany Beach, then a hiking trail. He mentioned that this trail is a hidden gem, a way for me to experience "the real Fenwick." Funny, he used the same phrase as Star, two such disparate people, making the same claim. I wonder how much their versions of the real Fenwick coincide, if at all. So many things touched me tonight, but I keep returning to one exchange, when he expressed such a staunch belief in my talent, 'you are a great artist, bring to life what you've already created.' When he said that, I felt an unexpected, irrational anger at Tyler, that I didn't consciously appreciate until right now, falling asleep. Why? Tyler always respected my career as an editor, and expressed deep fondness for my art. There was nothing chauvinistic in his attitude or behavior. I have no reason to feel that he slighted my professional existence or creativity...or do I?

...Chicago in May reminds me of New York, springtime so greedily engulfed by the relentlessly eager humid clutch of the summer. The spring semester at University of Chicago has just ended, and Tyler is frisky and carefree and determined to fool around. Paradoxically, I am extremely preoccupied with work, overwhelmed with a densely academic manuscript. I also have a raging headache that cares nothing for my looming deadline, and am rummaging for an aspirin inside my crammed night table drawer. I see the cherub card he bestowed on me the night our destiny in Chicago became fixed, and I wonder if I should be thankful or mad that I followed him here into this rewarding but often taxing phase of my career.

Even the title of the manuscript is cumbersome, "An Historical Investigation of the Execution of the Russian Imperial Romanov Family: Plumbing the Depths of History, Fiction, and the Perpetual Puzzle of Reality." Tyler repeats the title as I search in vain for the aspirin, and he starts laughing, much to my annoyance. "Sorry, it's just that it's a little emasculating being rejected in favor of this boring book." I want to scream, are you fucking kidding me? Mr. Linguistics, devoted to what is probably the most boring and self-importantly useless of all liberal arts disciplines?!? Instead, I ignore him, giving up on the aspirin and any further discussion with him. Playful pinches then, and puppy dog eyes, "I'm sorry, honey, I just miss you." Yes, like I have missed him whenever he's been coldly engrossed in his career tasks. No, he's not going to win me over by playing that card. I stay silent and remote, and he continues to pet and fondle me, trailing off into a sleepy monologue. "One day, hopefully soon, I'll win the Nobel Prize for my humanitarian application of speech genesis in third world countries, and we'll be rich, and you'll never have to work again. I'll take care of you and our beautiful family forever."

Chapter 22

It was barely dawn, and Petra stirred under her cool sheets, the air conditioner at full blast all night because her white-hot re-imaginings of Peterson had necessitated her being frozen into sleep. She was smiling into a restorative yawn when she idly reached for her phone. "Peterson," she whispered aloud, her grin instantly evaporating when she read his message. He had texted in the middle of the night, cancelling their plans for the day, without any further explanation. "I'll contact you when I can." Her hand reached up to her face, her cheek actually smarting from the slap of every indifferent word. Trying to diminish the abandonment she was feeling, Petra rationalized that this was just another example of his ambivalent behavior, a confirmation that he was struggling against something dangerously powerful. She'd been here before with him, this was nothing new, and yet, something was telling her that this latest slight was somehow more brutally neglectful than the others.

Her eyes wandered to the off the shoulder floral dress draped over the vanity chair, the one she had expectantly chosen the night before for their mid-morning breakfast date. She had planned to wear it over a cropped tank and fitted shorts, so that she could effortlessly transition to their idyllic sounding hike. Climbing into her bed the night before, she had envisioned them in a secluded glen, Peterson lifting the dress off of her, the two of them glowing with anticipation for their sequestered trek, culminating in a naked romp under a ceaseless waterfall. "Asshole!" she screamed at the now offensive dress, seeing Peterson's face in its pink and orange blooms. She was about to pound it into the floor when she got the sudden sense that he was going to be at their planned breakfast destination, just without her. She tried derailing that train of thought, knowing it was a waste of time figuring out his motives; he was married, and that was all she needed to know. *Whatever, this whole thing has been insane, so what's a little more insanity?* She slipped on the dress, brushed her teeth, and headed determinedly to the Yacht Club.

She arrived at the restaurant's Bethany Beach location within fifteen minutes, and immediately felt foolish sitting in her car, stationed with a view of the entrance. The Yacht Club was located on an elegantly winding bay, beside a well populated marina. Boats sprinkled the sparkling waterway, and a steady stream of casually attired but obviously moneyed people were filing into and out of the white wooden eatery. *What am I hoping to see? He's either not going to be here, and I'll have wasted my morning staking him out like some pathetic psycho, or he will be here, with her, and then what? Seeing her is going to make me feel better? Rejection is rejection, does it matter if I'm younger and more attractive than her? I'll still feel passed over and frustrated that I've let myself become attached to someone unavailable.* Her rumbling stomach broke through her embarrassed dejection, and she decided to grab a coffee and a quick greasy breakfast at a McDonald's she had passed on the way. Turning on the ignition, she was about to drive off when she saw a white Mercedes coupe driving into the next row of cars. She held her breath as the vehicle pulled into a spot. *Is that his wife's car? Did that bastard really come here with her?* Her view was obstructed, but from what she could see, no one was getting out of the car. *Shit, I can't take this! Who the fuck is in that car?*

She was tempted to storm over to the car, her anger and curiosity momentarily outweighing pride and morality, when a familiar voice wafted through her open window. A sarcastic laugh, and then a sullen sounding "no shit" bounced into her ear. Without hesitation, a name rolled off of Petra's lips: "Star." Just then, the raven-haired teen strutted defiantly away from the restaurant's entrance and towards a line of moored boats, talking on her phone, and dismissively waving off someone's attention. Petra was straining to put all the pieces together, the possibility that Peterson was here with his wife, and if or how Star fit into this emerging mess. Twisting in her seat to get a better view, Petra saw a striking black-haired woman, in a white pencil skirt and black sleeveless camisole, calling after Star, and shaking her head in frustration. She had on sunglasses, and carried a glittering baguette shaped purse, and even from a distance, Petra could see the gilded light of perpetual money shimmering over her. The woman's tense posture abruptly softened as a male figure came over, warmly embracing her waist and walking her towards the restaurant. For a second Petra was so consumed with the surprise knowledge that Star was back in town, likely having breakfast with her apparently wealthy socialite mother, that the man's familiarity didn't compute, until it did in a cold rush. *Peterson.*

I didn't want to be right, but I was. He actually did go on our breakfast date without me. I know I'm the mistress in this scenario, not the one with the rightful place in his world, and yet I feel so betrayed. But I can't even process that fully now because I'm still coming to grips with Peterson being Star's dreaded stepdad. His wife is her mom. Morningstar Glory…Gloria Jane… Lori. I did not see that coming. He deliberately misled me into thinking he's had one wife. Why? No way is that younger and even sexier Catherine Zeta Jones the mother to someone my age and a grandmother. She barely looks old enough to have Star. That's not even the most confusing lie. I waited for them to leave the Yacht Club, stewing in fury and rejection, knowing I had to follow them without caring to understand why. They didn't get on the highway as I expected, but instead took scenic backroads that I had been on before, with Peterson. I had never noticed the names of the streets before, so giddily wrapped inside our time together, but now I was seeing this cosmic thread running through the signs—Sunset Terrace, Andromeda Court, Lunar Circle. And then we were on Starlight Way…his address…only they stopped at the mansion he had twice taken me, supposedly his friend's house.

I stayed in my car, parked down the street from this house, once so impressive and mysteriously romantic to me, now a concrete monstrosity inhabited by ugly secrets. Sitting there was torture, but my eyes and mind were fogged in by teary sadness, and it was almost an hour before I was able to drive away, back to my own beach cottage hell. Shasta ran to me as I disembarked from my car, the whirl of her licking and shedding fur reassuring me that I wasn't the ghost my haunted emotions were suggesting. Bennie and Terrie walked over, figuring out everything in a glance, and placing me in between them, they brought me into their home, feeding and sheltering me, and letting me sink into a pleasantly forgetful sleep.

*****

Petra awoke the next day, the dim tug of placid light rousing her, seeping through unfamiliar sunflower embroidered curtains. *Where am I?* she tiredly asked herself, when through half-closed eyes she noticed a note on the table next to her love seat cradle. "Went for a beach run with Shasta. Breakfast is in the oven. Love, B&T." The events of the preceding day flooded over her at once, and she retreated back into the sofa pillow, still too listless and confused for the coming day. A steady knock at the front door soon started, apparently heedless of her malaise. If it was a package, they'd probably just leave it, otherwise, it couldn't be anything important. But still the knocking, and then the voice, "Petra, are you in there? I'm worried about you." *Shit, it's him.* Struggling not to make a sound, she carefully reached for her phone, and saw that while it had been on silent mode, Peterson had called and texted numerous times. The knocking and calling out unnervingly continued, and Petra remained stubbornly silent, wanting him to shoulder some of the self-doubt and unanswered puzzlement she had been forced to endure. "Fine, I'm going to call 9-1-1, and have them do a wellness check," he yelled through the closed door. Angry at his persistence, she stormed to the door, not even self-conscious of her puffy, ragged appearance.

"What are you doing here?' she demanded as she wrenched open the flimsy door.

"You look like hell, what's going on?" Hearing no reply, he continued, "You haven't answered any of my calls or texts since yesterday. I drove over here, and saw your car, and when you didn't come to your door, I was scared. I walked around your place, the blinds were all open, but there was no sign of you. Then I figured you must be here. Are you mad about yesterday? I wanted to see you, but something unavoidable came up."

"Yeah, your wife. At least you still managed to get to the Yacht Club."

"You followed me there?" he questioned in sneering alarm. She said nothing, and started to slam the door in his face when his hand reached up to stop her, fixing the door in its place. "Just answer the question."

"No, I didn't follow you there. I just had a feeling you'd be there, with her. It was obvious she was the reason you cancelled."

"So much for not intruding in my life," he snickered.

"I was hurt and frustrated and I just needed some answers."

"No, you were satisfying some morbid curiosity, and it was unnecessary. I already told you everything you *need* to know. I'm married and that's not going to change."

"Told me everything? Ugh, no. That woman is clearly not the mother of your thirty-year-old son, unless she had him when she was ten."

"Okay, so?"

"So?!? Why did you deliberately mislead me into thinking you've been married to the same woman all these years?"

"Mislead? Look who's fucking talking."

"Okay, I wasn't honest when we first met, but we already went through that. Why didn't you just tell me you're remarried?"

"I told you right away that I was married, so what difference does it make if she's my first or fifth wife?"

"It mattered enough that you lied to me. Why?"

He took a deep, irritated breath, and then began, sitting down on the front stoop, and staring off into the road. "My first wife died, in an accident. My son blames me for her death. It's the main reason he wants nothing to do with me. I was a lousy husband. Never unfaithful to her, but so preoccupied with my own stuff that I wasn't there for her or our son. After she died, I had so much guilt and regret to sift through, I pulled away even more from my son. Darla became his surrogate mother, she had actually been my wife's babysitter, and they remained close. At least she gave my son some sense of normalcy. Without her, he might've wound up in foster care for all the good I was." Turning around and looking up at her, "There, you happy? I didn't want to revisit that part of my life. Now you answer me, what is really bothering you?"

Fidgeting, and then sitting down next to Peterson, Petra stumbled through her thoughts before speaking, "I don't know. It's just from what you said, I imagined a matronly, cold, bridge playing type, not JLo. I saw you, holding on to her in the parking lot, and I felt meaningless to you right then. Superfluous. And that hurt."

Her words seemed to enter into him, momentarily muting his smug disapproval. "I may not have been completely forthcoming, but what I said was true. There isn't much between me and my wife. But she's young and beautiful and very sexual and we connect on that level. Honestly, I've had deeper conversations with you in the span of a week than I've ever had with Lori. That's been nice, sharing music and art with someone, and you and I are undeniably attracted to each other, but that's where it begins and ends Petra. Did I indicate we were progressing into something? I don't think so, and I apologize if I did. What did you think was happening here between us?"

"I don't know, but I felt like it was something. I didn't think it was just a disposable affair."

"What do you want me to say? You want me to lie? I like you; I do; I've enjoyed being around you, but I don't know what version of us you've created. I can tell you, though, it's not realistic."

She wanted to act cool, as if his practical dismissiveness was not shattering her, but Petra was still desperate to find a hidden route into what she still believed was the real Peterson, painfully innocent and vulnerable like her. "But you're not happy with her. How can you settle, when you could be—"

"Happy with you?" he interrupted. "Hmph, you don't know anything about me, just like I know nothing about you. Now we're suddenly destined just for each other? Come on."

His words stung, and she attempted to allay her pain and embarrassment by focusing more on his subterfuge than her own misguided perceptions. "Okay, but why did you lie to me about your house? You pretended it was your friend's, but it's really yours."

"And how did you realize that?" he asked, becoming condescendingly impatient.

"I told you I had your address before I arrived here, but I hadn't passed by until yesterday. I followed you after I saw you with her. I hadn't noticed the street signs the times we went there, and Bethany Beach threw me, I was expecting a place in Fenwick Island."

"The mailing address is Fenwick Island, sorry that this postal discrepancy interfered with your investigation."

Ignoring his arrogant sarcasm, "Why the cover story?"

"I don't like people judging me by that house, wanting to get close to me because they think I'm rich. It was freeing meeting someone that just wanted to know me for me. Anyway, it's more her house than mine. She's very wealthy. I'm not. It's her name on the checks."

Noticing he was getting ready to leave, Petra tensed, still attached to him even in her hurt anger, and so she proceeded, "And why does Star hate you?"

"Holy shit. I don't even want to know how you know *her*."

"I had no idea she had any connection to you until yesterday. I met her at Coffee, we ran into each other at the beach, and she mentioned that she hates her stepdad. Why?"

"I don't owe you any explanation."

"Fine. I just assumed her stepfather abused her."

"Please, I can't stand that little bitch, but I never did anything to her. She always hated me, was jealous that I came along and occupied her mother's time."

"Well, she seems to have more against you than that."

"Oh, you're a shrink now?"

"No, but I can put two and two together. Something awful happened between you."

"I'm not fucking my stepdaughter, if that's what you're insinuating. I'll tell you what happened. She walked in on me screwing her French tutor. The vindictive cunt ran to her mom, and I denied it, said she always had it in for me. It was easier for Lori to believe my version, and Star felt betrayed. Serves her right. You know how many things that witch did, that I hid from her mother? She's been screwing her brains out and doing drugs since she was twelve, and I never ratted her out."

Becoming increasingly disgusted by both her own pathetic codependence and his unapologetic depravity, biting insults began easily rolling off her tongue. "Admirable. How big of you. Ignoring her obvious problems because you're too lazy to be a parent. No shock, since you abandoned your own son."

"Don't get sanctimonious with me, sweetheart. You come after me, stake me out, with some crazy notion of 'finding yourself'? Even after I tell you I'm married, as soon as we meet, you don't go anywhere. I could tell you were just waiting, ripe for the picking."

"Keep mocking me. I've made myself an easy target, telling you the truth about what brought me here. But what about you? I'm not the only one here with demons. It's obvious you are in hiding, cutting yourself off from your identity as an artist. What are you running away from?"

Sneering at her, "I didn't ask to be analyzed by some fucked up girl."

"Okay, you're too scared to turn your lens of judgment on yourself, so keep deflecting your fears onto me. It's weak, but understandable."

His lip quivered in anger, but then a sadness dripped grayly over his face. "My first wife... I stopped painting after she committed suicide."

"Holy shit, I'm sorry. I didn't mean to...."

Hardening up again, his voice rising, "The hell you didn't. You're in some premature 'midlife crisis,' and you want to share your misery with me, pull me down with you. Well, don't bother to reserve a double bed in the looney bin. You're going there alone."

Petra opened her mouth to speak, but his cruelty paralyzed her vocal cords, and she just looked down at the ground with unveiled aching.

"Ugh, don't act wounded. You came after me, you manipulated the situation. If anything, you used me. Here's some therapy for ya. Clearly, you have real Daddy issues, and you thought you could work through them with me. What did you think, we were going to ride into the sunset together? Please. Maybe I should've walked away, but I'm just a man, and I don't think *anyone* in my situation would turn down the opportunity to have a fling with a gorgeous, smart young woman who's vulnerable and practically screaming to be fucked." His anger dissipated then, mutating into offensively blatant lust. "And I do like fucking you. Now you know where we stand, so there's no reason we can't still enjoy each other. Let's go next door right now." His fingers trailed over her hand as he cockily gaped at her, defying her to resist him.

She stared back, momentarily petrified inside a whirlpool of conflicting needs and emotions. Her hand was almost responding to his touch of its own accord, ready to reach out for him, when one of his statements repeated inside her mind. *I'm just a man.* She remembered similar words spoken by one of her dream versions of Peterson, and all of these aloof, inconsistent apparitions reappeared before her, sneering and smug just like the one touching her now. Petra wondered if the nightmare iteration currently beside her was flesh and blood after all, or merely a hallucination that had somehow dragged her into hell? Becoming conscious that this nearby specter was now kissing and licking her neck, she abruptly jerked away from him, and stood up.

"Get the fuck out of here!" she screamed, her voice throbbing with rage.

He looked at her with surprise, a flicker of sorrow wafting over his face before his features became an inhuman mask of concrete, hard, lifeless. Shaking his head at her with impassive distaste, he walked to his pickup, and drove away, the cloudy fumes he left behind soon evaporating into stale nothingness.

All I want to do is read my book. It's a British young adult novel that has been banned as indecent in the US, but my cousin Connie stumbled on a bootleg copy, and gave it to me. The main character is about to lose her virginity. I am eleven, and of course I know what that means, but not completely, and I am beyond curious. It's another hazy summer, spent with my grandparents, and Mom and Grandma have gone food shopping. Normally, I would go with them, making sure

to stealthily place Entenmann's cupcakes and Chips Ahoy in the cart, but I am engrossed in this book, and eager for time to read it away from the loving but prying
eyes of my mom and grandmother.

They have left me with Grandpa, and he is usually distracted these days,
so I was looking forward to undisturbed reading time. But he is strange today, he
keeps laughing for no apparent reason, and muttering gibberish that I can't understand. I'm trying to ignore him, to lose myself in the book and wander far away
from his awkward presence, but he keeps coming over to me, patting my head and
leaning down to kiss me as I recline on the couch. His kisses are slobbery, and I
am wiping away their intrusive wetness when the honey-colored liquid in his glass
splashes onto me. "Grandpa! You're making a mess!" and he looks ashamed and
sorrowful, and I feel awful. "Forgive me, sweetheart, I'm getting clumsy in my old
age," and now he is Pop-Pop again, sweet and loving, normal. He places down
the glass, and sits next to me. I hide the book in the folds of the couch and he beckons me to his lap. I know I am too big to sit on top of him like I did throughout the
earlier years of my childhood, but he looks so vulnerable and harmless, I obediently go to him, my back instinctively rigid as I sit facing away from him.

He is quiet and still, but I am very uncomfortable, and am about to pretend that I need to use the bathroom, when he speaks in a faraway tone, "Oh, how
I love my Junebug." Junebug? I'm confused and then I remember this is something
he occasionally calls my grandmother, a leftover endearment from their erstwhile
courtship. "Mmm, your hair smells like heather," and his nose is now pressed into
my scalp. Something is suddenly stiff against my thigh, and his hands are pressing
my lower body into him. Whatever this is, it's bad, and I don't want to be anywhere
near him. I desperately squirm out of his lap, and he is calling me back to him. He
immediately rises up from the couch, and I speed into the backyard. Where is my
mother? Please come back soon!! He is outside now, with an expression that my
preadolescent mind cannot fully apprehend. His face is disconcertingly childlike,
almost innocently intense, but also violently determined, and he is lurching towards
me. I need to get away. I am running around the pool, the concrete unbearably hot
under my bare feet, and I hear his breathing fast and hard behind me. I need to
get to the front of the house, to find a neighbor, I am running faster, my feet are on
fire, I look behind me to see how close he is, my foot hits against something, I am
falling down, fast into quiet blackness.

Chapter 23

Petra woke up with streams of sweat rolling down her back and chest, having nearly soaked her sheets. Her head was ringing and her legs and arms were trembling and sore. It was as if her running dream-self had sprinted into her sleeping body, infiltrating her with all its perspiring, frantic fear. Her stomach began heaving, and she ran to the bathroom, barely lifting the lid of the toilet seat in time to throw up. Gathering herself to look in the medicine chest mirror, the face staring back was red and blotchy, and had a battered but toughened and resolved look she didn't recognize, like someone who was now on the other side of a long-fought battle, bracing for the hard road ahead, not exactly hopeful, but not dead either. "Stop being so dramatic Petra. You weren't abused. That was just a nightmare, it never happened." Petra looked at the familiar but strange beaten face saying these rational words, but she didn't believe them, no matter how much she wanted to. Her kindly, soft-spoken, cultured grandfather a perverted monster? It was too awful to comprehend.

She sat on the couch, running through all the reasons her dream was false, but finding only suggestions it was real. Her memory loss from that summer, Calli's nervousness whenever the alleged diving accident came up, never returning to visit her grandparents' house after that summer. So much sketchiness, and now it was all beginning to make sense. Another jolt of memory, and Petra saw herself with her much-adored pediatrician, Dr. Duke. Calli always had gotten visibly rattled whenever the doctor asked Petra if any of her memory had come back, and when Dr. Duke had suggested Petra see a therapist being that her post-accident affect was so uncharacteristically sullen and reserved, Calli had refused, and whisked Petra out of the office, promptly finding her a new pediatrician. *How did I miss this*? Her mother's skittishness about having her back at the house to clean out her grandmother's things was another red flag, as was the nervous awkwardness shown by both her mom and her aunt when she did show up. Most glaring were the weird, uncomfortable images that sometimes flashed during her sleep of her grandfather drinking, infrequent but now impossible to overlook. "It's true, it happened. I have to get out of here."

*****

Within an hour, she was showered, dressed, had gotten all of her things together, the car was packed up, and she was putting the bungalow key in the lock-box. She wanted to say goodbye to Bennie and Terrie, but dejectedly changed her mind. The vacation was over, for better or worse, and full of dangerous loose ends that no friendly words of departure were going to neatly tie up. Seeing the paintings in the car, done by she and Peterson on a recent afternoon an eternity away, she grabbed them and left them on Bennie and Terrie's porch. Taking a memo pad from her purse, she quickly scrawled a note thanking them for their delicious food and drinks, friendship and motherly attention, leaving it between the two portraits, hoping that those two now joyless pictures would reclaim some brightness within Bennie and Terrie's warm homey walls.

Driving out of Fenwick, Petra felt angry and wasted, just a burned-out mess of trauma and betrayal, past and present reprehensibly united in abusive chaos. She was about to pound the steering wheel in frustration when she noticed the lighthouse ahead. Suddenly she felt soothed, the white tower like a pillar of radioactive Vicodin, buzzing calming, hypnotic rays into the airspace. In a haze, she got out of her now parked car, leaving it idling, walking towards the gate that Peterson had so gracefully opened for them. She remembered their last night there together. *Our place, that's what you called it Peterson. Maybe in some way, some permanently lost or misunderstood facet of us. But today, and for every tomorrow, we don't need a place that's just for us.* And that was the last and the nicest thing she'd ever say to that bastard.

She slowly walked around the gate, to the area of the lighthouse with the carved heart in the brick. Kneeling down, she said a prayer for the mason and his lost wife. If anything Peterson said had been true, she hoped it was that tragic romance, two souls so in love that reunion in death was better than life apart.

Imaginary or not, the love he described was real, at least somewhere, and for right now, that was enough reason for Petra to get back on the road, stay calm, and brace herself for the painful tumult surely awaiting her. The star-crossed lovers loomed ahead of her like road flares directing traffic after an accident, fiery beauty on the outskirts of a tragedy. For even if they weren't real, living only in Peterson's imagination and her memory of that, they represented all lovers in pain, struggling to connect, and wasn't that everybody in the world, she thought? Half of your own broken heart lying in someone else's chest? Her plight couldn't be pointless if its pain and recovery resided in her own shattered twin somewhere, fragmented and searching just like her.

*****

As soon as Petra hit the highway, she knew where she was going. It wasn't someplace she wanted to go, but it was the only place she could confirm what she already feared was true. The drive to her mother's home in Maryland would take her two and a half hours without traffic, but for once, the prospect of bumper-to-bumper cars and a sluggish, stop and go pace was beautifully appealing, and as Petra made her way for the 404, she was practically praying for the route to be paved with stationary cars. The volume of traffic remained light, though, and despite purposefully driving well below the speed limit, she found herself pulling up to her mother's quaintly charming brick house in the expected timeframe. It was almost two o'clock, the sky bright with harmless fluffy clouds, and Petra knew exactly where Calli would be. Walking into the backyard, she felt she was stepping inside one of the many pictures her mother had sent of the Zen garden, the manicured retreat seeming almost too perfect to be a real place. Calli was standing in front of the effervescing fountain, in a textbook Yoga tree pose as preternaturally idyllic as everything else in this fabricated fantasy world Petra found herself loathing. The site of her mother so placid made her rageful, and she wanted to smash all the clean peace into rotting oblivion.

"There was no diving accident, was there?"

Startled, Calli nearly fell to the ground, her tree pose splintering apart into decayed twigs.

"Petra! I can't believe this. You're here!" Seeing Petra's furious expression, she nearly choked on her own breath, and then as if hearing Petra's antagonistic question in a delayed echo, asked "What?"

"Don't play dumb, Mother. I remember. I never had a diving accident."

"Oh, my goodness, what's happened?" She moved towards her daughter, readying for a hug, but Petra stiffened and backed away.

"Well, you've been lying to me for almost two decades. Why don't you tell me what the fuck really happened?"

"Honey, what do you think you know?"

"Stop the bullshit!" she screamed. "Your father was a fucking deranged pervert and you left me alone with him. How could you? And then you make up some bullshit diving story. You have the fucking nerve to tell me during your last visit that I 'self-sabotage,' mentioning junior high bullshit, and all the while you knew that I was abused and you did nothing, absolutely fucking nothing, to protect or to heal me. And you claim to love me?"

"I do love you, so much," pleading through tears, "please let me explain."

"Fuck explanations, Mom, it's a little late for that. Bad enough Dad is an asshole, now I have two deadbeat parents." The sound of the back door sliding open interrupted the buzzing wrath filling the once serene garden, and Petra turned to see her stepfather Beau trotting decisively towards them. "Oh, here comes the other moron. Dumbass Cubby himself, predictable and boring as white bread. Why don't you both drop dead in this stupid Zen garden!"

"Petra, enough!" Beau demanded loudly, and Petra shivered slightly, never having heard his voice so incensed and sonorous. Speaking more quietly, but still with obvious displeasure, he continued, "I know you don't like or respect me, and maybe I haven't done enough to earn either, but you will not yell at your mother. Whatever is going on here, it's none of my business, but I will not watch the woman I love be disrespected under any circumstances. You can stay here as long as you want Petra, but any further discussions you have with your mother will be courteous. Calli, let her be for a moment. We'll be in the house Petra, you come inside when you've calmed down."

Calli turned to her daughter with a pained look, but seeing that her anger had a stubborn foothold, she followed Beau back into the house, leaving the sliding door slightly open behind her, despite the lack of a screen and all the late summer insects clamoring for entry. Petra stared into the narrow opening, wanting to squeeze in and hide inside her mother's soft, perfumy arms, but she was too mad at everyone, including herself, to enter into that cozy, waiting haven. Feeling the unwelcome vulnerability of tears she ran to her car, finding sadistic comfort in the unforgivingly hot leather seats.

I want to kill that stupid Cubby. Who the fuck is he? I was molested by my grandfather, damn right it's none of this idiot's business. My mother, my best friend, my protector, she failed me. Of course, I'm pissed. Shouldn't I be? I'm getting out of here. Where are my stupid keys? Oh, I left them by that fat, self-satisfied Buddha. To hell with him and his Zen bullshit. Let me just get the keys, and hit the road. Maybe I'll just keep driving, one nameless, shapeless town after another, until I too am nondescript, at home everywhere and nowhere. Okay, back in my car, let's get going. Why won't this stupid car start? Shit, I'm out of gas, now what? I wish I was dead, I have no one left to count on, no one to trust, least of all myself. Fuck, fuck, fuck!!!!!!!!!!!!!!!!!!!!!!!

"Petra! Stop banging on the horn! Get out of that car, you can't drive like this. Honey, even if you hate me right now, you can't go anywhere until you rest. I am begging you. Come with me. We don't have to talk if you don't want to."

Petra was about to go on foot if she had to, anything to get away from the sense of betrayal and exploitation she was experiencing, and she was preparing to bolt out of the car when she heard her name being whispered. She looked at her mother, silent with fear and shame, and realized that the voice hadn't been Calli's, but it was entirely familiar. Baffled, she slumped back in her seat, and then a large dragonfly fluttered in from the passenger window, nearly brushing against her nose before exiting through her window. She would've thought it was a mirage, but Calli turned to follow the flying form, watching it escape into the wide-open air.

"Grandma" they said in unison, a remembrance and a wish all at once. They looked at each other, and Calli's trembling hands and wet, desperate face, along with the palpable sense of her grandmother's spirit, challenged every bit of anger Petra clung to, and she bounded out of the car, falling into Calli's waiting embrace. Two hours, several cups of tea, and almost a dozen butterscotch oatmeal cookies later, they began talking.

Calli put down her cup, and steadied herself with a deep breath before speaking. "Petra, since I first learned I was pregnant, my whole existence has been about loving and protecting you. I'm not perfect, I make mistakes like anyone else, but I always try to do what's best for you. Are you ready to hear everything?" Petra nodded, and Calli began. "That summer, when we last stayed at my parents', I noticed right away that something was off with my father. He was moody, distracted, drinking more than usual. I mean, none of it was excessive, just out of character for him. I asked Grandma, and she said that he was frustrated about being forced into early retirement. She didn't confide in me how bad things had gotten, I guess it was her misguided way of protecting him and his dignity, and protecting us from being afraid. When I left you with him that day Petra, I had no idea what he was capable of. In Grandma's defense, from what she admitted to me later, when I obviously was incensed with her and my dad, she had no way of knowing, either. As much as he had deteriorated, he hadn't," pausing, and exhaling as her gaze shifted to the floor, "done anything like what he did that day."

"Oh my god, it really happened. I thought you admitting it would make me feel better, but now I feel sick, actually sick to my stomach. He was touching me, ugh, running after me. I don't understand. You mean to tell me overnight he became a pedophile?"

Reaching over to lightly clasp her daughter's hand, "Before that awful thing with you…no…he never did anything like that. I know I shouldn't have left you alone with him given the changes I did see, but you must believe me, this was nothing we…I mean, it was beyond anything my mom and I could've imagined. When Grandma and I came home, and found you passed out, and him, standing there, looking disheveled and crazed, with an…oh, I can't tell you how crazed I was, with anger, with worry. I rushed you to the hospital, and thank God, you were all right physically. To be honest, I was always glad you didn't remember, I didn't want you to live through that again. But maybe that wasn't the best thing for you. Maybe that horror was dwelling inside you somewhere, still hurting you subconsciously. I'm so sorry, Petra, can you ever forgive me?"

"Oh, Mom," now placing her other hand over her mother's, "I'm not mad at you. Him on the other hand, I hope he rots in hell."

"Ah sweetheart, you should know, there's a reason for his awful behavior. It probably won't take away your disgust with him, and I still struggle with my resentments after all these years, but in actuality, it wasn't truly his fault."

Abruptly taking her hand away, Petra said, "Oh, please, don't try to tell me that there's an excuse for this. Plenty of men get aged out of their jobs and feel misplaced, but they find a hobby like golf or putting miniature ships into bottles.

They don't become inebriated degenerates, preying on their grandchildren."

"Petra, I mean that he had an actual illness. They found it after his autopsy. It had been undiagnosed, but he had frontotemporal dementia. It's a form of memory loss, but it also includes altered judgment and sexual disinhibition. I think the alcohol was his way of self-medicating, but unfortunately, it made his symptoms worse."

"Okay, I'm sorry he had an illness, but he should have gone to the doctor, instead of being in denial that there was something wrong with him. I can't forgive him, Mom, I just can't."

"Honey, I'm not asking you to forgive him. Like I said, as wonderful a father as he was, and knowing he was sick, I still can't completely get past what he did. If he came to life right now, I think I'd want to choke him. But for your own sake, I want you to not be filled with hatred and repugnance where he's concerned. He did something horrendous, he put you through hell, but you are still here, stronger than ever, and you need to get past this, not hold on to any of it, so that you can once again be free and happy."

"I know, you're right, but right now, I can't help it, I hate him. I still can't understand how he didn't seek help. Even if his mind was going, he had to have lucid moments when he realized something was off. Yet, he did nothing about it."

"Not until it was too late." Calli then nervously stood up, appearing to want to change the subject. "I think we could both use a snack. Sweet or salty? What are you in the mood for?"

"I'm not hungry. What did you mean, Mom, 'not until it was too late'?"

Walking into the kitchen, "Nothing, just that he didn't get help in time to stop from harming you. All right, I think I could go for pizza bites, what do you think?"

Shutting the freezer door after Calli opened it, "No, no pizza bites, no stalling. What did you mean?"

Calli opened her mouth to speak, and then awkwardly stopped, running her fingers through her hair, and nervously chuckling, "This humidity is murder, I'm going to grab a scrunchie."

As she turned to escape, Petra grabbed hold of her mother's arm, and shrieked, "Enough! What are you still hiding from me?"

"He killed himself, all right!!" Calli shrieked back, the eggshell-colored walls nearly cracking from her volcanically erupting voice.

Calling from upstairs, Beau asked with concern, "Cal, is everything okay down there?"

"Yes, Cub, no problem," she said with forced sunniness. Speaking softly, holding back a seeming avalanche of sobs, Calli began, "Petra, Aunt Chloe and I didn't tell you or your cousins because we didn't want to traumatize you. We let you think it was an accident or a heart attack, I mean Chloe and I were so upset, we could never get our stories straight, so it became that he had a heart attack while driving. But he killed himself, with a shot gun in the garage. He left a note. I'll never forget what it said, 'This isn't me anymore. I need to go. I'm sorry.'"

They sat down at the kitchen table, both without words for long minutes, too mutually stunned and hurt to be mad at anyone, least of all each other. Finally, Petra spoke, her body and mind too exhausted to reach over to her mother with a hug, but needing to do what she could to bridge the pain separating them. Her voice scarcely audible, and cracking with barely restrained tears, "Mom, I'm so sorry you had to go through all of this. I have definitely been struggling underneath the surface, but you've had to carry this horrible burden silently all these years."

"Well, I've had you to be strong for, and I can't think of anything more precious to keep me going."

Chapter 24

And now the healing begins. Or so I hope. I stayed with my mom for a few days, even spent time in her damn Zen garden, which I have to admit was actually pretty therapeutic. Hmm, therapy, I am probably going to need actual therapy, not just the kind that comes from Buddha statues and symphonic backyard fountains. Mom did everything she could, as usual, fattening me up, taking me shopping, sending me for a much-needed haircut and mani/pedi, but when she brought up finding me a counselor, encouraging me to stay with her indefinitely, I knew I had to get home. I can't regain my strength and composure by clinging to Mommy. I will enter counseling, but in my own way, in the midst of my shattered life—career, relationship, sense of self, all broken—and I have to be willing to face every bit of the wreckage if I am to move forward.

Cubby turned out to be a pleasant surprise. Once he put me in my place, he actually stayed out of my way, letting me and Mom have our private time, purposefully declining our invitations to join us for dinner and movie outings. When he was around, he didn't treat me with kid gloves, like I am some damaged mental case or bratty, unruly child, though I am probably a little of both. He was unguarded and spontaneous, freely disagreeing with my politics and musical taste, refusing to stop playing his flavorless Perry Como albums while we ate dinner, despite my eye rolling. He's not all bad, there are certainly worse stepfathers out there, as I've come to know. Poor Star, living with that nightmare. Fucking Peterson, that sexually depraved, sociopathic narcissist. But that's a subject for therapy, whenever I get around to going. I don't want to revisit our affair right now. To be honest, as horrible as he turned out to be, I'm still missing the closeness and the fun that we seemed to be having, and I hate myself for admitting that...

Anyway, Beau revealed his final gesture when I got home, in his typically self-deprecating, humble style, which I used to find annoyingly contrived, but now am beginning to appreciate. Slipped into my packed bag was a letter, with a check for five thousand dollars. "I recently sold a house in the Adirondacks that I inherited from my parents, and I made more money on the deal than I had anticipated, so this really isn't a terribly generous gift. It's just a small attempt to be of assistance. I know you haven't been working, and I just want to make sure that money issues don't become a distraction for you. Focus on yourself. The only repayment I expect is you living the happy and full life you deserve."

Well, I'm tired, enough journal writing for now. I'm here, in my dusty, noisy, stale and empty apartment, lonely and adrift, but aware, finally, and that is something...

Catching up on her mail, while eating instant oatmeal, Petra reached for her phone, suddenly remembering that she was overdue for her yearly gynecological exam. She was about to call for an appointment when she received a text from Delaine, joyfully announcing that her drawings were ready to be picked up, the attached picture showing the beautifully scratched frames now regrettably filled with Petra's secondhand renderings of Peterson's work. Petra meant to respond that she would come soon to retrieve them, but instead unplanned yet seemingly necessary words spilled from her texting fingers.

"Beautiful, they are absolutely just as I envisioned. Thank you so much, Delaine, but I really think you should keep the sketches, do whatever you want with them. I don't need them anymore. I'm sorry for troubling you. I hope to see you soon, regardless of everything."

No response came back, and fearing she had offended Delaine, she forgot about the OBGYN appointment. She instinctively reached for her sneakers, figuring a run would settle her nerves and prepare her for the coming weeks of therapy that she would surely need to face. Running out the door, she tripped over a newspaper mistakenly left for her. Aggravatedly picking it up, she queried aloud "The NY Post, who reads this garbage?" As if in answer, a flyer fell out of the thin newspaper, an advertisement for a concierge service. "We run so you don't have to," it chipperly announced, photos of a blonde ponytailed woman happily grocery shopping, picking up dry cleaning, and choosing arts and crafts supplies, while on the opposite side an attractive female enjoyed a manicure, frolicked in a pumpkin patch with her children, and did an art project with her son—all her leisurely activities allegedly made possible by the concierge service. "When the hell does the perky blonde get to relax? Who's running her damn errands so she has time to stroll through a friggin' pumpkin farm?" Petra mused sullenly. Throwing the paper and the ad down the hallway, she suddenly felt disinclined to run herself, and reentered her apartment.

Now what? she wondered as she stripped off her sneakers and settled into her couch. Running. She had been doing a lot of that for too long, and she was overdue for confrontation and clarity. Reaching for her phone, she began scrolling through a google search of Manhattan psychiatrists. Clicking on some of the profiles, she noted the focus on pharmacology, and not wanting to be zoned out on antidepressants and anxiety meds, opted for nonmedical counseling. *I'm not jumping off a bridge, no need for Prozac and Thorazine, but Vicodin, that's another story, no no no, I don't need any of that, just a safe space to talk through things, with someone not emotionally attached to me, a professional, just a regular therapist.* Looking through the many names of counselors that came up, everything from PhD psychologists, MSW's, and hypnotherapists, to spiritual advisers, energy healers, high priestesses, and past life regressionists, Petra was overwhelmed and dismally convinced that all of New York City, and perhaps the world, was nothing more than a breeding ground for emotional ills.

She was about to give up the seemingly futile search when she came across a name that riveted her attention. Elijah Tobias, Master's degree in psychology, specializing in grief counseling. His name sounded Biblical and sturdy, and she imagined him sitting in a sedate, unpretentious office, a linen and cedar scented candle burning perennially, making the room comfortably unbound by the relentless passage of time, a reliable and seasonless haven. Admittedly, her most recent death-related loss was her grandmother several years back, and perhaps a grief counselor was not the ideal therapeutic choice. Still, there was no denying that she was in grief, and something felt right about seeing this particular therapist. Dialing his number, she held her breath until a polished, phone-ready voice picked up.

"Dr. Payne's office, please hold," and before Petra could say anything, the melodic voice disappeared.

Waiting for almost a minute, she became increasingly frustrated, afraid that Elijah Tobias had moved his practice to somewhere predictably sunny like Palm Beach, and that she would never find the right therapist. *Dr. Payne, like I'll see someone with that name…pain…what the fuck, sounds like a sadist.* "Where is she? Come on already. Shit."

"Excuse me?" the friendly voice asked, though with a little less friendliness.

"Oh, sorry, I stubbed my toe. I'm actually looking for Dr. Tobias, uh, I mean the grief counselor, Elijah Tobias."

"Yes, he actually moved down the hall. I can give you his number? Oh! Please wait a second." Her voice got lower, but Petra could hear her saying "Hi" to someone, and a male voice saying something too faint for her to make out.

"More damn waiting, just what I fucking need," Petra irritably heckled, sadly reminding herself of Star.

"Yes, well, no more waiting for you. You're in luck. Eli just dropped by to get his mail. I'll put him on."

"This is Eli Tobias."

"Oh, hi, I'm Petra. I was hoping to make an appointment with you, for therapy. Well, obviously for therapy, you know that already. Um, I know you're probably booked up, but I would like to see you as soon as possible. Is that okay? Obviously, your regular patients are your priority, and new ones if they're suicidal or I don't know, having a psychotic break. I mean, I'm none of those things, so it's not an emergency, but I really…"

"Petra?" he asked with calm, polite severity.

"Yes?"

"I'm sorry to interrupt you. I don't make a practice of that. Forgive me if I'm overstepping, but I want you to pause for a bit, take some deep breaths, slow down, okay?"

"Mm hmm." Taking several deep inhalations as suggested, she did feel less jittery. "Thank you. I'm sorry, it's been a rough time."

"No problem. Well, that'll be $500. We can add it to the cost of your first visit."

"Oh, you're considering this a consultation?"

"I'm kidding Petra. More proof that you do need to relax. Listen, my schedule has been a bit tight lately, but I just had a cancellation. I'd be more than happy to see you later if you have the time."

"Yes, definitely. Thank you."

"No need to thank me. I look forward to meeting you. Three o'clock. I have an hour and a half blocked out, so you don't have to come early to fill out paperwork. I'm on the Upper West Side, 2200 Broadway, at 74ᵗʰ Street. You're familiar with the city?"

"Yes, I live here."

"Great, see you later. I've got to go now, but I'll hand you back to Clarissa. She'll tell you my suite number and give you my phone number as well."

*****

Petra arrived promptly at three o'clock, and entering the door saw a small waiting room with no receptionist. Walking out from the office in the back was a bookishly handsome man, late forties or well-preserved fifties, with thick, dark, ungrayed hair, wearing glasses and a bow tie. There was something dichotomous about his appearance and bearing, for he projected a sober, learned temperament that suggested he read the Smithsonian for idle fun, but his tanned skin gave him the look of someone who weekends in the Hamptons and enjoys running bare-chested on the beach. For Petra, he conveyed a certain Richard Gere quality, post-*Officer and a Gentleman*, pre-*Unfaithful*. He also had an easy confidence and elegant artfulness in his gait that uncomfortably reminded her of Peterson. She was here though, and sick of running, so she would have to stay.

"Petra?" he asked with professional warmth, extending his hand. She nodded, and he waved her into his office. "Please, make yourself comfortable. I left the forms and a pen on a table next to the couch. I have to run down the hall for something, but I'll be right back."

She filled out the forms quickly, having no psychiatric history, and the head injury and memory loss being her main medical episode. *"Do I mention the miscarriage? Not ready to discuss that. Or that I occasionally smoke pot? It's legal now, so who cares, right?"* Her fingers reflexively began writing in Tyler's name as her emergency contact, getting as far as the "l" when her mind reached the tip of the pen, demanding a hasty scratch out which was replaced by Calli's name and number. Once finished with the paperwork, she surveyed the office, finding no burning candle as imagined, and a bright peach and yellow coloring motif unlike the darkened, subdued palette his scholarly name had evoked. Petra was staring into the bare walls, noticing irregular outlines of pictures or other artwork that were now vanished, when Elijah walked back into the room.

"Forgive the appearance of my office, I recently moved in," he explained as he sat down beside an end table in the deskless room. "It gives off an abandoned nursery school vibe. The woman who rented the office before me was a lactation specialist. I've been peeling teddy bear and baby elephant decals off the walls for days. Can I get you water before we start?"

"No, I'm fine." Again, she saw flashes of Peterson, in the way he smiled, and that bridge he effortlessly inhabited between vital youth and aged maturity, distractingly handsome. Throw in Richard Gere, and she was regretting she hadn't opted for a female therapist.

"Is something wrong?"

"Well, yes, um, that's why I'm here."

"No, that's not what I meant. You were looking at me like you were trying to figure something out."

"Oh, yeah," sighing with slight discomfiture, "you remind me of some-one, two someones, I mean two people, actually."

"Who?"

"It's stupid."

"Now Petra, you seem like a smart person. Even if you've only seen ther-apists depicted in movies or books, you know nothing is stupid or irrelevant in therapy, it all means something. So, tell me." Seeing her reluctance to speak, he continued. "Cat Stevens?"

"What? Is that a person?"

"Yes, he was a singer in the '60s and '70s. People have told me I resemble him. But I guess they were much older than you."

"I was thinking of a celebrity, someone else, but also a person I know, knew I mean, but I don't want to talk about him."

"Well, then maybe we should. If it makes you uncomfortable, it might be helpful to discuss it." He said it in a way that was both firm and gentle, making her want to say more, but she was afraid to get sidetracked by her ill-fated affair with Peterson when she had much bigger issues to address.

"Later, not yet. Actually, I don't even know where to begin. There's a lot I need to discuss, but I don't feel ready to talk about any of it. Maybe I should just come back another time."

"Sure, if that's what you want, but why don't we try something first, okay? If I were to ask you how you feel, right now, what word jumps to mind?"

"Lost."

"Okay, when was the last time you weren't lost?"

She hesitated before answering, not sure she had an answer. Putting her hand to her forehead, she absentmindedly smelled the lavender lotion on her arm, and then smiled, called back to Tyler's sweet Easter basket, futilely wishing herself back into its lovable oblivion. "This past spring, Easter with my mom and my boyfriend at the time. He gave me the cutest gifts, Mom and I cooked together. It was nice."

"All right, this is a good starting point. We can go slowly, and work backwards through what has made you feel lost since that day, and along the way, if it gets overwhelming, we can revisit that Easter, dropping by there to refresh you and remind you of what's possible."

"That sounds wonderful, but it won't work, not for me. I know it won't. I'm sorry, but you don't understand."

"Then help me to," his tone and expression unpressured and genuine.

"I can never go back there, to that Easter. I wasn't even really there to begin with. That happiness was a lie. A shattered mess held together by flimsy glue."

"What first shattered everything?"

"My father."

"How so?"

"No, I meant my grandfather."

"Did you?"

Her voice infused with undisguised annoyance, "Yes, I very recently uncovered a repressed memory of something horrendous my grandfather did to me. That's actually why I came to see you."

"All right, we will talk about that, but what is your relationship with your father?"

"Nonexistent."

"Do you want that to change?"

"Is this how it's going to be? You tell me what we should be talking about, despite what I want to say? I'm out of here, I don't need another smug, dismissive asshole in my life. Thanks for nothing." Rushing to the front door of the office space, she noticed a pink giraffe affixed to the yellow painted wood, an overlooked fragment from the office's previous life, momentarily reprieved from its certain doom in the next wave of renovations. "Better you go now, poor thing," Petra whispered to the adorably awkward creature, scratching it off onto the floor before she slammed the door behind her.

Epiphany. I love that word, but I hate how people throw it around carelessly. Rianne realizing that her latest romantic entanglement is just another unhealthy fiasco is not an "epiphany," as she'd like to believe, especially since next week, she'll be involved with another carbon copy loser. No, a true epiphany is something rare, profound, divine...life-changing. Maybe I, too, am grasping for depth and meaning in my absurd, trivial life, but I feel I am in the midst of a true epiphany. There wasn't a voice from heaven, and I haven't instantaneously become wise and peaceful, but a shift is taking place, perhaps small, but still dramatic in its impact. Elijah, Eli, whatever, he certainly did piss me off, but I think he was on to something. He forced me to start seeing things of which I had been totally blind.

I have acted like my father is a nonentity in my life, as unnecessary as an appendix, but now I see how that appendix has long been infected, seeping unknown into areas I thought it could never taint. So simple, and yet those are the things that are often the hardest to discern, hiding in plain sight. My father never gave me the approval I needed. I felt so loved and acknowledged by my mother, that I told myself my father was superfluous. I didn't need him. But I did, I still do. Tyler and I as a couple clearly had wonderful aspects, but I think there was something decidedly unwonderful about my relationship lens, what I projected onto him and expected him to provide me. He unwittingly was a stand-in for my remote father. I wanted Tyler's approval, no matter what, which is why I continually uprooted myself for him, putting aside my desires and professional happiness for his fulfillment. I also stayed in denial about my past, pushing any hints of its creeping truth down into my deepest subconscious, not just for me, but for Tyler, to be his pleasing, perfect, good girl.

What happened with my grandfather was its own distinct horror, but it developed and persisted in the vacuum of male abandonment that my father's inattention created. When my grandfather first began showing me undue attention that ill-fated summer, I felt uncomfortable, but in a way, was so starved for the paternal care held back by my father, that I said nothing, not even to my mother. I'm not an expert in child psychology, maybe my reticence to speak up would've been the same even if I had a more involved father, but I suspect his emotional absence was at least one ingredient in my passivity. I returned home, with a healing concussion and memory loss that was likely more psychological than somatic, and my father became even more closed off from me, likely knowing the truth about my injury from my mother, and maybe feeling guilty for our own fractured relationship. So many secrets and hidden feelings, my own, my parents' and grandparents', and they all spun together to keep me in the dark from myself.

But nothing stays secret forever. When Tyler proposed, the emergence began. I had long lived within an unknown cloud of betrayal and hurt and lack of male trust, and any joy in his proposal was immediately rained out by all those latent tears. Once my carefully crafted world of denial began imploding, it became inevitable that I would meet Peterson, this man existing at the crossroads of all my frustrated hopes, aspirations, and veiled trauma. He provided me with the artistic approval I never got from my father. And in some truly creepy way that I will probably need years of analysis to fully process without cringing, I think I must have noticed that Peterson was close to the age of my grandfather when he first became ill, and abusive to me. Maybe I subconsciously felt that I could sublimate all of that past psychic pain by creating a new relationship with a seemingly harmless substitute for my grandfather. Ugh, Freud always did make me uncomfortable sexualizing everything, but maybe there's a reason he's still the most famous psychoanalyst in the world. I wonder what I was really thinking that summer in the weeks preceding my "accident," daydreaming in front of Peterson's sketches in my grandmother's den? Did I sense what was about to happen? Was there some premonition that this mysterious artist would occupy a strange but undeniable place in my future, perhaps my hoped-for link to the precious innocence that my granddad was about to wrest from me?

Chapter 25

The morning after her curtailed therapy session arrived with hazy sunshine, and Petra desperately wanted to visit her father. It had been more than three years since she had seen him, and almost a year since she had communicated with him, whether by phone call or text, she couldn't recall. Casual friends and acquaintances often assumed her father was deceased or living in some distant part of the globe, because he was rarely around and she never spoke about him. Yet, he was alive and living about an hour away in Connecticut. Without calling ahead to him, Petra checked the schedule of trains leaving for Stamford, and within ninety minutes, was seated and on her way to see her dad. She had forgotten to grab a book, and her only available reading material was a pamphlet on fire escape gardening that a homeless man had illogically passed to her as she boarded the train. She inwardly chuckled thinking about all the times she and Tyler had risked frostbite, mosquito attacks, and public indecency charges cavorting on many different fire escapes in their NYC life, and all the tomatoes and basil leaves their sexual acrobatics would have crashed onto the sidewalk if they actually had a fire escape garden.

The train ride was less than an hour, and Petra was feeling last minute jitters about seeing her father. Sitting on a bench outside of the station, she felt frozen in place. So much was riding on this visit, confronting the ghosts of her past, and starting to heal, so she could move forward in a healthy relationship with him, and herself, and eventually a man, perhaps even Tyler. Thinking of all these contingencies, she was panicked, wondering if she'd be worse off if her father continued to be neglectful and cold. She was wrestling with the possibility of getting on a train back to the city when a taxi pulled up to the nearby curb.

"Did you call for me?" the driver asked imperatively.

Looking around before she answered to make sure he was addressing her, "No?"

"You don't sound like you're sure, lady. Did you or didn't you?"

"No, I didn't, but if you're available, I do have someplace I want…that I *need* to go."

"Okay, get in. Where to?"

"1111 Domino Road."

*****

Standing in front of her father's modest Tudor home, she felt mildly sad, realizing she had only been at his house once in the five years that he lived there, heavily encouraged by Tyler to make a Christmastime visit. It wasn't sadness at not having spent much time with him, but rather that she didn't consciously *want* to be in his company. She slowly but affirmatively walked towards the front door, knowing that she had to confront their distant relationship if she wanted any chance at a peaceful, whole existence. Just as she was about to ring the bell, the door opened, her father slipping on a windbreaker and holding his keys. His face fell into shocked stillness, and he stared at her without speaking, shaking his head in unbelief.

"Hi, Dad," she said, silently pleased that her presence was causing him discomfort. "I guess it's a bad time. You look like you're on your way out."

"No, I was just going to the grocery store, but that can wait." Still shaking his head, "Wow. You're here."

"Yep. Can I come in?"

"Of course, I'm sorry, um, I just can't believe you're standing at my front door. This is, uh, incredible." Ushering her in, he closed the door behind him, and pointed towards the kitchen. "I just finished lunch, are you hungry?"

"No."

"How did you get here?"

"Train, then a cab."

"You came here to see *me*?" he asked with an obvious trace of nervous hope.

"Well, I don't know anyone else in Stamford, so it looks that way."

"Sit down. I'll get you something to eat."

"I said I don't want anything."

Trying to ignore her antagonism, "This is so surreal, I was sitting here thinking about you. I was rummaging in my basement, and found your senior yearbook. You were voted most likely to succeed, remember?"

"Well, we all know high school is nothing but bullshit."

"Maybe so, but I think it was an accurate assessment of you. Still is."

"Yeah?" Her sarcastic tone loudly evident, "I'm jobless now or didn't you hear?"

"Yes, your mom told me, but that doesn't change all that you've accomplished, and will accomplish in the future."

"I've been contemplating a career change, maybe pursuing art, but we both know you don't consider that a real profession, so I guess I'm not that much of a success after all."

"Petra," large nervous gulps of air staggering his speech, "you… you… whatever you put your mind to doing…you can do."

"Thanks, that is really helpful, you would have made a swell guidance counselor."

"Petra, I know we don't have the best relationship, but if you're going to be this defensive, I don't see what good this visit is going to do either of us."

"Huh, so you want me to leave, already? So much for unconditional love. Take care, *Dad*," her snide emphasis on the last word collapsing him like a popped balloon.

Shrinking into his refrigerator, "Hey, I do love you, more than I love anything in this world, and I want you to stay, but I'm not going to keep trying to talk with you if you're determined to shut me out. There is a reason you came here, and I don't think it was to give me sarcastic insults, so why don't we try to put aside the tension, and just talk, if not as father and daughter, then like cordial acquaintances, or basically anyone you aren't about to stab," reaching for a nearby fork, and jokingly poking it into his chest.

She glowered at him for a moment, stifling laughter until she couldn't hold it in another second. "Okay. Anyway, that fork looks dull. I'd need something much sharper. So where is this yearbook? Mom made me wear a pearl necklace and an updo for my senior picture. I looked like a middle-aged librarian."

*****

Hours later, they were picking at the remnants of chicken tikka masala and almond basmati rice from their take-out meal, and still laughing over Petra's ridiculous graduation photo. Things were more relaxed, but they hadn't yet addressed their difficulty relating to each other over the years, and neither one appeared ready to do so, or able to forget it, so they pretended to still be eating while nervously avoiding eye contact.

Sick of playing with the same scrap of chicken, Petra finally dropped her fork, and sat back from the table, "Well, that was delicious. Who knew Stamford has better Indian food than Manhattan? I'm stuffed." Wiping her mouth with one of the flimsy napkins that accompanied their meal, "I'm gonna go wash my hands."

"Sure, I'll clean up."

Walking down the hallway, Petra stopped at a framed painting, so memorized and yet long ago seen that it clung to the wall like a piece of ancient history digging itself up from desertion. It was her own prizewinning watercolor painting of the Ferris wheel, scoffed at by her father so many years ago. Now it was hanging proudly on his wall, with no other pictures in sight, as if it were the only memento that merited being on display. It hadn't been there when she visited previously with Tyler, and she wondered if her desperately fragile psyche had placed it there and not her father's own hands.

"Hey, do you want some dessert? I have Chips Ahoy cookies and chocolate ice cream if you want, or…" and her father stopped speaking once he saw her transfixed by the painting. "Oh, yeah, I hope you don't mind that I have it. I mean, technically it's yours, so if you want it back, I understand." Turning to look at the painting, becoming as lost in it as his daughter, "I love it, though. It's my only piece of art."

"I can't believe you have this. You didn't even seem to notice it when it was first painted."

"Petra, I'm—"

"No, Dad, honestly, I didn't mean that as another insult. I'm just genuinely shocked that you want it, that it means something to you. I'm not even sure how you got it, but thank you."

"Please, I don't deserve it, the thanks or the picture." His eyes appeared wet and ready to spill tears when he began quietly laughing.

"What?"

"Your mom gave me such a hard time about this painting. Remember the flood in her basement a couple of years ago? She and what's his face, Rhett Butler or whatever his name is, they were salvaging what they could, and she found some things of mine that she accidentally took when we separated. I went over to get them when I was passing through Maryland visiting some friends, and I saw she had a whole corner of her living room dedicated to your artwork. Must have been at least ten of your sketches and paintings. But this one, the Ferris wheel, it broke my heart, because of how I, you know, didn't make a fuss over it. I asked her for it, one painting out of all she had, and she refused. I don't have to tell you how stubborn she can be. So, when she left the room, I grabbed it off the wall, and got the hell out of there. Her and that stupid husband chased me into the street, screaming and yelling. It was like an episode of *Dukes of Hazzard*. I felt like some damn fatso sheriff was gonna nab me before I hit the state line. I never did get the stuff of mine she found, she probably burned it after I left. But it was worth it."

Petra was crying, in laughter, sadness, and gratitude, and it was the first time she saw her father as a real person, flesh and blood, imperfect but not a monster, human and complicated, just like her. "Seriously, *the* dumbest thing I've ever heard, but so freaking entertaining. Beau's been exceedingly kind to me, but I have to admit, I still get a kick out of him being tormented."

"Yeah, he probably doesn't deserve it, but that makes it all the more satisfying to piss him off. Terrible, I know. I guess you get that mean streak from me." Pausing in thought, "You know, until you were five or so, you were so attached to me, your poor mother developed an inferiority complex."

"What?!"

Elbowing her playfully, "Don't sound so shocked. I don't have an altar to Satan, you know."

"I'm sorry, I just don't remember. Tell me."

"Well, basically, you only wanted me. I had to be the one to dress you, feed and bathe you, put you to bed. On nights that I was working late, I'd come home to find your mom with a vodka martini and a compress on her head, saying that you screamed yourself to sleep because I wasn't there to read you a bedtime story."

"Wow. Umm, what changed?"

"Well, your mom started taking you to these mother-daughter art work-shops, which I encouraged because I knew you both needed to bond with each other. It worked, so well in fact, that you two developed this whole shared world that I wasn't a part of, never could be. I'm strictly a numbers guy, nothing artistic about me. I think I always resented your artistic talent because I felt I lost you to it."

"I'm so sorry, Dad, I had no idea you felt slighted."

"Petra, I was the adult, it was up to me to get past it, not you. I'm the one who's sorry." Chuckling again, he was momentarily caught somewhere else, hold-ing his chin, and staring into the background of the Ferris wheel painting, as if he were inside its pastel-colored amusement park.

"What is it now?"

"I was so relieved when that brain dead jock, Kenny, moved next door to us. He had an absentee dad, and shooting hoops with him made me feel useful, that I wasn't a total waste as a father. I think I caused him to hate you, though."

"What do you mean?"

"I was always bragging to him how smart and creative you were, all the academic and art prizes you won. Must've pissed him off, he'd practically tear the basket off with some of his shots after I got through listing your accomplishments. I've always been so proud of you, Petra, I'm sorry if I never showed you."

*****

A short while later, they were sitting in front of his house, waiting for the car he had insisted on ordering for Petra to take her directly door to door. The late August evening air was neither summer nor fall, as if wading undecided between two colliding waterways. The crickets seemed to be the only steadfastly defiant thread of summer. Petra and her father were in their own transition, not belonging to past or future, sure of only their tentative moment.

"I want to hug you, Dad, and say that everything is perfect between us, and I can't tell you what it means to me that you've opened up about our relation-ship, but I'm dealing with a lot of things right now, and I'm just not ready. But I will get there."

"Petra, I'm already happy, just having you here. I'll accept whatever you are willing to give me."

A navy Kia pulled up just then, and they both stood, reluctant and relieved to say goodbye. They held hands for a brief moment, and Petra walked away, turning back when she sensed her father wanted to say something. She looked at him, sentimental and strong, mouth unsure, but arms locked tightly against his chest. She knew he was struggling, trying to be sensitive and tough, vulnerably open and soundly reliable, all at once, and she felt for him, wanted to comfort him as much as she needed her own reassurance.

"I love you, Dad."

"I love you more, kiddo."

She smiled as she entered the pine-scented car, finally knowing it was true.

Chapter 26

Petra was sifting through her closet, looking for the fall and winter clothes she would soon require, when Tyler's journal fell from the upper shelf, and she marveled at how it was like a mercurial garden gnome, popping up everywhere, always in some unexpected location, ever-present and still unknowable. It had traveled from the hall closet to her bedroom closet, and in between had materialized by her couch and even in the bathroom, and she didn't recall placing it in any of those locations. Shoving aside her sweaters and scarves, she picked up the journal, and sitting down in her cluttered closet, opened it. Thumbing through, she saw a lot of absurd, nonsensical doodles, and laughed, saying out loud, "I am definitely the artist in the family, not him." The word "family" reverberated inside her, and she felt surprised and, in a peculiar way, soothed, that it was still her default instinct to consider him family, even though he seemed stubbornly resistant to occupying that role any longer.

She passed over several pages of written thoughts, feeling like a voyeur for glancing at words he probably never intended anyone to see. But then a title caught her eye, "Lost Boy," undated, but written in small, shaky lettering that was so overtly plaintive, she could actually hear his younger voice echoing out from the page. Petra began reading it out loud, reading it with him, the Tyler of the past speaking alongside her in the present.

People see him,

So clearly,

They say.

Smart, athletic,

Talented,

They say.

Future so bright,

Nothing of the dark,

They all say.

He sees too,

Through them,

Back to himself.

He sees nothing,

He is lost,

Not to them,

Only to himself.

She stared at the words for what seemed like days, uncomfortably crouched on the hard, cold wood of her closet, but unable to move, implanted inside Tyler's long ago, wintry pain, wanting to stay there with him, packing it together with all her own angst, and then trudging through it with him, until they were both so numb from ice-covered grief that they could be at peaceful rest until the summer thaw welcomed them to new life. How had she never seen this side of him? Was this the authentic him, not the placid, assured person she had come to expect? Maybe he revisited this anti-Tyler when he sat reading his Wordsworth poems, stepping back into his own fragile poet's soul. Her brooding quiet was disturbed by the harsh ringing of her phone, unintentionally raised to its highest pitch, and she grabbed it, her fingers trancelike as she accepted the call.

"Hi, Petra? This is Daphne from Dr. Farren's office. We have the results of your blood test from the other day. I'm going to connect you with the doctor now, hold on."

Petra had forgotten all about her OBGYN visit the other day, finally making the appointment only when a raging migraine headache caused her to raid her medicine cabinet for the prescription ibuprofen Dr. Farren routinely prescribed, and sadly realizing she was all out. The blood and urine tests were routine, especially since Petra hadn't been examined since nearly a year and a half before, so she was surprised to be receiving a call. *That married, perverted SOB gave me syphilis. Or gonorrhea. I hate him.*

"Petra, it's Dr. Farren. How are you?"

"Fine, just a little concerned that you're calling. Is everything okay with me?"

"No cause for alarm. But there are two things we need to discuss. Firstly, you have a mild case of anemia. And also, you're pregnant."

"What? No, I can't be. I'm still on the pill."

"Well, no birth control is one hundred percent effective, and you are not my first patient to experience a pregnancy while on the pill. But you are definitely pregnant, and I advise you to stop taking the pill at once."

"This can't be happening."

"Petra, I know this is a surprise, so I want you to just sit back right now, process this the best you can, and then come see me tomorrow. I'll give you my lunch hour because I really want to see you. We'll discuss all your options. Come at 12:30, is that okay?"

"Yes, I'll be there."

*****

Tyler stared apathetically up at the ceiling, lying unusually motionless and naked on the latest in a series of temporary beds, various friends and work colleagues all providing shelter while he supposedly looked for his own place. It's not that he relished being permanently nomadic, but simply that committing to an apartment or condo seemed to be committing to a life without Petra, and though he openly admitted no wistful desire for her, he couldn't deny it in his interior silence. His physical and mental disinterest was in stark contrast to the restless body beside him, full of undisguised uncertainty, gently but insistently tapping on his arm, waiting for his acknowledgment.

"Tyler? Where are you right now?"

Turning towards his beautiful, dark-haired companion, "That was awful."

"Gee, thanks."

"No, you're absolutely amazing. I'm talking about myself, I'm sorry, I wanted to be into it, but I'm distracted. There's something wrong with me lately."

"Ex-lover, not so ex?"

"Did Isaac tell you anything?"

"Only that he had a great guy for me to meet. I'm officially firing him as my matchmaker."

"I deserve that," and he shrugged back into his vacant stare at the ceiling.

"No, neither of us do, but that's life. I could sense some phantom girl hanging over you from the moment we met, but I came here anyway, so I'm at fault too. I'd ask you to tell me about her, but I'm naked and rejected, and I'd like to make it out of here with some dignity and self-esteem, so I'll get dressed and be on my way."

Within minutes, she was out the door, going back to wherever she lived, and Tyler feeling like an insensitive heel for not even having asked. They met at a bar he had selected, she was gorgeous and friendly, and after a brief and casual conversation, and half-finished drinks, they were in a cab going to his provisional abode. In the door, and in his bed, in dissolute, disappointing seconds. "What am I doing?" he wondered aloud. Images of the past few weeks careened inside his head: drunken sex with his ex, Lexi, more drunken sex with a visiting literature professor from some European country he couldn't recall, and now this latest escapade. All lovely women, somehow dissolving into one regretful mistake, none of them Petra, the woman he despised and most painfully, the only one he loved. They weren't together, and she was the one who ended the relationship, but the rumpled sheets were indicting him as a cheat, a betrayer of his own heart. His phone beeped then with a text from Lexi, a red heart, and he winced. "Shit," he cried, remembering that the night he'd been with Lexi, they had momentarily shifted back into relationship familiarity, and no protection was used. "What if she's pregnant? Please, no."

Getting up to grab a much-needed beer, he nearly tumbled over a bin sitting abandoned on the outskirts of the living room. It was their travel mementos, his and Petra's, that she had brought with her that last day he'd seen her, at the Bluebird Café. He still couldn't bring himself to look through it, but it followed him from apartment to apartment, always the first thing he carried into each new dwelling place, and still the last thing he could handle seeing. He vividly remembered that day, how defenseless Petra had seemed, as breakable as their throwaway shell necklaces, grasping for life in that bin she had so cluelessly offered him. Of course, he wanted all of those stupid trinkets, precious reminders of their beautiful life together, but not as a eulogy. He wanted that life still, that day and even now, with the scent of another woman clinging to him, a woman whose only obvious flaw was not being Petra.

When Petra sat there in the café, mournfully wrapping their years together in a neat little box, a future that she mutated into a past, he wanted to cry, and hug her, and beg her to stop destroying them both with denial and fear. But his intense pain and bruised ego would only allow him to sneer at her, to be cruel the way she had been cruel in killing something that seemed to be alive even before they met. When he yelled at her, he could see her shaking inside his fury, and he stormed out, not because of his anger, but because if he stayed a second longer, he would have needed to cradle and soothe her, because her pain hurt him more than his own, and he was too wounded to show her that. So instead, he left, and he waited in a doorway across the street, hot, floury air from a bakery clouding his sinuses in the impatient summer heat of late June. He needed to make sure she was okay, and he waited until she left, her face visibly sad as she emerged, but her dancer-like gracefulness evident enough that he knew she was all right. He saw that her hands were devoid of his old red sweats and the box of their travel knickknacks, so when Petra had turned the corner, he reentered the café, reclaiming what he had only pretended to leave behind.

Now

I haven't had any dreams in several weeks. I had a phone session with Elijah, he says it's not unusual for the sleeping mind to need a break when major psychological cleansing is happening in the waking hours. I'm glad to be making progress, but I miss the comfort of my nontraumatic nocturnal wanderings, so safe in moments, prior and imagined, that stretch out, immune from the present.

Wow, I have written a lot these past few months. Scanning through it now, I can't believe I've lived through all this, or that I survived, and even managed to have some fun along the way. So much happiness, pain, revelation, more pain, good and bad surprises, old friends, new ones. Passion, sex, near misses, disasters. Traumas, imagined, forgotten, pushed away, then rediscovered, unfortunately all too real. Family. Grandma and Mom, forever. Dad, once again, and even Cubby, kind of. And always me, here, learning, growing, or at least trying to.

I've imperceptibly slipped back into my editorial position, reading my dream logs and journal entries as if they are part of a manuscript, from an edgy up and coming author that everyone is talking about, and I was lucky enough to land. This insecure, but headstrong, buzzed cut beauty with a nose ring, pearl neck-lace, and sweater set, half Miss Oklahoma, half Sinead O'Conner, is sitting in my sky-high office, telling me how every bit of this is real: it is her story, it really hap-pened. Listen honey, I tell her with patronizing but sincere care, channeling my old boss, Melanie. We can't market this as a memoir. True or not, it reads like fic-tion, as do all the best and worst life stories.

Okay, enough poetic avoidance, time to address the as yet invisible but still enormous elephant in the room. I am pregnant, and I'm scared but absolutely thrilled. Let me not get ahead of myself, I was here before, and it didn't turn out well. But something tells me this is really my baby, the one that's going to actually leave heaven in favor of this crazy world, to be loved and protected by me. By me. I can't believe I'm having that bastard's baby. I don't want him to ever know that we conceived a child together. But can I do this, keep him in the dark, and prevent this child from knowing its father, even though this "father" is an absolute disaster to his son and stepdaughter? I was so angered at my mom for not telling me what happened with my grandfather, and yet I am going to keep my child from knowing his or her own father? Do I pretend he died, or that it was a one-night stand and I never got his full name? Lies, too many lies in my life already, things misrepresented or hidden or omitted, I can't add to this, and yet, right now, I see no other way.

Phew, this is a lot. I should probably speak with Elijah again soon, he encouraged me to make another appointment, he must think I'm a basket case… repressed memories, incest, lots of outdoor sex-capades, raunchy affair with a married man, unplanned pregnancy. Wow, I always thought of myself as a stable, regular person, but that does sound like the makings of a Hollywood ready, icepick wielding, sexy femme fatale. Yikes. But honestly, I feel relatively normal these days, and I actually don't have anything to say right now to a therapist, or maybe I have too much to say, and it's just easier not to say it, to deal with it on my own. I'm no longer in denial, so I don't feel in danger of backsliding just because I'm not willing to lie on a couch for ten years and revisit potty training traumas as a means of supposedly becoming whole. I told Eli about my grandfather. I know what hap-pened, I have to make my peace with it, and with him, but I honestly don't want to talk or think about any of that now. That awful event stole enough from me, I don't want to lose anything else. And now I have something more important than any-thing else to focus on, a baby, my baby.

I left out one essential part of my odyssey. Tyler. I know I said I wasn't really in love with him, but that's not really true, or maybe it's accurate but not in the way I originally meant it. Even in our perfect moments, we were never perfect people, never can be, and that's okay. The parts of him I did see, the ones that made me happy, that protected and excited me, as well as the aspects that left me marginalized, passed over, pissed off, they are all fragments of a sublime complicated whole that I think I am willing to spend a lifetime getting to know, if he's willing to get to know me, the entire Petra that I am only now starting to know myself. What we had wasn't fake, it was just an incomplete picture. I wonder how he's doing now. Is he thinking about me, about us? Is he done, and too scared or angry not to be? He's not a pig, but he likes sex too much to be celibate for long. Who's sharing his bed these days? Boringly wholesome Lexi? One of those deceptively prudish Linguistic professors, all glasses and tight bun in the classroom, and then ravenous, leather-clad hellcat in the bedroom? Let me stop, I'm pregnant with a married man's baby, no one's nominating me for sainthood anytime soon.

Mmmm, the baby, this blameless, innocent being, created in such deceptively beautiful but truly ugly circumstances, their birth possibly stirring up even further struggles. For me, whether I involve Peterson or not...for him, Lori, even Star, if their house of cards comes tumbling down...and for Tyler, himself mostly blameless in all this. Even if we can wade back to each other through all the wreckage of the past few months, could he ever look at me the same way, giving birth to a child that was supposed to be ours? Any reunion between us would surely feel tenuous at first...could it survive the revelation of this baby? Would my undeniable glee about this miracle eventually filter inside of him, softening any of his resentments, or would it be a daily slap in his face, a constant reminder of our time apart, made even more palpable when this baby arrives? I suppose it all gets back to who Tyler truly fell in love with in the first place: idealized, faultless Petra, who never existed, or the always imperfect one, sitting here today, and for every day to come.

So then, who am I? On any given day, lots of different people. A nice girl, a bitch, grateful, impatient, content, sad, hopeful, depressed, carefree, lonely, pleased, preoccupied, tired, excited, quiet. But most importantly, alive, to experience all the good and the bad, and that's amazing. I don't think I'll ever go back to being an editor. Been there, done that, no need for a second look. Art is a possibility, but I think I've gotten what I needed from it, at least for the time being. It forced me back into a hell that I could only escape from by reentering. I don't feel inclined now to draw or paint my feelings, I am happy just to feel. Writing, that's something I like, more than I ever did before. I might want to do this, to write my own books instead of editing someone else's. New Mexico. For some reason, I see myself there, in an adobe shack, dusty but clean in the hot, dry sandy air, typing away on a vintage typewriter that is somehow younger than me, thirty years old but experiencing so many little deaths and rebirths that I am ageless. Perhaps Tyler will be there too. I've followed him where he needed to go, maybe he will want to follow me now. Isn't the Painted Desert near there? That sounds so beautiful, a painting that's real life.

I've been reading and rereading Tyler's journal, and I've never felt closer to him or further away. The voice in these pages is so different from the Tyler I remember, and yet so achingly similar to the person I'm slowly realizing I've always been. Vulnerable and broken but somehow intact. I've gone over our relationship countless times. What kind of a couple were me and Tyler? We looked so ideal, and it felt so most of the time, but was any of it true? If I was hidden from myself throughout our relationship, did that invalidate our connection? Was he only in love with a false, emotionally sanitized version of me? And if I couldn't present my true self to him, could he really be his genuine self with me? I see him, sitting in our living room, lost in his book of poetry. What are his demons? Will he ever delve inside of them? Will he take me with him? How reliable was anything between us? Isn't psychic energy relational, the law of attraction and all that? Did my emotional veil naturally engender his own disguise? Or maybe our lack of perfection actually proves how deeply our love ran, and maybe still does. If two people, unknowingly haunted by buried pains and unexplored resentments, can find joy and harmony with each other, doesn't that speak of transcendent love? And isn't that what everyone wants their love to be, something grounded in the ordinary, that grows from pleasure and pain, dwelling in reality while lifting you out of it?

My grandmother always told me that the cure for a bad day and the gratitude for a good one lied in one small exercise: go to sleep thinking of your sweetest truth. What is a sweetest truth? I asked when she first told me. 'Oh, honey, if you're asking, maybe you are too young for me to have told you. You'll figure it out. I can tell you this. It changes over time, it can be different people or things, a pet, an experience. But whatever it is that day, it'll just roll off your tongue as you fall asleep.'

I am tired, but I already feel something riding atop every cell of my body, latent, percolating, eager but patient. All in time.

Tonight, now, what is my sweetest truth? Sweet. Maybe bittersweet, but that's okay.

I think I like that better.

...Tyler...